# As Close
# as Sisters

Books by Colleen Faulkner

JUST LIKE OTHER DAUGHTERS

AS CLOSE AS SISTERS

Published by Kensington Publishing Corporation

# As Close as Sisters

## COLLEEN FAULKNER

KENSINGTON BOOKS
www.kensingtonbooks.com

KENSINGTON BOOKS are published by

Kensington Publishing Corp.
119 West 40th Street
New York, NY 10018

All Kensington titles, imprints, and distributed lines are available at special quantity discounts for bulk purchases for sales promotion, premiums, fund-raising, and educational or institutional use.

Special book excerpts or customized printings can also be created to fit specific needs. For details, write or phone the office of the Kensington Special Sales Manager: Kensington Publishing Corp., 119 West 40th Street, New York, NY 10018. Attn. Special Sales Department. Phone: 1-800-221-2647.

Kensington and the K logo Reg. U.S. Pat. & TM Off.

eISBN-13: 978-1-61773-519-6
eISBN-10: 1-61773-519-1
First Kensington Electronic Edition: November 2014

ISBN-13: 978-0-7582-5571-6
ISBN-10: 0-7582-5571-3
First Kensington Trade Paperback Printing: November 2014

10 9 8 7 6 5 4 3

Printed in the United States of America

*For my sisters; you know who you are. . . .*

# ❦ 1 ❧

# McKenzie

I don't understand why I have to write this. Why *I* have to keep the journal. I'm the one who's dying.

We always keep a journal of our annual stay in Albany Beach. But I hate writing it all down as much as Aurora, Lilly, and Janine hate it. And I'm the one who's bald and spends a good deal of my time in the bathroom puking or wishing I could puke. I would think my friends, my *dearest* friends, my closer-than-sisters, could cut me a break.

They won't.

According to Aurora, the unsanctioned leader of the gang, I should keep the journal precisely because I *am* dying. If my doctors' predictions are accurate, I won't be around next July to write the damned thing. Aurora thinks I should take my turn while the option's still available.

I don't understand why Aurora's vote always seems to count more than mine, Janine's, or Lilly's. Actually I do. We all do. It's always been that way. At least since August 17, 1986.

But I'm getting ahead of myself.

I need to start at the beginning. But not the very beginning. I don't have that much time. *Literally.* So I'll start at the beginning of this chapter in our lives. I'll start with my arrival at the beach house.

I arrived at the beach house, for what is to be my last summer, a day earlier than the others. I planned it this way. I wanted to settle in. I wanted to get a good night's sleep and be rested when *the girls* arrive tomorrow. (I don't know why we still, at forty-two years old, call ourselves *girls*. We just do.) The two-hour trip from my house in northern Delaware to the beach has exhausted me. I don't want to be exhausted when they arrive.

I also wanted to get here first so I could open up the house. This is a gift to Janine, Lilly, and Aurora. We all hate closing the house up at the end of our summer stay, but we hate opening it up more. Those first few hours always take us back too close to that August night. Each time we arrive, the ghosts have to be resurrected, then folded out of sight with the sheets and tablecloths we use to protect the furniture. The nightmare that was that night has to be swept away with the spiderwebs and mouse droppings.

No one comes to the house but us. Ever. Janine's mom wanted to have it bulldozed. Or sold; it's probably worth a lot of money. Two or three million, because it's oceanfront. But she respected her daughter's wishes and deeded it to Janine instead.

As I got out of my Honda, I looked up at the two-story Cape Cod built on pilings. I'd parked in the back; the front of the house faces the ocean. The cedar shingles have weathered to a lovely gray, but the white trim is flaking and needs painting. I grabbed a duffel bag off the backseat and leaned against the car to catch my breath. I breathed deeply, and the salty breeze stung my nostrils and revived me. Most of the windows of the house were covered with curtains or blinds, but two on the second floor weren't.

I felt as if the house were watching me.

I took another deep breath, heaved my bag onto my shoulder, and crossed the short distance to the staircase that led up to the back deck and the back door. Beneath the house, there was a clutter of things: old rope, a bicycle leaning against the outside shower, a stack of bushel baskets from previous years' crab feasts. I dropped my bag on the bottom step and looked for the key in a pile of empty flowerpots under the staircase. I have no idea why the flowerpots are there. No one ever stays long enough to plant flowers. Not since 1986. Could they really have been there that long?

I found the key in a Ziploc bag inside a terra-cotta flowerpot. It was on a Dolle's keychain. Dolle's is an icon on the Rehoboth Beach boardwalk. Saltwater taffy is their specialty, although they make caramel popcorn and other beachy treats. Janine and I both worked there when we were in high school and college.

Fingering the key, I went up the steps, half carrying, half dragging my bag. It didn't seem this heavy when I put it in the car.

The beach cottage was built, circa 1935, on pilings that had saved it from more than one hurricane and nor'easter. Janine grew up in this house; lived here until she was fourteen. Her maternal great-grandparents had built it.

It seemed like a long way up the steps, and I was out of breath by the time I reached the top. A lousy dozen steps. I panted, trying desperately to fill my lungs with oxygen, knowing my lungs wouldn't cooperate. I had portable oxygen in the car. "Just in case," said my oncologist. "Just in case," said my mother. I was afraid I was going to need it.

Technically, I have thyroid cancer, but those Machiavellian cancer cells had traveled down into my lungs. I was breathing at about forty-one percent capacity right now. It beat not breathing at all. At night, I used nebulizer treatments, which relaxed the muscles around my airways and made it easier to breathe. I've been putting off the supplemental oxygen albatross as long as I can, knowing my reliance on it was inevitable.

Leaning on the rail, I took long, slow, deep breaths. Shallow breathing didn't work; it used only the top half of the lungs. Slowly, I walked across the deck to the back door. A foot seemed like a mile. The door, an oasis. I opened the screen door and slipped the key into the doorknob. Then I hesitated.

Did I really want to do this? Did I really need to scrape the scabs off these wounds *yet again?*

It wasn't too late to cancel. I could play the Cancer Card and go home to my cozy little college town of Newark, Delaware. I could call my twin daughters, play the Cancer Card *again*, and insist they stay with me for the summer instead of their father. I could do that. I'm dying. I'd learned since my diagnosis that I could pretty much do and say anything I wanted and people would put up with it. But I couldn't do this to my friends or my daughters because . . . because they have to go on living when I'm gone.

Jared and I have the typical custody arrangement; our seventeen-year-olds live with me during the school year. They see their dad every other weekend, a few weeknights a month, and he gets them for most of the summer. He lives in Rehoboth Beach, within biking distance of the boardwalk. I think that when we divorced four years ago, he realized that living in a cool place might make the difference between seeing his girls once they got older and not seeing them at all. He wasn't smart about a lot of things that year (like cheating on me with the cashier from Home Depot), but I give him credit—he thought through his move to the beach before he made it. He used to do construction in Wilmington. Now he has his own company in Rehoboth Beach. He's doing well, well enough to pay hefty child support for our girls and keep his new wife and baby comfortable. The baby's name is Peaches. Honest to God. It's on the birth certificate. Who names a baby *Peaches?*

I'm digressing again. I'd like to say it was the drugs I'm taking that make my thoughts wander, but that would be a lie. Ask my staff at the University of Delaware, where I used to be the head librarian. (Theoretically, I'm on *hiatus*. That's what employers say when they let you go home to die.) I was like this before I had an entire pillbox of medicine to take every day.

I turned the key and pushed the door open. I was assaulted by stale air and crushing memories. I picked up my bag and stepped into the laundry room that would soon be a catchall for stinky running shoes, wet bathing suits, *and* dirty clothes. It was late in the day, and the yellowing curtains over the window made the room dim.

Panic fluttered in my chest. I steadied myself against the washing machine. I felt a little dizzy. Weak-kneed. I wanted to blame that on the cancer, too. Couldn't. Every summer I felt this way the first time I stepped into this house.

I closed my eyes.

Every year, I wanted to slough off this feeling as quickly as possible, but not today. Today, I stood there and took in the whole experience: the flutter of my pulse, the faint nausea, the clammy palms. Because, feeling pain . . . feeling fear, I'd learned, meant I was still alive.

I'll never do this again, I thought. *I'll never walk into this house for the first time. I'll never feel the way I'm feeling at this instant.*

It passed. Quicker than you'd think it would. Another thing I've learned over the last year is how adaptable human beings are. What seems unimaginable quickly becomes perfectly acceptable. The first time I said, "I'm dying," I could barely manage the words; now, I say it like I'm telling the time.

I exhaled slowly. I inhaled.

Again.

I opened my eyes. I grabbed my bag, walked through the kitchen into the big living room (that also served as the dining room), and dropped it near the staircase. It was hot in the house. Did I turn on the air or try the windows first?

I went to the floor-to-ceiling windows that ran along the front of the house, and I pushed back the long, white tulle curtains. I unlocked and slid open the windows and let the cool breeze from the ocean fill the stifling room. The late afternoon sun cast shadows on the front deck. I gazed out over the dunes, speckled with dry sea grass, intersected by a zigzagging sand fence. The ocean rippled. Pulsed. I heard the waves hit the shore. I felt them. I closed my eyes, and I really *felt* them.

This moment passed, too. I didn't feel the waves anymore. I just felt silly standing there with my eyes shut.

I reached for the nearest dustcover, a pink, flowered sheet. I gave it a yank and uncovered a rocking chair. I moved from piece of furniture to piece of furniture. The living room, like the rest of the cottage, was decorated in shabby chic. It had been a group effort. I bought the white end tables and coffee table at a yard sale years ago. Janine contributed the two matching Ikea couches, covered in unbleached canvas. An ex-girlfriend had bought them. Janine didn't want them at her place, but she wouldn't just donate them to the Salvation Army, either. They were practically new.

I pulled a blue sheet off a faded, flowered recliner. I have no idea where it came from, but it has been here for years. I tossed the sheet in the growing pile on the floor and seriously considered sitting down in the chair. It looked so comfy, so inviting. But if I sat, I was afraid I wouldn't get up again today. Usually my energy petered out by three. It was four thirty, and I was still feeling pretty . . . okay.

I went to the fireplace and opened the flue, afraid if I didn't do it now, no one else would think of it and the house would fill up with smoke when we lit a fire some night. It had happened the previous year. Maybe the year before that, too. The hinges screeched, the flue opened, and I rubbed my sooty hand on my jeans.

Lined up across the mantel, at nose height, were framed photographs of us. The Fantastic Four. There was one of us in the seventh grade. Career Day. My mom took it. I reached for the five-by-seven photograph in a WE WERE FRIENDS frame.

Lilly was wearing a white lab coat and the school nurse's stethoscope. She couldn't get into medical school; she became an optometrist. Janine was dressed like a cowgirl, but she was wearing a shiny sheriff's badge; now she wore a police badge. I studied myself in the photo: dark red hair pulled into a loose ponytail. Not unattractive looking, just . . . awkward.

I miss my hair. I resent my hair loss. It's petty, I know, considering the fact that I'm about to lose my life, but I miss it anyway, and still spent too much time obsessing over it.

In the photo, I was wearing some sort of Lois Lane getup and holding a pen and a pad of paper. I had wanted to be a novelist back then, but I hadn't known how to portray that. My mom had made me a newspaper reporter instead. At the time, I remember thinking it was a dumb idea but had gone with it for lack of a better one at seven a.m. the morning of Career Day.

Aurora, with her blond hair, was at the very edge of the frame, wearing her school uniform, a French beret, and sporting a tiny black mustache she'd drawn above her upper lip with eyeliner. She'd wanted to be an artist. Her dream had come true. Aurora always got what she wanted.

I rubbed the dust off the top of the frame with my finger and put it back on the mantel. There was more dust. There were more pictures, pictures taken after August 1986. After Buddy died. After Janine cut her hair. After Lilly lost her mom. After I became the ordinary person I never wanted to be. But I didn't linger there any longer. We'd be here a month; there would be plenty of time to dust and reminisce.

I grabbed my duffel bag to take it into the front bedroom. We'd already agreed, in e-mails going back and forth, that I'd sleep here. Janine's parents' bedroom. It looked nothing like it did when *he* slept here, but it still creeped me out. I would rather have slept upstairs in the little room Lilly and I had always shared. But the girls were right; that made no sense. Stairs and cancerous lungs—oil and water. I left my bag on the floor, just inside the doorway. I went back into the living room and stared up the staircase. I didn't know why, but I wanted to go up. Now? Later?

Now.

I took two more deep breaths and slowly attacked the stairs, one step at a time. I longed for the days when I could run up these stairs. Hell, two summers ago I'd chased Lilly up, then back down, when she stole my cell phone and was reading sexts from my then-boyfriend aloud to the others. The relationship hadn't lasted. In retrospect, I realized I hadn't liked him as much as I had liked the *idea* of him. It was a big deal when he broke up with me. Not such a big deal now.

My chest was tight. I had to pause. I felt as if I was physically breathing, but there wasn't enough oxygen getting to my cells. *Was this what it would feel like to suffocate?* That was what everyone with tumors in their lungs feared. Suffocating. It's the way it happens—lung cancer death—though no one wants to come out and say it. That's the kind of information you find on the trusty Internet.

I put one foot up on the next step. I leaned heavily on the rail. I told myself I was almost there. A lie. I kept going.

There were three bedrooms and a bath on the second floor. My intention, halfway up the stairs, had been to open all the rooms. But as I struggled to reach the landing I thought that maybe I'd wait until morning when I was more rested. I still had to get the food and booze and my nebulizer bag out of the car. And I was badly in need of a glass of pinot grigio. I'm not supposed to be drinking with my medication, but I have a glass of wine when I feel like it. Why not? What's it going to do? Kill me?

I was really sucking wind by the time I reached the top of the staircase. It was so damned hot. Hotter upstairs than down. The whole heat rises thing, I guess.

I bent over, hands on my knees, as if I'd run a seven-minute mile.

The thought made me laugh. Or I would have laughed if I could have gotten enough air. Never in my life, even when I was at my fittest and considered myself a runner, could I have run a seven-minute mile. I leaned against the big, square, white newel post. My hand hit the carved cap on the top, and I knocked it off. It rolled across the hardwood floor and came to rest against the wall near the first bedroom door. I stared at the cap. It seemed so far away.

It's been unattached for as long as I've been coming here. I'd knocked it down the hall, down the steps. I wondered why none of us ever got some wood glue and reattached it.

I caught my breath, which seemed to take forever, then walked over to the newel cap and slowly leaned over to pick it up off the floor. I returned it to its rightful place, slipping the stripped threads of the post over the screw. How many times had I touched this cap? How many times more would I do it?

It was weird to constantly see things in finite terms where I had once seen them in infinite ones.

As I went down the hall, I thought I heard a sound downstairs. I stopped. Listened. I didn't hear anything. The wind, maybe? Had I left the back door ajar?

I pushed open the door of the first bedroom. Janine's room. I flipped the switch on the wall, and the overhead light and two bedside lamps came on. For a second, I didn't see the pale blue walls and white trim or the blond wood floor. I saw the room as it was that night. Pink walls, beige carpet. I saw the bed against the wall to my right, not where it was now.

My gaze fell to the place on the floor where Janine's father had lain dead. I remembered what his blood smelled like. (Who knew blood had a smell?) How thick the puddle of blood seemed, the way it sat on top of the carpet rather than being absorbed. It had looked fake, like from a B movie.

It wasn't.

I swallowed hard. Fought the nausea. I had taken my medication two hours ago. Sometimes it made me nauseated. But it wasn't the cancer medication making me sick to my stomach right now; it was Buddy McCollister. Sergeant Buddy McCollister, Albany Beach Police Department.

I wasn't ready for this. I leaned against the doorframe. I thought I was, but I wasn't. I couldn't clean or make Janine's bed. I wondered if I should start with my own room downstairs.

I backed out the door, turning off the lights. But instead of going downstairs, I headed for the bedroom Lilly and I used to sleep in. I reached the bathroom. The door was open, the starfish shower curtain pulled back to expose the claw-foot bathtub and shower combination. I walked past the bathroom, past the next closed door. My hand was on the doorknob of our bedroom when I stopped. Something wasn't right. I retraced my steps. I went back to the bathroom and reached around to turn on the light. Nothing was amiss, except that there was a towel hanging on the towel rack. We never left towels out when we closed up. Dust. Mildew. I didn't know how long it had been since Janine or one of the others had been here, but we never left towels out or beds made. Maybe Janine had used the towel when she'd stopped by earlier in the week to turn on the hot water heater and the water. I fingered the turquoise towel. Was it damp? It couldn't be. It had to just be the humidity.

I caught a glimpse of my reflection in the old oval mirror over the sink. I barely recognized the woman looking back at me. I'd aged ten years in the last eighteen months. I was wearing a blue and green paisley head scarf—hippie style, not charwoman, mind you. I was wearing the silver starfish earrings my girls had given me and a green malachite pendant that hung beneath my thyroidectomy scar. Kind of classy.

But anyone who looked at me could see the big *C* on my face. My reddish brown eyebrows are penciled in. My eyelashes are barely existent—just a few stubbles. But my freckles are still there, and I could still see my old self in my green eyes. My red hair was always my best feature; I'd worn it long my whole life. Until it started falling out, in clumps. Now I think my eyes are my best feature. The greens and blues in the scarf played them up nicely. Somehow, I found a smile for myself.

I shut off the light and went back up the hall, passing Aurora's room, to reach the one Lilly and I always shared, at the end of the hall. I pushed it open tentatively. I flipped on the light switch. No lights came on, which was weird. I walked to the nightstand and turned the switch on the lamp, which was draped with a pretty scarf. The light came on. I grabbed the scarf, gave it a shake, and returned it to the shade. The walls were pale teal. I painted them three summers ago. My single bed, next to Lilly's, was new . . . new to me. Bought at a secondhand store and repainted the same summer. I loved my beach bed. It had a high headboard, and at the top was a carved, fluted seashell. I wished I could sleep in it tonight. Maybe I'd be the rebel for once and insist on sleeping here. But that wouldn't be fair to Lilly, to make her listen to me wheeze all night. And it wouldn't be fair to make one of the others sleep downstairs. In *his* room.

I yanked the white chenille bedspread off my bed, revealing the bare mattress, and tossed it out the door. I'd wash tonight . . . or maybe in the morning. As I turned back, my toe hit something under the bed. Something soft, but with form.

I lifted the dust ruffle and pulled out a navy rucksack. It looked like it had seen better days. It wasn't mine. I opened the bag: T-shirts, jeans, a wide-toothed comb, a toothbrush. I dropped the bag on the floor, suddenly afraid. Was someone staying in the house? A vagrant maybe? It happened. People know most of the houses along this beach are only occupied during the summer.

I listened carefully, wondering if I just heard something downstairs again. Water running?

I was suddenly dry-mouthed. My heart was pounding. Where was my cell phone? Did I leave it on the car seat? In my handbag? Did I lay it down somewhere downstairs? I couldn't remember. I always kept my cell phone with me . . . in case one of my daughters needed me. In case I needed to call 911. Because I'm dying.

I patted the front pockets of my jeans that hung on my hips. No phone. My back pockets. No phone in the left . . . but in the right, a lump. I almost sighed I was so relieved. I stepped quietly into the hall. Listened.

I didn't hear a thing . . . except for my own labored breathing.

I walked down the hall. Still nothing. I stopped at the top of the steps and listened, my iPhone poised. I was ready to dial 911.

I heard nothing. I was beginning to wonder if I imagined the sounds. There was probably an explanation for the rucksack under my bed. I crept down the staircase. Down was easier than up.

There was no one there. There was no homeless guy camping in the house, I told myself. That was silly. I'd just go out to the car, get the rest of the things, and lock up for the night.

The final step at the bottom of the staircase squeaked. I froze. Nothing.

I walked through the living room, past the downstairs bathroom, into the kitchen. My gaze went first to the back door in the laundry room. It was closed. I was so relieved that it took me a split second to realize I wasn't alone in the kitchen.

The dark figure, backlit by the sunlight filtering through the kitchen window, turned toward me. I almost dropped my phone as I started to thumb the numbers on the keypad. Then I saw her face. "Aurora!" I gasped. My hand went to my chest. My heart was pounding.

She held open her arms, an amber bottle of beer in one hand. "Expecting someone else?"

I laughed, but I wanted to cry. I hadn't seen Aurora since April; she'd been out of the country. We talked on the phone, we Face-Timed occasionally, but it wasn't the same thing. I'd missed her so much. Missed her strength, the enormous presence she brought to a room. I hurled myself into her arms.

Everything would be all right now. I knew it in my heart's core, "*ay, in my heart of heart*" (Shakespeare's words, not mine). I could do anything if I had Aurora at my side. I could even die.

She hugged me, and I held on to her tightly. I didn't care that she was still wet from her swim. Her body was cool against my skin.

"How are you, babe?" she murmured against my temple. Aurora was tall. Taller than me, taller than any of us. She was a six-foot blond Amazon. "You're wasting away."

I didn't tell her that weight loss was the one thing I secretly liked about having cancer. It was too embarrassing to admit, even to my best friends. "I'm okay."

She smelled of the ocean, briny and clean. "Yeah?" she asked, still hugging me against her wet body. She was wearing a red one-piece swimsuit she'd had since she was a lifeguard when we were in college. I couldn't believe she could still fit in the suit. Almost more unbelievable was that she still had it, twenty-some years later. I didn't get it. She could afford to buy a new swimsuit for every day of the year. She could buy a suit, wear it once, and toss it. Aurora is what my mother calls *filthy rich;* Mom speaks the phrase as if it's something deplorable. I wouldn't mind trying it. Especially now, with my timer about to go off.

Aurora stepped back and tugged off her faded blue swim cap; long, shiny blond hair fell down her back. She tossed the cap on the counter. Her movements were graceful; everything was art with Aurora. She could have been a dancer.

She cocked her head and pointed with the beer bottle. "What's with the scarf?"

My hand went to my head. It seemed like a silly question. I whispered, "I'm bald." My gaze locked with hers. She had big, brown, expressive eyes. You didn't expect brown eyes from a blonde.

"Let me see."

I shook my head, feeling the contours of my skull beneath my fingertips. "No."

"Oh, come on. It's me. You have to show *me*. You have to show *us*." She pursed her perfectly pink, full lips. Natural. No Juvé-derm injections. "It's not like you're going to go around wearing a scarf day and night for the next month."

Honestly, I had considered it.

For me, my baldness was the ultimate substantiation of my vulnerability. I didn't want to be vulnerable anymore. I didn't want to feel scared anymore. I wanted to feel like Aurora must feel every day of her life. Invincible.

Aurora held my gaze for a long moment, then took a step toward me again. "Come on," she whispered, covering the hand on my head with hers.

I looked down at the floor.

"Just a peek," she cajoled, putting pressure on my hand. "I'll tell you if it's awful. You know I will."

*True story,* as my daughters would say. Aurora was the one who told me not to marry Jared; she said he'd be unfaithful. She told me not to major in literature in college because I would never become a writer that way. She also told me when it was time to start dyeing the gray in my red hair. And when to call it quits on the marriage she'd warned me against years before. And she never said, "I told you so." Never once. I trusted Aurora. Above all things, she was honest. Even when it hurt.

I let her push the scarf off the back of my head. I balled it in my fist and dropped my hand to my side. I felt like I was standing naked, with my C-section belly scar and deflated breasts in front of a stranger.

Aurora looked at me, smiling. She rubbed her palm over my almost-shiny pate. "It's already growing back in."

I tried to smile. I tried to be thankful. *Whoopee.* I may not be bald by the time I'm laid in my coffin.

"I like it." Aurora gave my head a final rub as if it were a genie lamp. "You have a nicely shaped head," she added.

I rolled my eyes. "Am I supposed to thank you for that?"

She shrugged. Sipped her beer. The brown bottle was sweaty in her hand. I bet that if I opened the refrigerator, there would be half a case of Dogfish Head 60 Minute IPA inside. There wouldn't be any food, beyond a hunk of aged cheese and some expensive bubbly water, but there would be plenty of microbrewed beer.

"It's coming in red. You know I'd give anything to naturally have hair the color of yours," she said.

She and I have had this discussion a million times over the years. She says she always wished she had a curvy body and auburn hair like me. I find that hard to believe. Who wouldn't die to have her natural thinness and gorgeous blond hair? Okay . . . maybe not . . . die.

Funny how your perspective changes.

"What are you doing here already?" I slipped the scarf back on and adjusted it. I still had to go out to the car and get my things. I certainly wasn't going to let the neighbors see my bald head. "You're not supposed to be here until tomorrow."

I was a little disappointed I wouldn't have time to myself now. When you're dying, people tend to gang up on you. I feel like I'm never alone. My girls, my mom and dad, my neighbors, my colleagues, they want to surround me day and night. They don't want me to be alone in my last hours, I suppose. And maybe I don't either, but I would like to catch my breath once in a while. Maybe pee without someone knocking on the bathroom door and asking if I'm okay.

"I was bored with the scene in Rome," Aurora told me with a sigh only the truly privileged could emit. "I got here Monday."

So the towel in the bathroom *was* damp. I wondered why her rucksack was in my old bedroom rather than hers, and why she'd been sleeping in my bed without any sheets, but I didn't ask. I found it interesting that Aurora had been here five days and there was no more evidence of her presence in the house than a damp towel and a tiny bag. No car. Who knows how she got here? (Probably hitchhiked. She did it all the time. So far, no Dean Koontz crazies have kidnapped her and held her underground in a beer barrel.) She was rich, but no one would ever know it. She was a vagabond. She rented out warehouses for studios, slept in hotels or on people's couches. No fancy cars. Few jewels. No property. I had no clue what she did with her money.

"Bored with the scene in Rome," I repeated, walking over to the sink to open the window over it. The kitchen was stifling. I wondered how she'd stayed in the house for five days with the windows closed and the air-conditioning off, but I didn't ask that, either. I was too preoccupied with the Rome pronouncement.

I've never been to Rome; I'll never go. We talked about taking a trip to Italy, together, the four us, but it never happened. It never will happen now, will it? I opened my arms wide, gesturing wildly with my final words, trying to understand her. "You were *bored* with Rome?"

"I needed time alone. To think. I've got a new project simmering." She tapped her temple and then downed the rest of the beer. "A commissioned work. An enormous chandelier piece. For the Museum of Fine Arts in Boston." She wrinkled her pert nose. "Or maybe it's Chicago. I don't remember what my agent said."

Aurora is an internationally celebrated sculptor. I mean she's *big*, like cover of *Juxtapoz* magazine big. Her medium is metal, her tool of trade an oxyacetylene torch. She works in her studio in hot pants, a leather apron, and a welding mask that looks like a medieval torture device. Or some kind of crazy sex game mask. She creates enormous sculptures of mixed metals to stand in reception areas of corporate buildings and in parks. Her work amazes me and scares me a little. It's beautiful and brilliant, but defies interpretation by my pea-sized librarian's brain.

"You've been sleeping here all week?" I asked. "You should have called me. Mia and Maura have already been down here with their father for two weeks. I've been sitting at home watching eight seasons of *Dexter*. I could have come sooner."

She didn't answer me. She's like that. She just doesn't answer questions she doesn't want to. She also hangs up without saying good-bye and goes to bed without a good night. I like to think it's the artsy dreamer in her; my mother says she's just plain rude. Can't remember if I said this—Mom doesn't like Aurora. Never has. When we were sixteen, Aurora was arrested for smoking weed in a Dunkin' Donuts while drinking a latte. Not even in the bathroom. Right at the table. My mother decided I shouldn't associate with Aurora anymore. She tried to forbid me to see her. It didn't work.

I'm doing it again. Digressing.

"You just get here?" Aurora opened the cabinet under the sink and tossed the empty bottle into a bucket. It clinked against other bottles. Beer for sure. Probably a gin bottle, if she's been here since Monday. "Stuff in your car?" she asked.

"Yeah. You mind getting it?" I plopped down on a kitchen stool, chest tight. I took a couple of deep breaths. "I've got groceries and wine. I'll make you dinner," I called after her, but she was already on her way out the door.

Aurora carried everything in. She put away the groceries and lined up the bottles of wine on the counter near the refrigerator. Our makeshift bar since the days when we had to acquire our alcohol illegally. She even took the pillows I brought from home and the black nylon case with my nebulizer to the bedroom. She grabbed a quick shower upstairs, but she was down in ten minutes. Speed showering; she couldn't possibly have shaved.

Aurora didn't let me do anything but open a bottle of pinot grigio and pour a glass for each of us. We chatted while she made a veggie stir-fry. At first, we talked about unimportant stuff. Not *unimportant*, exactly. Everything is important to me now. But the stuff that isn't emotionally charged. Even though we're best friends, more than best friends, it always takes a little while, after we've been apart, to get warmed up.

Aurora didn't mention my cancer while she'd chopped vegetables, and I didn't bring it up. It was nice. Almost as if I didn't have cancer. At least for a few minutes. We talked about how my girls did in school this year, and I showed her their junior prom pictures on my iPhone. Aurora told me about a Portuguese sculptor she dated in Rome. I learned that his name was Fortunato and that he'd had a big wang. Her word, not mine.

When the stir-fry was ready, we carried the plates, our glasses, and the bottle of wine (we were on our second glass by then) out onto the front porch. There was a cool breeze coming in off the ocean; there almost always was. I sat in a big Adirondack chair. My Adirondack. There were four of them lined along the front porch, one for each of us. Mine was bright green. Aurora's was white.

She refilled our glasses, and we both sat back to enjoy our dinner: asparagus, snow peas, hearts of palm, mushrooms, and zucchini, all in a thickened peppery vegetable broth.

"Lilly texted earlier. She'll be here by noon tomorrow," I said.

"She driving over alone"—Aurora stabbed a mushroom with the tines of her fork—"or is *he* bringing her?"

*He,* meaning her husband. They've been married nine years, but Aurora doesn't like Matthew any better now than when we met him. She finds him stuffy and boring. Aurora thinks he stifles Lilly. That he keeps her from reaching her full potential. I disagree. Not all of us can be famous, globe-trotting artists sleeping with the Fortunatos of the world. Some of us have to be librarians, cops, and in Lilly's case, optometrists. I like Matt. He's good to her. A hell of a lot better to her than her first husband was.

"I assume she's driving over herself." Lilly lived in Annapolis. She and Matt, also an optometrist (they met at a convention), have an upscale office there. "And Janine will be here right after work tomorrow. No later than six, she said."

While we're all equally close, I'm the *administrator* of the group. I'm the one who keeps everyone connected with texts, e-mails, and phone calls. I always make the arrangements when we get together. I coordinate arrival and departure times. I make the dinner reservations and settle minor disputes.

Aurora set down her plate and reached for her glass. She'd barely touched her food. "We can talk about it if you want. Get the clumsiness out of the way."

I looked up from my plate, having no idea what she was talking about . . . for a second. Then I smiled. "You're a funny one."

She looked at me from over the rim of her glass, tipped it, and drank. She was wearing a tight white T-shirt with something in Italian on it (I don't speak Italian. I can manage a little conversational *Español,* but that's it. I was always going to learn to speak Italian. Once I finished my doctorate in library science. Once Mia and Maura were older. Guess I put it off too long.) and a pair of baggy men's athletic shorts. Her hair was still damp from her shower, her face bare of makeup.

"So you want to talk about it or not?" she prodded. "You don't have to. We're going to have to rehash it all tomorrow night. But I thought you might—"

"Want to take a *dry run?* Is that what you're asking me?" I've set my plate aside. I thought I was hungry, but after a few bites, I wasn't. The new medication did that to me. She drew her knees up to her chest. "Now who's the funny one?" She gazed out over the dunes. She looked so serious.

Together, we watched the waves tumble in, one after the other. The tide was coming in. From the waterline on the beach, in relationship to the little picket fence in the dunes, I guessed that high tide would be in another two hours. Nine-ish. I made a mental note. I marked my days here at the beach house by the rise and fall of the tides.

I remembered, from a family vacation in Hatteras, my dad showing me a tide chart. I was nine or ten. He explained how the gravitational attraction of the moon caused the ocean to bulge toward the moon and how, on the other side of the world, it was doing the same thing. There are twelve hours and twenty-five minutes between each high tide. It would be low tide around three tomorrow.

My gaze caught Aurora's. She was watching me now. Waiting.

"We don't have to talk about it," I said. But I realized that I did want to. Maybe I *did* need a dry run. Tomorrow night would be the first time we'd all been together since the death knell officially began. Last summer we'd all been so hopeful. We thought I just had a measly little case of thyroid cancer in my thyroid.

Tomorrow there would be tears. A flood of tears . . . hugs all around . . . several times. Maybe I needed to tell the story without the tears. This was something else I can always count on with Aurora; she wouldn't dissolve. I couldn't decide if that was because she was such a selfish person or such an unselfish person. Could you be both?

Aurora sat back to listen.

"Not a lot to say." I feel like I've told this story a million times.

"After I had my thyroid removed, we thought I might be in the clear. I wasn't. The cancer cells drifted into my lungs," I explained. They say it that way. *Drifted.* Like it wasn't an assault.

I was quiet for a minute. So was Aurora. I went on. "It's thyroid cancer, but in my lungs. The scans look crazy. Little starbursts of tumors, filling my lungs." I took a sip of wine. "That's what's making it hard for me to breathe. The tumors are filling up the space where air should go. There's no cure. No treatment. Eventually the tumors will fill my lungs and then . . . then they'll kill me," I added matter-of-factly.

"What about the nuclear radiation pill you took when it was in your throat?" she asked.

I shook my head. "A no-go. Thyroid cancer cells are, apparently, tricky. They know how to morph or something. I still don't quite understand." I raised my hand and let it fall. "The cancer cells are somehow different now that they're in my lungs. The nuclear stuff can't find them, so it can't stick to them, so it can't kill them."

"Fuckers," Aurora muttered.

I smiled.

"So now?"

"So now, the doctors will make me *comfortable* until I die." I exhaled, looking into my nearly empty glass. Aurora gave me a refill. We were both quiet. Another thing I've always loved about Aurora. She doesn't feel the need to constantly talk.

I swirled my wine and watched it form a tidal pool in my glass. I sipped it. I was waiting for the question *How long?* How long do you have to live? How long before I need a dress for your funeral?

But Aurora didn't ask. She just gazed out at the ocean. She probably already had an appropriate black dress.

I took a deep breath and relaxed in my chair. The sun wouldn't set for more than an hour, but it was well behind us now and the sky was darkening.

After what seemed like a very long time, Aurora said, "I'd take it from you if I could." Again she was quiet. Then, "Your cancer."

My eyes felt scratchy behind the lids. I'm not a crier. What tears I had, I tell people, I've already cried. As if we're born with a certain number of tears in our eyes, like eggs in our ovaries. Maybe I was just afraid that if I started crying now, I'd never stop. I didn't want to live out the rest of my days, however many there were, crying.

"I'd die for you," Aurora said. "I'd do it. I wish I *could* do it," she added softly.

"I know."

My mother said the same thing when I told her that I was terminal. She cried buckets. She said it wasn't fair that she was old and useless and I was still young, with children to raise. But there was something different about Aurora's tone when she told me that. It was as if . . . she was more than willing to die, that she . . . I don't know . . . she really wanted to. Which made no sense. She had a perfect life: famous, rich . . . and then there was Fortunato and his wang.

I realized my thoughts weren't making sense. It was probably the wine. I was feeling tipsy. The combination of the wine and the meds. I was most definitely not supposed to have three glasses.

I looked at Aurora. She seemed so sad.

This was one of the most difficult things for me about having cancer. I felt as if I were making so many people sad. Hurting so many people. Me, I got to die. They—those I love—have to stay. They have to carry my death with them for many years to come.

"I . . . haven't told anyone this," I heard myself say. "But . . . I'm taking part in a drug trial."

She shifted her attention to me again.

"At UPenn." I set my glass down. "They're hoping the drug will slow the growth of the tumors. Maybe even reduce their size."

Aurora unfolded her long legs and stood, holding a finger up, telling me to hold that thought.

She was back in two minutes with another bottle of wine and the corkscrew. "So the doctors have had good luck with this drug?"

I shook my head. "It's a drug *trial*, meaning the doctors are basically taking a wild stab in the dark and need some human guinea pigs." I stopped and started again. "Not exactly. The whole process for creating a drug and getting it approved by the FDA is very complicated and takes years. There's been some evidence—in lab rats probably—that this drug I'm taking might have an effect on this type of cancer growth."

"So it might work?" she asked.

"Someday. For someone. I know it's too late for me, but I agreed to be a part of the study because I like the idea of possibly helping someone else, someday."

"Why haven't you told anyone?" she asked as she stripped the foil from around the cork.

"I can't."

She waited.

"Nothing else has worked, Aurora. This isn't going to work. It's a drug trial, not a cure." I shook my head. "I can't tell you how many second opinions I've gotten. How many oncologists I've seen. I can't do that to my parents, to my girls. I can't do it to Lilly and Janine. I can't give them hope, not when there is none."

Aurora held the wine bottle between her bare thighs and used a simple plastic corkscrew—the kind you picked up at the counter in the liquor store and carried in your purse. She pulled on the cork, and it came free with a delicious *pop*. "But you can crush *my* hope?"

"I'm sorry." I glanced at my hands resting in my lap. "It's just that you're the strong one. The brave one. I guess . . . I needed to tell someone, and I know you . . . you won't act crazy and start planning my fiftieth birthday or anything."

She raised the bottle to offer me another glass.

I covered my glass with my hand. I'd had enough. "I'm sorry," I said again. Now I felt bad. "I didn't mean to dump this on you."

I hesitated and went on. "Please don't tell them. Lilly and Janine. Or my girls."

"You know I won't."

"I know." I watched her pour herself another full glass of wine. And these were big glasses. The kind without the stems. "You're good with secrets. You never told anyone I made out with Kandy Delacroix at her sixteenth birthday party."

Aurora grinned. Raised her glass in toast. "That's because I made out with her that night, too."

I laughed. Hard. The kind of laugh that comes from deep in your belly. I didn't know why that delighted me, but it did. We were sixteen. We weren't lesbians; we were just *exploring our sexuality*. And our drinking limits. I wondered if either of my daughters has ever made out with a girl. I knew I'll never be able to ask them. We get along well, for a dying mother and her daughters, but there were lines we will never cross. Asking them if they ever kissed a girl would be over the line.

I laughed until tears came to my eyes. "I'll be right back," I said, getting out of my chair. I needed to use the bathroom.

"Then maybe a walk on the beach?" Aurora's dark eyes were on mine again.

"A *short* walk. Maybe just down to the water. I'm not much of a walker these days."

Aurora rose, glass in hand. She had already drunk half of it. "I'll carry you. If you get too tired."

I grinned, resting my hand on the doorjamb. "I know."

## ✎ 2 ✍

# Aurora

She's dying. *Stroke. Glide.*
She's really dying. *Stroke. Glide.*
I could see it. *Stroke. Glide.*
Her bald head. *Stroke. Glide.*
I lifted my head to breathe deeply. The tangy, ionized air filled my lungs.
My face hit the cold ocean water again.
But it wasn't her hair. *Stroke. Glide.*
It was her eyes. *Stroke. Glide.*
I saw it in her eyes. *Stroke. Glide.*
McKenzie was really dying. *Stroke.*
I breathed again.
My strokes were always choppy when I first hit the water. I was more a crawler than a breaststroker, but tonight, I was feeling it. Needing it.
Slowly, I found my rhythm. My breath. I cut through the dark water, under the dark sky. I was fifty feet off the shoreline. Invisible in the darkness. I liked the invisibility.
*McKenzie was going to die.* The thought drifted from my head, down to my shoulders. I pulled at the water, and the thought drifted out from my fingertips.

*Well, fuck me.* McKenzie was really going to die.

*And then how would I live?*

For a moment I let my emotions wash over me like the salt water. The pain. The fear. Sadness so deep that it took my breath away. But I could only hold on to the feelings for a second and then they're gone. Not my own anymore. They drifted below to the great deep.

Everyone died sometime, I told myself. I was going to die.

I closed my eyes. I pulled myself through the water. I tasted the salt in my mouth. It stung my eyes, even with goggles on. *Stroke. Glide. Stroke. Glide.*

And I did it again.

I swam faster. Lifting myself in and out of the water, I propelled myself through the dark, cold water. The ocean was the only place where I could really think.

I dove off the yacht in the Venice lagoon. Pretty ballsy. Even for me. It was probably close to a mile swim. Which wouldn't have been a big deal except that I had been drunk and sleep-deprived. And I might have done a line of coke. I'm not sure, even now. It was a miracle I had made it to shore without being chopped up by a boat's propeller.

I wondered what Fortunato and his brother thought. When they came back to the cabin in their black leather pants and masks. Found me gone. Not in the bathroom. Not up on the deck. Gone. Over the side. Into the dark, silky water.

I laughed at the idea and gagged and spit. Broke my stroke. Picked it up again.

I could have died. In that filthy water that night. Christ knew what was in that water. Sharks, probably.

But I couldn't have stayed on the yacht. Not with the human sharks. They were way too coked out. I had let things go too far. Kinky sex was one thing. *That,* what they wanted, was another.

I could have died on that boat. It had been smarter to risk it with the sharks and the boat propellers.

McKenzie was going to die.

If I had died on the yacht, would McKenzie have been spared?
*Stroke. Glide. Stroke. Glide.*
I did it again and again and again.
I wondered how far I'd swum. How much time has passed.
McKenzie would be pissed if she woke up and found me gone
from the house in the middle of the night. Maybe even scared.

But she knows that I have to swim. I swim or die.

# ❦ 3 ❧

# McKenzie

My one-piece swimsuit (dark blue—I was living on the wild side two summers ago when I bought blue instead of black) was a little baggy in the butt and boobs, but I had put it on. It was the only one I had.

As I tugged on my University of Delaware ball cap, I wondered if I should get a new suit. There were plenty of boutiques and swim shops in Albany Beach. There was a nice boardwalk; smaller than in Rehoboth, but it might be fun to go shopping one day. The four of us, for old times' sake. But that would be a waste of money, wouldn't it? I always bought good clothing, intending to wear it for years. I wasn't buying new clothes these days.

It was ten forty when I walked into the kitchen. I'd slept in. Bad night. Aurora and I didn't go to bed until one. Then, like every night, my alarm went off on my phone at three a.m. and I took my drug trial medication. It had to be taken on an empty stomach at least an hour after I've eaten, with no food for an additional hour. Two doses, twelve hours apart. I fell asleep right after taking the harmless-looking little beige pills, but I woke an hour later feeling as if I'd had three bottles of wine instead of three glasses. The bed had been spinning. The waves of nausea washed over me. I didn't puke, which was a nice surprise. But I was deathly nauseated. It was so bad that the thought went through my head that if I walked (or more likely, *dragged* myself) out into the ocean, I'd be too weak to swim. I could just let myself go under. . . .

Wouldn't my mother love *that* phone call?

I'd never do it, of course. I wasn't suicidal. This cancer was going to kill me, but I'd fight it to my last breath. My last glass of wine. The last smiles of my daughters. The hugs of my friends who should have been born my sisters instead of the dud I got.

There was fresh coffee in a French press on the counter. Aurora. It smelled heavenly. A dark roast. She'd ground the beans this morning; the grinder was still on the counter, surrounded by little brown specks. But I didn't dare have a cup. Coffee doesn't stay down first thing in the morning. I needed tea, lots of hot, sweet tea. I added water to the teakettle and sat on a stool at the counter and waited for it to whistle.

I wondered where Aurora was. She wasn't in the house or out on the deck. I called to her when I got up. A morning swim maybe. Or she might be hitchhiking to Mexico City. Either way, she wouldn't leave a note.

I would never leave the house without leaving a note. Maybe it was the mommy in me.

The kettle whistled, and I took a tea bag from the box I'd brought. Barry's Irish Breakfast. Janine had sent it to me. I smiled. She'd sent me four boxes. She knew how I loved my morning tea.

"Mom, pick up. Mom, pick up," my phone chirped.

My daughters set my ringtones.

I checked the screen before answering. I heard the same ringtone no matter which girl was calling. An image of Mia, sticking her tongue out at me, was on my phone screen. "Hey," I said.

"Hey."

"So what are you guys up to today, Mia?"

"It's Maura."

I rolled my eyes. "I told you guys you can't do this to me. You know I can't tell your voices apart on the phone. My phone says *Mia's* calling. I expect *Mia*."

"I can't find my phone," Maura said.

I pushed the tea bag around with a spoon. The mug was in the shape of a woman's curvy torso, wearing a hot pink bikini. Not my favorite cup (we all have our favorites), but the one closest to me when I opened the cupboard.

"I warned you. I'm not paying for another phone," I told Maura. She'd had two since Christmas. I was lying, of course. If she needed a new iPhone, I'd buy it today. A new Maserati? Coming up. A dying mother's prerogative—to spoil her daughters.

"It's upstairs, somewhere," Maura said dismissively. "Or at Sondra's. Is everybody there yet? Aunt Aurora?" My girls, particularly Maura, adored Aurora. I knew Maura wished that she were their mom instead of me. She had as much as said so. Aurora was beautiful and cool. She sent good gifts: FAO Schwarz toys when they were younger, Italian shoes and handbags now. And she would never get cancer and die on them. "Aurora's here, but not here right now. Lilly will be here soon. Janine tonight. When are you coming over to say hi?"

"Mia! Mom's on the phone! You wanna talk to her?" my darling daughter hollered.

I held the phone a few inches from my ear.

"I don't know," Maura said, now talking to me again. "I work 'til ten tonight, Saturday, and Sunday night. We're going to Sondra's house tonight. So I guess Monday or Tuesday."

"Your father making you stick to your curfew?" I fished the tea bag from my mug. I added sugar but not milk. I couldn't do dairy, not since I started the drug trial. That was a guaranteed express train to Barfsville.

"Of course we're keeping our curfew." She was using her "sweet Maura" voice.

She was lying. I knew she was lying, but what was I going to do about it? Soon Jared would be her only parent. I had to trust him.

I closed my eyes for a second, standing too close to that abyss. Teetering on the edge of an emotional black hole I visit too often.

*You can't think about this*, I told myself. I repeated my mantra. *You can't think about it.*

I couldn't let worry about my girls dominate my last thoughts, my last days. Mia and Maura would be okay. I'd raised them for seventeen years. I could trust them, even if I couldn't trust their nitwit father. How could you trust a man who names his baby Peaches?

"Hey, Mom. Having fun?" It was Mia now. I only knew that because I heard her take the phone from her sister while complaining that there was no cream cheese for bagels.

"Hey, honey. I *am* having a good time." I took my cup of tea and walked out of the kitchen, into the living room. "It's just Aurora and me right now, but Lilly and Janine will be here later today."

"Aunt Janine bringing Fritz?"

Janine's German shepherd. Mia adored animals. They both did. But Mia wanted to be a vet. Maura, on the other hand, aspired to be an NBA player's wife. Needless to say, I was a little concerned about her career path.

"I imagine she is."

"But not Betsy?"

"Not Betsy," I repeated. Betsy had been Janine's partner for five years. They had broken up the previous summer, got back together, then broke up again. For good, this time. I thought.

"Guess she's really gone. That's too bad," Mia said. "I liked her. I thought she was good for Aunt Janine. She made her laugh. Aunt Janine doesn't laugh enough."

I walked out onto the porch, carrying my tea. "I liked her, too."

"Did Maura tell you about the guy she met last night? *Viktor*," she sang loudly, obviously for her sister's benefit . . . or detriment.

"I told you not to tell!" I heard Maura holler.

"He's one of the Russian guys who just started working with us at the pizza place. *Viktor*," Mia said again, using her Natasha Fatale accent.

I slid into my green chair and set my tea on the arm. I loved these moments with my girls. I kept thinking about how much I'd miss them. But would I? When I was dead, would I know I was dead? Who do you ask?

"If we're going to the beach, come on," Mia yelled to her sister. Then to me, "Gotta go, Mom. Call you tomorrow."

"Have a good day. Wear sunscreen," I said. "Make your sister wear sunscreen."

"Bye. Love you."

"Love you!" Maura echoed.

"I love you." I gripped the phone. "I love you both so much." My voice was shaky. Luckily, Mia had already hung up. She didn't hear my desperate words.

I sat on the porch and drank my tea. With no sign of Aurora, I went into my creepy bedroom to grab a book. I'd brought a whole canvas bag of them. In the year and a half since my cancer diagnosis, I'd been trying to make better choices about what I read. I'm a librarian, for God's sake. I should be reading the classics. Banned books. Books that have impacted the world. There are actually lists on the Internet of books you should read before you die.

I laid my hand on *Moby-Dick*, then a sweet Amish romance caught my eye. I hesitated, then chose the skinny paperback instead of the hefty, *loftier* book. It felt deliciously wicked to leave Melville behind.

I made another cup of tea, grabbed a towel from a basket in the living room, and returned to my chair on the porch. The towel smelled slightly mildewy. I made a mental note to throw the whole basket of towels in the washing machine later. Right now, that wasn't how I wanted to spend my limited energy.

It had come down to this in my day-to-day life, making decisions as to what was physically or emotionally worth my effort and what wasn't. People were worth the energy: my family, my friends, even the lady at the post office. Usually, *things* just didn't seem worth the bother.

I spread the suntan-lotion-stained blue and white towel on my chair and sat down. As I opened the cover of my book, I considered going down to the beach. But from here, the seventy-five yards seems like seventy-five miles. My *busy* morning had tired me. More likely the trip from home. The excitement of seeing Aurora again. The walk down to the ocean last night. And the long walk back, slogging through the sand.

I felt like I wanted to close my eyes and just enjoy the heat of the sun. But I was afraid to. Afraid I'd fall asleep and waste the morning. A morning I'd never get back again. Instead, I watched the way the sun sparkled off the ocean's surface and then I read the first page.

I didn't look up again from my book until I heard the sound of a car. I was too caught up with what was going on with the Yoder sisters in Kent County. I loved the series, partially because it took place locally, but mostly because the simple life of the Amish families took me far from my own life, which was definitely not simple. No Yoders were dying of cancer. At least not so far.

I put down my book, crossed the porch, and went down the steps. I followed the narrow footpath around the side of the house to the backyard, which was really just a sandy parking lot. I spotted Lilly's car, tugged at the brim of my ball cap, and hurried, hoping to surprise her.

I was the one who got the bigger surprise.

Lilly spotted me and grinned ear to ear. She's pretty, our Lilly. Maybe not beautiful in the conventional sense of the word, but she has an amazing presence. Heads turn when she walks by. Her mother was Japanese, her father is Somalian; she has gorgeous sun-kissed skin, black hair, and the blackest eyes. I always thought she looked like a shorter, healthier version of the supermodel Iman.

"McKenzie!" She threw open the door of her Mercedes and popped out in a sweet floral sundress and a baby bump.

A *big* baby bump!

I stopped so fast that I practically slid in the sand. I stared at her, unable to believe what I saw. I'm rarely struck speechless, but I was, just for a second.

Her hands went to her belly, and when I met her gaze, her dark eyes were brimming with tears.

"You're pregnant," I said, knowing it sounded stupid, considering that was obvious. I said it anyway.

"I'm pregnant," she repeated.

I opened my arms to meet her and hugged her tightly, reveling in the feel of her taut, round abdomen against my bony hips. For just a slip of a second, I remembered my own big belly and what it had felt like to carry life inside me. As I hugged her, I tried to feel that life, life that would carry on beyond not just me, but my Lilly, too.

She had to be six months along.

I found my voice. "Lilly, I'm so happy for you." Her arms were warm and secure around me. She smelled of gardenias. She'd started using the perfume years ago when I thought she was too young for the scent. Now, anytime I smelled gardenias, I thought of Lilly.

I savored her embrace another moment longer, then took a step back, grabbing her hand. Unwilling to let her go, yet. "Why didn't you tell me? I only saw you, what? A month ago? Six weeks?"

She slid her big, white sunglasses that were perched on her head down over her eyes. "I don't know how you didn't notice. I was already out of my clothes, covering it with tunics and baggy jackets. But two weeks ago, I really popped out. There's no way I can hide it now." She laughed and stroked her belly. "I don't know how those girls in that reality TV show have babies without knowing they're pregnant. I feel like I swallowed a watermelon."

Lilly was a Chatty Patty. Especially when she was nervous . . . or happy or sad. Lilly had always been the talker. She was the one who used to get detention all the time in school for talking.

Of course one of us would inevitably get detention, too, because she was always talking to us.

I looked into her eyes. I was a little disappointed that, for the last six months, I haven't had the enjoyment of knowing she was pregnant. I've had some pretty lousy days. Days when I could have used something cheerful to think about. Lilly had been trying to have a baby for years. First with husband number one, then husband number two. (Sounded like a game show.) Polycystic ovary syndrome. She's had five miscarriages. I thought she and the hubby were considering adoption.

"Why didn't you tell me?" I didn't mean to sound whiny, but it came off that way.

She made an apologetic grimace. "Didn't want to worry you, I guess. Not until I was sure." She searched my gaze, her eyes still teary. "I'm sorry, McKenzie. I didn't mean to hurt your feelings." She squeezed my fingers. "I was just . . . trying to protect you, I guess."

I took my hand from hers and smoothed her dress over her belly. I stared at it, at the wonder of it. "Boy or girl?"

"We don't know." She shook her head. Laughed. She was giddy. "We want it to be a surprise."

I was still rubbing her belly. I couldn't get over the magic of it. A baby. At forty-one years old. Our Lilly was going to have a baby. In all these years, I was the only one who'd ever had children. And kept them. I was immediately excited to have this connection with Lilly. Being mothers. And for a moment, the years that will follow flash in my head: being in the hospital when Lilly gave birth, going to the baby's birthday parties, comparing her experiences to mine so many years ago.

Then I remembered. Would I even make it to the baby's birth? What if I took a turn for the worse?

"When are you due?" I asked, refusing to feel sorry for myself right now. I'd do it later, when I was alone and could hide my shameful thoughts.

"I'm twenty-seven and a half weeks. Almost seven months. October fourth."

October fourth. *I can make it until then.* I wasn't even breathing that hard right now. With Lilly about to have a baby, I had to make it until then.

"Let me help you carry things in," I said.

She gave me a look, a *Lilly look*. "You shouldn't be carrying anything. You need to save your strength to get better."

Lilly didn't understand that I was dying. Or refused to believe it. I wasn't sure which. From the beginning of my diagnosis, she'd been Miss Polly Positive. Even when the lab results, lung biopsy, and specialist consultations turned out to be less than positive. I'd tried to talk to her about it, about my chances of survival. Or lack thereof. But she hadn't been willing to listen. And if I was honest with myself, I guess I hadn't been totally forthcoming with information, as of late. It was that guilt. Feeling guilty about disappointing her. Anyway, the good thing was that since she didn't think I was dying, she didn't treat me like I was. She babied me like I was sick, but not like I was headed out the door.

Of course I was going to have to talk to her about it. I had to make her understand. But I didn't want to. I was going to make her cry. Sob. Aurora and I talked about it last night. Aurora said I needed to make Lilly understand. She said I couldn't just die on Lilly without her knowing it was coming. I thought it was interesting that Aurora had put the burden on me. Why didn't *she* make Lilly understand?

I eyed Lilly through the lenses of my sunglasses. "I want to help you," I said. "I can carry a bag to the house." Now, I actually *was* feeling a little out of breath. If I could hear it in my voice, she could, too.

She looked at me for a second too long, then leaned into her car and pulled out an enormous handbag. Lilly had always had a thing for expensive handbags. And shoes. Sometimes, I got her hand-me-downs. The bag I was carrying now was an old bag of hers. But it wasn't this big.

Her white bag felt heavy as she dropped it into my arms. She grabbed a big wheely case from the backseat and lowered it to the ground. "We'll get the other stuff later. Am I the first one here?" She headed for the back steps, pulling her designer luggage behind her; she was light on her feet, despite the big belly.

"Nope. I got here last night. I wanted to open things up for everyone. I didn't get a lot done," I confessed, following her. "And Aurora was already here. She's been here for days. Apparently, *she got bored in Rome.*"

Lilly threw me a different *Lilly look;* she had a whole repertoire of them. She climbed the steps, dragging the suitcase. "Bored in Italy. We should all be so lucky." She grinned over her shoulder at me.

I grinned back.

"She here now?"

"Nope." I took the steps one at a time. Riser, foot, foot, riser, foot, foot. I was really winded. But I wasn't going to give in to it. I wasn't. My Lilly was here. With a bun in the oven. I wasn't going to crawl into my bed and pant the day away. "She was gone when I got up."

"Ah. So who knows when we'll see her? Janine?" Lilly held open the door for me and waited.

"Working today." I stopped at the top of the flight of steps and took a couple of breaths before forging ahead. "She'll be here as soon as she gets off."

Lilly led the way through the laundry room to the kitchen and left her suitcase next to the dishwasher. "I'll be right back. I have to pee. I'm not going to tell you how many times I had to stop between Annapolis and here."

When Lilly came back from the bathroom, she heaved a sigh of relief. "That's better. Anything to eat here? I'm starving."

"I brought a few things." I had set her handbag on the counter and taken a seat on the nearest stool. "I thought we'd plan some meals, then go to the market together. Tomorrow, maybe."

She opened the refrigerator. "Any word on that lawsuit

against Janine? She e-mailed me earlier in the week, but didn't mention it."

I shrugged. "She was cleared for duty. I can't imagine it will come to anything."

"It's so unfair. The whole abusive cop stereotype."

I wanted to say that there was almost always a reason for stereotypes, but I didn't. Lilly believed in the best in all of us, even when we didn't deserve it.

Lilly took out a ball of mozzarella cheese and a tub of pesto from the refrigerator. "You bring fresh tomatoes?"

"From the farmer's market." I pointed to a wooden bowl by the sink. Aurora had put the peaches, bananas, and tomatoes in it the night before while she was making dinner. I didn't tell Lilly that I didn't actually *go* to the farmers' market. A neighbor in Newark had brought them to me. That little detail wouldn't mean anything to her; for me, it was another chink in my armor. "Bread's in the cupboard."

"I really hope that's the end of it. The thing with Janine. Matt read in the paper that there were videos." She grabbed the bread and carried all the ingredients to the counter in front of me. "You know, like cell phone videos from witnesses on the beach." She retrieved two Fiesta dinnerware plates, one lavender, one yellow, and started making sandwiches. She didn't ask me if I wanted one. Lilly had always been the mother of the group. She mothered us all. "What kind of woman eight months pregnant would get into an altercation on the beach?"

I smiled at her innocence. "The kind who gets into fights with state troopers?"

"But to accuse Janine of police brutality." She shook her head. Her shoulder-length hair was pulled back in a sleek ponytail and bobbed back and forth. "That just seems crazy."

"Crazy times," I said. "I'm sure the woman is just looking to make a buck. I'm sure Janine's family history doesn't help."

Lilly sliced a tomato. "You think? That was a long time ago. And Buddy wasn't a state trooper. He was just a *town* cop."

"He was still a cop." He had been on unpaid leave that night. Waiting to go to trial for the attempted murder of the young black man he'd beaten half to death; the case was dropped when he died. Over the years, I had wondered about Lenard Moore. Did he go on to have a happy life? Become a schoolteacher? Or had he succumbed to a life of crime? Was he even alive?

"Chips?" Lilly asked cheerfully, a bag of Old Bay flavored potato chips in her hand.

"You better hide them from Janine or there won't be any." It was an old joke that wasn't really that funny, but we both laughed, and I wished Lilly's laughter would go on forever.

## ❦ 4 ❧

# Janine

I pulled in behind Lilly's fancy Mercedes, but I didn't cut the engine in my Jeep Cherokee. I just sat there. Hands on the steering wheel. I stared at the house through the mirrored lenses of my sunglasses. I sat there so long that Fritz stuck his nose between the seats and gave me a nudge.

"Back it up. Your breath smells like ass," I told the German shepherd that cost me more money than some people paid to adopt a kid. I bought him in Germany from a world-renowned breeder. Had him flown over as a puppy. Trained him myself. He was a perfect specimen: strong and agile. He was my best friend. At least after Mack, Aurora, and Lilly.

When that thought went through my head, I realized I still wasn't sure where Chris fit in. Was I in love or just lust? Jury was still out. And if I was in love, then what? Did I stay and try to make it work? Did I take off before I screwed it up the way I've screwed up every other romantic relationship I've ever been in?

So much to think about. So much, that sometimes I just wanted to put the heels of my hands to my temples and crush this stuff out of my head.

At my command, Fritz scooted back on the seat. He continued to watch me. He tilted his head the way a dog does when he thinks you're not following what he's saying. I knew what my dog was saying. He was giving me permission. He was telling me it would be okay if I backed out of the driveway. Went home. We lived in a town house five miles inland. Chris would be there.

Fritz knew I hated this house. I mother effing hated it. But I kept coming back. I couldn't let it go. Why couldn't I let it go?

Chris had a psychobabble explanation. Chris has a psychobabble explanation for just about everything. Being a psychologist and all. When we first started dating, I thought it was kind of hot. This morning, at breakfast, when we talked about my coming here and the feelings that would come with it . . . not so hot.

But right now. Being here. It felt worse than usual. Why did it feel worse? Because McKenzie was dying?

Too simple. It was something else. Something this bastard of a house had in store for us.

*God damn it!* I slammed my hand on the steering wheel. Fritz didn't even flinch. I hated feeling this way. I hated that Buddy could make me feel this way twenty-eight years later.

I looked up at the back deck. Closed my eyes. I had to go in. By now they knew I was here. Lilly was probably looking out the window. Waiting. Telling Aurora and McKenzie how hard it was for me to come in. Even after he'd been rotting in the ground all these years.

Mom and my brother. They had wanted to have Buddy cremated. I wouldn't let them do it. If I'd had my way, they wouldn't even have had him embalmed. At the time, when he died, I had liked the idea of worms eating his guts. How sick was that for a fourteen-year-old? At forty-two, I still liked the idea.

He deserved worse than he got.

Fritz whined, and I opened my eyes. Aurora was standing on the back deck. She leaned on the rail, her blond hair tumbling over one shoulder. She was looking down at me. My window was open, but she didn't call to me. Aurora, my angel. My protector.

"Come on, Fritzy," I said. I opened my door. His manners were too good to climb over the seat. (Which was more than I could say for some of my fellow troopers.) He waited for me to open the back door and jumped down. He was enormous: on the very top end of acceptable height and weight for his breed. He waited for me. I grabbed my old green duffel off the seat. It had my name stenciled on the side. J. McColl. They had left off the last five letters. That was the army for you.

I slung the bag over my shoulder and headed for the steps. Aurora watched me. She smiled faintly. The most beautiful smile. I thought so even before I knew I liked girls. Aurora and I were never lovers, though. I always thought we were too close for that.

"Hey," I called up to her.

She just stood there, leaning on the rail, looking all lazy and way too cool to hang out with someone like me. "Hey, sweetie."

Fritz trotted over to a tiny patch of grass. Did his business. He didn't raise his leg like most male dogs. I'd taught him to just squat and pee. Pee like a girl in fatigues in Afghanistan. He bounded up the stairs after me.

At the top of the steps, I stopped. Bag still over one shoulder. "You're a sight for sore eyes," I told Aurora.

"Your hair," she said. "You're growing it out." She reached out and ran her hand down one side of my face, stroking my hair and my cheek at the same time. "I love it."

I glanced at the open door, embarrassed by the attention. I'd worn my hair short since the morning after . . . after Buddy. I had cut it myself. Then my mom took me to have it cut properly for the funeral. I'd been wearing it short ever since. Well . . . until about six months ago. It looked shaggy now, but it was almost long enough to pull into a little ponytail if I used bobby pins.

"How's she doing?" I whispered the words. I looked tough. I acted tough. Like a woman who'd seen men die far from home. But I wasn't tough. Standing here right now, thinking of McKenzie dying, it was all I could do to keep my knees from buckling under me.

Aurora nodded. "Good. She's tired, but . . . she's good. For now, at least," she added.

I didn't know how to respond to that, so I didn't. "How about you?"

Fritz dropped to sit beside me. He was dying to greet Aurora. To run around the deck and smell the smells. But he wouldn't leave my side until I gave him my okay. And even then, he'd watch me. The minute I called him, he'd come.

"You know me." Another Aurora smile.

"Exactly," I murmured. My gaze met hers. Her eyes were brown, but there were golden specks in them. Like a lion's eyes. I saw her that way. A tawny lion. "Which is why I'm asking."

We were both quiet for a minute.

I was close to all three of my girls, the sisters I never had: McKenzie, Lilly, and Aurora. No one relationship was more or less important. How could it be? It would be like saying one arm or one leg was more important to my body. To function, to live. But my relationship with Aurora was unique. I didn't *get* her most of the time. She didn't think like me. She didn't think like anyone I'd ever known. But she was the one who saved me from that hell that was Buddy McCollister. I believed in my heart of hearts that Aurora saved my life. And for that reason, in my eyes, she could do no wrong. There was nothing she could say that I would criticize. I loved her more than I loved myself. Which she said was wrong.

"Italy was okay," Aurora said slowly. "It got . . . a little crazy."

I could tell there was more to the story. She actually looked worried . . . or scared. Which seemed impossible because Aurora wasn't afraid of anyone or anything.

I glanced at the door and shifted the duffel on my shoulder. "I guess I should . . ."

"Yeah."

I let Fritz lead the way.

# ❧ 5 ❧

# McKenzie

I couldn't stop smiling. They were all here. *We* were all here. Sometimes I felt like I spent my whole life just passing time, waiting to be with Aurora, Janine, and Lilly again. Which was silly, of course. I had a life separate from them. Sort of. And even when we were apart, we were still together.

Later, on my laptop, I'd record my impressions of this first evening together. I would not only be responsible for the when, what, and how of the month we spent together, but also the why. The thoughts. Those expressed and those that bubbled just under the surface, waiting to spill over.

As I looked from one face to the next, I wondered what exactly we were to each other. I mean, I knew, but . . . how did I express it?

*Friends. Sisters.* None of the words I can think of really describe what we were. How did we get here? Could we have ever gotten to this place, found this closeness, without being together for days, weeks on end?

And then there was the tragedy that has shaped and reshaped our lives over and over again. Like it or not, there was no denying that Buddy had brought us closer together. This house, this refuge that was hell and heaven at the same time, had made us more than the sum of our parts.

Pretty deep thinking for a Friday night.

We sat on the front porch, the parts of me: Janine, Lilly, Aurora. The sun was setting behind us, behind the house. Dinner was done, and the plates were piled in the sink for someone to deal with later. Now we sat, lined up along the porch in our Adirondack chairs. But not our own. I was in Aurora's white chair, she was in Lilly's pink one, Lilly was in Janine's blue one, and Janine was in mine. Fritz sat on the edge of the stairs, gazing out at the ocean, beyond the beach, the same way we are. I couldn't tell if he was sitting vigil or considering making a run for the water's edge.

Lilly was telling a funny story about being pumped up on IVF baby-making hormones, fighting a man for a parking space at the Annapolis Mall. It was a long story with a lot of gesturing. Janine and Aurora were laughing with her. I looked from one face to the next. I never realized how much I missed them, missed *us*, until we were all together again. Why was that? Was it because the pain would be too great if we fully realized it? Could we physically not survive if we felt the true depth of our desolation when we were apart?

I was so happy to be here with them. Who was I kidding? I was happy to be here at all.

I took a slow, deep breath, the way I had learned to do in my yoga-for-healing class. I inhaled the salty air. Oddly enough, my breathing seemed to be a little better this evening. I couldn't imagine why. It was such a relief to have made it here again, to all be together at last . . . this one last time. In the weeks leading up to my arrival, I'd worried something bad would happen and I wouldn't make it. My immune system was poor. I caught every cold, every stomach bug that went by. Last week I became almost paranoid about germs, washing my hands constantly with antibacterial soap. I was afraid the universe was going to turn against me, that lightning was going to strike, that something awful was going to happen to prevent me from seeing my Lilly, my Janine, and my Aurora.

But here I was, at last.

Lilly's story came to an end, and she drank water from a glass. Her bracelets jingled on her wrist. She was delicate, our Lilly, even with her big belly. Her hands were small. Her wrists were small. I'd always been envious that she could wear bangle bracelets, and I, with my big manly hands, could rarely find any that fit.

I reached for my glass of wine. I was only going to allow myself one tonight. I was hoping to avoid a repeat of the previous night's bed-spin.

Everyone was quiet for a moment. There was just the chirping of insects in the beach grass below and the rhythmic pulse of the waves. I could vaguely hear the whirl of the exhaust fan, left on in the kitchen.

Aurora sipped her gin and tonic. She and Janine had moved on to the hard stuff as soon as we ditched the dinner plates. For Aurora, it was gin. For Janine, Jack Daniel's. The girl can hold her whiskey like nobody's business.

A minute or two passed before I realized that everyone was looking at me. At least stealing glances. I felt uncomfortable, and I adjusted my bony butt in my chair.

Aurora rose and went to sit on the porch rail, balancing on it, butt and feet on the narrow, white beam. "Okay, McKenzie. You might as well get it over with," she said, not looking at me. "Tell us what's going on with the tumors."

I sensed she left the phrase open to give me a choice. I could tell them about the drug trial. Or not. I was standing with my decision. I wasn't going to tell them. I wish I hadn't even told Aurora. That was what I got for drinking too much.

That didn't mean I didn't feel a little guilty about it. I couldn't make eye contact with anyone. I settled my gaze on the slatted sand fence that protruded from the dune in front of the house.

I'd been having so much fun all day that I didn't want to ruin it. I didn't want to talk about me. About *it*. I just wanted to be here together with them and talk and laugh and pretend nothing had changed. That nothing *would* ever change. I wanted to pretend that we'd all be back next summer, and the summer after that. I wanted to go down to the beach where the sand was soft, dig a big hole the way I used to when my daughters were little, and stick my head in it.

"She doesn't have talk about it if she doesn't want to." Lilly wrapped her arms around her belly the way pregnant women do. Protectively. Only I felt as if, somehow, she was trying to protect me with her arms.

Janine poured herself another two fingers and didn't say anything. I wondered how long it would be before she'd be drinking directly from the bottle.

I glanced at the German shepherd. No word from him, either.

I wrapped my hand around the stemless wineglass. Squeezed. Released. Someone had lit a citronella candle, even though there were no mosquitoes tonight, and set it on a little round table. I liked the smell. Some people didn't, but I did. It reminded me of this place. Summers here. Summers when we were all happy . . . at least fairly so.

I could feel them waiting. Compelling me to speak.

"There's not much to say." I looked down at my feet. I was wearing a pair of old canvas Toms that had once belonged to one of my daughters. I could feel the grit of sand between the big and second toes of my left foot. I took my time, pulling my foot out of the shoe and wiggling my toes. "The tumors are still growing," I said softly.

"You don't know that for sure," said Lilly.

"For sure," I answered, with little emotion. Was I just out of emotion? "My scans. They always compare them to the previous ones." I didn't identify the proverbial "they." It didn't much matter: Christiana Care, Johns Hopkins, Sloan Kettering.

Aurora cut her eyes at me. She thought I should tell them about the drug trial. But that wasn't her call. It was mine. She could give me the stink eye all she wanted.

"There's not anything anyone can do?" Janine's voice seemed to come from far away.

We were all staring at the dark water beyond the dunes and the stretch of white sand. I shook my head slowly and stole a glance in Janine's direction. "No."

Janine was looking tough, but I saw tears glisten in her eyes. "Surgery?" she asked. "You can't find anyone to cut the little bastards out?"

"They're not those kinds of tumors. The kind that can be surgically removed." I paused. Guilt washed over me to the same rhythm as the rising tide. How could I be doing this to them? To Mia and Maura? To Lilly and Janine and Aurora? "There are . . . too many of them," I said.

Lilly was crying quietly into a tissue. I noticed earlier that she carried them around with her; this wasn't the first time today she'd plucked one from the plastic pouch. Apparently, she cried a lot these days, with the hormone thing happening. More in my presence.

"You've done research? On the Internet?" Janine again. "Talked to people? I mean, just because doctors in the US don't—"

"There's nothing that can be done," I interrupted. I didn't want to talk about the *options* again . . . with anyone. Not even Janine.

I'd heard plenty about nonconventional treatments from everyone and their brother: acupuncture, salves, qigong. A nice enough girl from work wanted me to take some kind of vitamin concoction that had *proved* to cure cancer in South America. (Containing white-headed marmoset pee probably.) A gal in my hot yoga class wanted me to meet her spiritual advisor, who'd had good luck with healing mantras. (*Ommm*, kick this cancer's butt, *ommm*.) Apparently, he'd cured someone of brain cancer. Or so the gal with the big, fuchsia tiger tattoo on her shoulder had told me.

Lilly was sobbing now. I reached over and took her hand. "Oh, Lilly, don't."

"I just . . . can't . . . believe . . ." She was taking big, noisy gulps of air. "Believe this . . . is . . . happening to us."

I wanted to get up and put my arms around her, but honestly, I was too tired. Instead, I rested her hand on the arm of my chair and laid my cheek against it. She crumpled over and rested her face on my shoulder, her hair falling over my face. I liked the feel of it, and for a moment, I pretended it was my own hair. The fantasy didn't last long. Her hair was smooth and silky and smelled of expensive shampoo. My hair was longer, coarser . . . and I used Head & Shoulders. Or leftovers from the assorted bottles my daughters discarded on the floor of their shower.

Now Janine was crying. Crying without making a sound.

It was Aurora who broke the silence. She lit up a cigarette and sighed loudly with obvious pleasure.

Lilly popped up her head. *"Really?"* She sniffed, taking her hand from mine, and fumbled for the pack of tissues.

I leaned back in the chair and closed my eyes. I wasn't going to be able to stay up much longer. I needed to climb into my pajamas, into my bed. I needed a nebulizer treatment. I needed sleep.

"You're going to *smoke?*" Lilly demanded. "She's got lung cancer, and you're going to *smoke* five feet from her?" Her last words come out angry. Bitter.

I sometimes think that while Lilly loves Aurora, a part of her resents her. Resents what she did that night. The way it changed us all. The way it solidified our relationship, but broke us into little pieces, deep inside.

I patted her hand. "Lilly. It's okay."

"It's not okay."

I opened my eyes to see Lilly heaving herself up out of the chair. "Put it out, Aurora," she told her, pointing her finger.

Aurora drew the cigarette, held between her fore and middle fingers, to her lips and inhaled dramatically.

Lilly reached out and plucked the cigarette from Aurora's mouth.

Janine had gone from crying to laughing. No one messed with Aurora. No one but Lilly.

"I see a Tiger Mom in the making," Janine declared.

Lilly ground the cigarette out on the top of the empty Coke can Aurora used for an ashtray. "No more smoking in front of McKenzie. I mean it. You go out on the back deck if you want to do that." She pointed in the direction of the back of the house. The funny thing was, Lilly used to smoke.

I waited for Aurora to argue . . . or at least *say* something. *Do* something. I wondered if she'd light up again. Maybe blow smoke rings into Lilly's face. But she didn't. She just raised her glass to her lips and artfully deflected the attention. "Dating anyone, Janine?"

Lilly retreated to her chair. I was relieved to have been saved from any further discussion of me possibly taking a yak trip across Siberia to meet a medicine man.

"Actually, I am." She was drunk enough to talk to us about her love life. She gave us a half smile. She had this way of turning her lip up on one side. Kind of like an Elvis smirk.

I like her hair the way she's wearing it. Longer. It was less . . . severe. It was a pretty brown. Chestnutty. No gray. She'd worn it short since she cut it herself that summer. This was the longest I've seen it in all these years. I wanted to tell her how much I liked it but hadn't. If I did, I was afraid she might take the scissors to it again.

"Do tell," Lilly said.

Janine sipped her Jack. "Nah . . . I don't want to. Not yet. I don't want to jinx it."

Lilly's eyes widened. "Does that mean it's serious? After Betsy, you thought you'd never love anyone again. Janine, this is so exciting!"

"Always someone else out there to love." Aurora prodded Janine with her bare foot. "Right?"

Janine just kept smirking.

"Is she hot?" Aurora asked.

"Pretty hot," Janine agreed.

Lilly rolled her eyes and heaved herself out of her chair. "I've got to pee. Again. Don't say a word until I get back." She held up her finger.

All three of us held up our fingers at once, imitating her. And we all four burst into laughter.

# ❦ 6 ❧

# Lilly

I looked at her, lying on the bed in a small circle of light cast from the bedside lamp. I just wanted to cry. She looked so pale. So skinny. She'd always been curvy with nice breasts. The turban covering her head looked so . . . not McKenzie. All that beautiful red hair, gone. Eyelashes. Eyebrows. Gone.

I wondered if that meant *all* of her hair fell out . . . everywhere. Pubic hair, too? I didn't know why I cared, but I thought how weird that would be. It was such a part of our femininity, wasn't it?

McKenzie saw me in the doorway, in my pink nightgown, and smiled. "Hey," she said, closing her laptop. She sounded sleepy.

"Hey. I just came down to check on you before I went to bed." I couldn't stay up like I used to. I needed so much more sleep than I did pre-blimp. Janine and Aurora were still out on the front porch. Aurora was probably sneaking a joint, since I'd gone to bed. Which meant Janine was threatening to arrest her.

I hung on the doorknob, hesitant. Did McKenzie want me to come in? Was she too tired and just wanted to be left alone? I hated feeling this way, as if I didn't know her anymore. As if I didn't know what she wanted or needed.

"Journal?" I asked. It sounded lame. Like I was the new girl in the cafeteria or something and didn't know what to say. I'd felt this way my whole life. As if I never quite fit in. Even here, where I fit in best. I was so ordinary compared to McKenzie and Janine. And certainly compared to Aurora, who was practically a goddess.

McKenzie nodded. "I've learned the hard way to write every night, if I can. Otherwise . . ."

"I know," I commiserated. At first, I thought it was kind of mean, us making her write it. But then Aurora told me that she thought it was good to give McKenzie a job, something to focus on other than her cancer. That made sense to me. I acquiesced, which of course I always did when push came to shove with Aurora.

I glanced at the dozen or so brown plastic pill bottles with the white caps on McKenzie's nightstand. I saw the nebulizer on the other side of the bed. The hose. The face mask. I knew the treatments helped her breathe, but I hated the machine. I returned my gaze to her face. While she had certainly aged since her diagnosis, she was still beautiful to me. "Okay if I come in?" I asked.

"Of course. I know you guys are trying to be nice, letting me sleep down here." She stuck her lower lip out in an exaggerated pout. "But it's lonely."

I glanced around the room as I entered. For years, we just kept the door shut and never came in here. But eventually, when McKenzie had her girls and wanted to bring them down, we completely renovated it. We pulled out the carpet and had the hardwood floors refinished. We painted the walls a sunny yellow and added white curtains. White coastal-style furniture. It was a gorgeous room . . . but I'm still glad I'm sleeping upstairs instead of here. Just the thought of sleeping in the same room where Buddy McCollister had once slept gave me indigestion. Which I already had enough trouble with now, as it was.

McKenzie scooted over in the queen-sized bed, making room for me. Anymore, I feel as if I waddle instead of walk. I couldn't imagine how big I'd be at forty weeks. I already felt like a whale. But I was determined to enjoy my rotundness. This baby was a miracle and I knew it, and I didn't want to squander a moment of my pregnancy.

I waddled to the bed and sat down on the edge. She rearranged the pillows she'd been leaning against and patted the empty space on a pillow. I hesitated. Should I be lying in bed with her? Shouldn't I let her get her rest? She needed her rest if she was going to get better.

But the way she looked at me, I couldn't say no. I stretched out beside her. Our heads were side by side on the king-sized pillow. I felt her warmth and smelled her facial moisturizer. We stared up at the white ceiling. There was a ceiling fan. I watched it spin. Listened to it tick-tick.

"I'm sorry," I said.

"It's okay."

She knew what I was talking about. I'd been here all day, but we hadn't gotten to discuss it. Me not telling her sooner that I was pregnant.

We were both quiet again. The fan tick-ticked. Lying there beside McKenzie, I could hear her breathing. It wasn't labored. I wouldn't go so far as to say that, but it wasn't normal breathing, either. Shouldn't she have been breathing normally, lying in bed?

"I *wanted* to tell you . . ." I said finally. Then I hesitated. I hated to blame it on Matt. People thought I let Matt control me. I know Aurora thinks he does; she makes comments about him all the time. But what she didn't understand was that I only let him make decisions that I couldn't or didn't want to make. I let him do the things I couldn't or didn't want to do. I knew this was totally not acceptable in the modern feminist world, but the truth was, I liked having my husband take care of me. I *really* liked it.

"Matt and I talked," I went on, "and he . . . I was afraid that if the pregnancy . . . didn't continue, it would make you sad."

She rolled onto her side and propped her head up with her hand. I stayed on my back.

She looked down at me. "Of course I would have been sad if you'd lost another baby. But, *Lilly*, that's not how it works between us. We share the bad things, too."

"I know. I know." I felt my lower lip tremble. The floodgates were about to open. I'd cried three times already since I'd arrived. Of course I cried when McKenzie talked about her illness. But I'd cried earlier when Janine was telling us about a homeless teenager she found under a local bridge. I also cried when I saw a mom and dad on the beach with a little boy, flying a kite. Janine and Aurora looked at me like I was crazy. Even Fritz thought I'd lost it. But McKenzie . . . she understood. I guess because she was a mother.

I knew I wasn't a mother yet. But, I was, in a way. I was mom to all those little souls that had lived in my hostile womb for a brief time. I truly believed that.

McKenzie rubbed her hand over my belly, and I smiled, bringing myself back to the here and now. It was something I was working on. It was time to stop always looking to the future, Matt told me. It was time to live in the present. And he was right.

So I lived in the present, here at this moment in bed with McKenzie. Her hand felt good against my taut skin.

"I'm so happy for you," she said. "I'm mad at you for cheating me out of knowing all these months." She smiled, looking into my eyes. "But I'm so happy for you, sweetie."

Her turban had shifted when she rolled over to face me, and now it sat askew. I reached out to readjust it and cover the tiny bit of red fuzz beneath it.

She rested her head on the pillow again, and we just lay there.

"Lilly, I want to talk to you," she said after what seemed like a long while.

I realized I was drifting off to sleep. I needed to get up. I needed to go upstairs to my own bed. "Not tonight," I told her, opening my eyes.

I knew what she wanted to talk about. About her cancer. But

we *already* talked about it tonight. Of course, when we talked, it was in a general way. Like a recap of the information we already knew. I wasn't the only one who had cried. Janine had cried then, too. I saw her tears, even though she was trying to hide them. I'd always loved that about Janine. She could get her bull dyke cop on when she had to, but she could still be a girly girl with us. She could still cry *for* us. The way we've cried for her. The way I still cry for her sometimes for that night. For all of those nights we didn't know about, until after the fact.

"Lilly." McKenzie whispered my name. Her green eyes were so intense, more so now that her face is thinner.

"I know," I whispered back. "But I can't, honey. Not tonight." Then I sat up. Awkwardly. I kissed her forehead, right where the knit turban met her pale skin. "You okay?" I pressed my palm to her cheek and frowned. "Do you have a fever? Your . . . face looks red." I looked at her more closely.

She pushed my hand away. "I'm fine. It's . . . one of the medications. I get a little bit of a fever sometimes. If I get lucky," she joked, "maybe I'll break out in hives by morning."

I don't know how she can joke about this. If it were me with the cancer, I wouldn't be cracking jokes. I'd be curled up in a ball on the floor, unable to speak or function.

I made myself smile. "Okay," I said slowly. My gaze went to the nebulizer on the table beside her again.

My mom had died of lung cancer. She'd had a three pack a day habit in her prime. I knew my nebulizers. My oxygen tanks. I knew how a person with lung cancer dies. How their life slowly eked out of them with each struggling breath.

"Go to bed," McKenzie ordered. She gave me a push, but she didn't lift her head off the pillow. I think maybe she was so weak that she couldn't.

I paused at the bedroom door and looked back at her. She was lying there, half asleep, half smiling. I knew she was happy we were all here together. Happy, like the rest of us. It seemed like we lived our lives just waiting to get back here. To be together again, here. Just the four of us.

Kind of sick, when you thought about it.

*"Yoi yume o,"* I told her. Words my Japanese mother always said to me before she turned out the light.

"Sweet dreams," McKenzie echoed.

# 7

# McKenzie

"Get in." Lilly pointed.

I stared at the motorized grocery cart. I didn't want to *get in*. But they were all standing there looking at me, making me feel self-conscious. As if I didn't already feel that way, sporting no eyebrows. We were standing outside our favorite organic market in town.

"I can walk," I told her. "I feel good today."

"Get in the cart," Lilly ordered. She was wearing another sundress, this one pink and green, and the big white sunglasses again. The handbag that weighed a hundred pounds swung from her elbow. "We don't have all day. I want to sit on the beach."

"Come on," Janine urged, pressing her hand into the small of my back. "It's not a big deal."

"If she doesn't want to ride, she doesn't have to ride." Aurora went to the double doors, and there was that familiar pneumatic hiss as they opened.

Janine and Lilly stood on either side of me.

"You should save your strength," Janine said quietly into my ear. She glanced away, but kept talking, as if this was some kind of top secret summit. "You don't want to waste it on grocery shopping. We'll go swimming this afternoon. All of us. If you're up to it," she added quickly.

I couldn't see Lilly's eyes through the designer sunglasses, but I could feel her stare, boring into me. Her pink lipsticked mouth was in a pucker.

I sighed and threw up my hands, imitating one of my girls. "Fine. I'll get in the damned cart, but we're going to talk about this," I warned. "I'm not going to be treated this way. You guys aren't supposed to act like this. Not you guys." I sat on the black molded plastic seat of the cart. I always felt like an idiot when I used one of these things; they were for old people, handicapped people, not me.

Regrettably, this wasn't the first time I had used one. In March, I'd come down with a wicked case of bronchitis. I had barely been able to walk from my living room couch, where I had slept, to the bathroom. When I was well enough to go out again, I still couldn't walk from the car into a store without gasping for breath, so I'd been forced to ride in the damned things.

I twisted the grip on the right side of the T-shaped steering wheel, and the cart lurched forward. I took off at a snail's pace.

"What are you talking about? Act like what?" Lilly kept her voice low. Lilly didn't do scenes. Her mother had always insisted on a certain veil of decorum, no matter what. Even with a dead body. I still remember when the police had Lilly's mother come to the beach house that night to pick her up. She'd been so . . . polite.

"You know very well what I'm talking about." I hit the gas, full throttle, thinking I could zip away from them, but I was already at full throttle.

Lilly passed me at the "Free Beach Paper!" kiosk between one set of doors and the next. Janine continued to walk beside me. She looked like she was going to say something.

"Zip it," I warned.

"Everyone get what you want, and we'll meet at the registers," Lilly instructed. Inside the market, she handed Janine a plastic shopping basket and took one for herself. She didn't bother to give one to Aurora, who had stopped to check out sand shovels in a bin next to an artfully arranged table of local melons. "I'm making dinner tonight. Aurora, you're tomorrow night. When are the girls coming?" She turned back to me.

I was still racing to catch up. The motorized cart had a basket in the front *for all my shopping needs*. I wondered which aisle had handguns. "Monday or Tuesday. Probably Tuesday."

"I'll get stuff for chicken tacos for when they come. Of course we'll do the grill thing for the Fourth. Tonight, I think we'll have steamed shrimp, fresh broccoli, and baked potatoes." Lilly floated away in her white patent leather sandals. "Teens like tacos. I'll get some soda, too."

I slowly made my way through the fresh produce section, ignoring Janine, who had apparently been appointed my keeper on the outing. Lilly hadn't assigned me a night to make dinner. I wasn't a good cook, nor did I like to cook, so that was okay by me. I got two avocados, a sweet onion, and some garlic to make guacamole. One of my few specialties. When I started to stand up to grab a couple of limes, Janine reached over me.

"Two?"

"We better get three." I settled back into the cart. "Aurora will be ready for a gin and tonic by the time we get back to the house."

She chuckled, and I couldn't help myself. Even though I was still annoyed with her, annoyed with all three of them, I smiled. How could I be annoyed with Janine when she laughed at my dumb jokes? We headed down the dairy aisle. I debated getting some almond milk. Mia was lactose intolerant. As I reached for the carton, I realized it was silly to get it. I'd be lucky if my girls stayed more than an hour; Lilly would be lucky if they ate her tacos.

I crawled along next to the open refrigerated shelves in search of some Greek yogurt. Janine was clearly going nowhere, which was okay because I hadn't had a minute alone with her since she had arrived the afternoon before. I wondered if she wanted to talk about the lawsuit that had been filed against her; we hadn't really talked about it, even on the phone. But I didn't want to be the one to bring it up. It was like my cancer. She had to be desperate for a few minutes peace without the weight of it on her shoulders. The charges against her were serious. If anything came of the case, it might mean her career.

"So, how are things?" I asked, trying to sound casual.

"Good."

I cut my eyes at her. "Your mom?"

"Fine." She was quiet for a second before she said, "I guess." She picked up a hunk of cheese she had no intention of buying. "I haven't really talked to her much. Well, just a little last week. For a minute. You know, when Todd and Christie had the baby. She called to say that Christie was fine and all. That everybody was okay."

"So you're an auntie again!" I tried to sound cheerful, but it came out fake. Janine put the cheese back.

"I'm sorry." I grabbed her hand. Squeezed it and let it go.

Physical shows of affection were tough for Janine. No surprise there. But we'd never let that stop us. Just because it was hard for her didn't mean she didn't want it. And sometimes she was okay with a quick hug or a peck on the cheek. It just depended on whether or not it was "a Buddy day." Today, apparently, wasn't because she didn't pull away from me or tell me to fuck off.

I know she feels bad about not knowing her nieces and nephew better than she does. I think, in a different life, Janine would have had kids.

Her brother barely spoke to her, which meant she had very little contact with her nieces and nephew. Todd was an okay guy, but he was more screwed up than Janine would ever be. For various reasons. A big one was that he blamed himself for what happened to his sister. The fact that he had been a little boy, younger than her, didn't seem to matter. He blamed Janine, on some level, too, for ruining his life. And of course he was the number two fan in the I Hate Buddy McCollister Club. The crazy thing was, he had never faulted their mother. Something Janine still had trouble coming to terms with. It was like an invisible wedge that always stood between them.

"You have a picture of the baby?" I asked.

She reached into the pocket of her knee-length cargo shorts and pulled out her cell phone. She held it out for me to see a wrinkled face burrito-wrapped in a pink blanket. "Megan."

"She's cute," I said.

Janine put the phone back in her pocket without looking at the screen. "We're talking about me going down for Christmas. We'll see."

I nodded and inched forward in the cart.

"I guess it depends. On whether or not I can get off work." She picked up a package of shredded mozzarella. "You put the word *organic* on something, and it's fifty percent more expensive." She dropped it into her basket. She'd be making baked ziti. She always made baked ziti. "I guess it also depends on what's going on with the lawsuit. The lawyer says we're looking at December. If anything comes of it."

So she did want to talk about it. I spotted Lilly crisscrossing in front of us. She was headed our way, but clearly on a mission, sunglasses perched on her head, her grocery list in her hand. I don't know if she even saw us.

"Any word on the status of the suit?" I asked Janine.

She lifted her shoulder. Let it fall.

At the end of the aisle, I maneuvered the cart around a stack of packages of *natural* toilet paper and started down the next aisle. Was there *un*natural toilet paper?

"You think it will actually go to court?" I asked.

She scowled. "Doubt it. Female perp who filed against me has a rap sheet. Her boyfriend, too. Both for assault, among other things. And this wasn't his first tussle with cops. Resisting arrest charges were dropped on a previous case, but my lawyer's got a private investigator on it. I'm not worried."

I stopped and studied a shelf of beans: kidney, garbanzo, black, cannellini. I had no idea why. Beans weren't on my list. What I needed was corn chips, to go with my guac. "I'm sure it will all be fine," I said.

She stood beside me, hands hanging awkwardly at her sides. She stared at the beans. "You read what happened, I guess. Saw the news."

I reached for a can of pintos. "I did."

"I didn't shove her, Mack. I barely touched her. The baby daddy grabbed me, and *he* was the one who knocked her down. All three of us went down. He was big and I was—" Her voice caught in her throat.

I looked up at her, the stupid beans still my hand. A female voice came over the loudspeaker advertising a sale on steamed crabs seasoned with Old Bay. Three dollars each, but just for the next fifteen minutes.

Janine's gaze was distant, as if she were watching the incident in question. Watching herself. I found myself holding my breath.

"I was pretty scared. There were only two of us. My partner and me. We had backup coming, but—" She stopped and started again, still not looking at me. This time under her breath. "I didn't touch the pregnant woman. I didn't touch her even though the bitch put her hands on me."

The article I had read said the whole incident had been recorded on a cell phone. The newspaper had implied that the video would prove that Senior Corporal McCollister was guilty of the charges filed against her.

"Was there really a video?" I asked.

She nodded. "A guy in the crowd took it right before he took a swing at one of our troopers who was barely out of a training bra."

She took the can of beans from my hand and set them on the shelf.

She met my gaze, and I ached for the pain I saw in her eyes.

"I didn't do it, Mack. I'm not my father."

"I know you're not," I said, wishing there was something else I could say. Something better.

We were both quiet for a second. I heard the sounds of customers in the store, of life going on around us. Continuing without us, which made me feel tiny and insignificant.

"So what else do you need?" She walked away. "I'm going to get some chips to snack on down on the beach. And some flavored creamer. I like the fake shit. I'll probably have to go to Wawa."

I just sat there, watching her walk away. She was pretty, though she'd never thought so. Not model pretty like Aurora or exotic pretty like Lilly, but girl-next-door pretty. I liked her shiny brown hair longer. She never wore makeup, but she had the kind of face that didn't need it to define her features. She had gorgeous hazel eyes, nice brows, high cheekbones, and suntanned skin that never blemished. And her smile . . . I found myself smiling.

"Lost?" Aurora walked up behind me, her flip-flops slapping on the concrete floor. She was carrying a sand shovel and a big candle, the kind in a jar.

I glanced at the candle. Raised an eyebrow. Except that I don't have an eyebrow.

"Soy." She sniffed it. She was wearing short white shorts and a pale yellow T-shirt that hung off one shoulder to show a teal bikini strap. "It says it smells like the beach. It doesn't smell like the beach to me, but I thought it might be nice in the living room." She held it under my nose.

"Smells good." I hit the pedal on the cart, and it inched forward.

She walked beside me and glanced into the basket mounted on the front of the cart. "Anything I should get? For the girls, maybe?"

"I doubt they'll stay long. They're pretty busy with work and—"

"Guys," Aurora interrupted. "And then there's their tan to worry about."

"Exactly." I turned at the end of the aisle, bypassing the next aisle in my search of chips.

"You shouldn't let that hurt your feelings, them not wanting to spend much time with the *mom* when they're at the beach for the summer," Aurora said. "Remember how we were? I'd go days at a time without seeing my mom. And I was living with her."

"My feelings aren't hurt." Which was only half a lie. They were, a little, but Mia and Maura were doing what I wanted them to do; live their lives. They were happy and well-adjusted. They were certainly happier than I had been at their age.

"Should I get, like, some beer or something for them?" Aurora asked. "I could hit the liquor mart next door."

"For my *underage* daughters?"

She laughed. I didn't even crack a smile.

"You don't think it's better if they have a couple of beers with us?" She tucked a lock of blond hair behind her ear, and I fought the urge to check the position of my head scarf.

"You *know* they're drinking," she went on. "We were drinking at their age. Going to be seniors in high school." She made a sound. I couldn't tell if she was making fun of me or of how stupid we had been at that age. Likely both.

"I hope my daughters are a little smarter than we were." Spotting chips—they'd moved them since the last time I'd been here—I cut in front of Aurora.

"Hope," she said. "There's always that."

I stopped in front of a wall of corn chips and pointed.

She tucked her shovel under her arm and grabbed a bag. I shook my head, and she grabbed the blue corn chips next to them.

"Yup."

She tossed the bag in my basket. "Anything else?"

"Nope. You?"

"Got my shovel and my candle. I'll get a bottle of gin next door."

"What about your turn to make dinner tomorrow night?"

She laughed and walked away, headed in the direction of the cash registers. She raised the shovel over her head. "Takeout, baby."

# 8

# Aurora

"**Y**ou think she's okay? It's not too hot out here for her?" Janine studied McKenzie through her mirrored cop sunglasses.

We were both standing in the water, a few yards offshore, one eye on the beach, the other on the waves coming in behind us. Janine was chin deep; I was nipple deep. The water was warm, at least to me. But then again, I'd swum in the English Channel.

We bobbed up and down as the waves rippled in. "She's fine," I said. "She's got cancer. She's not a retard. She'll go inside if she gets too hot."

"The medication she's taking. She's not really supposed to be out in the sun. And it's *person with a mental disability*." Janine cocked her head toward me. "Or *person with mental challenges*. No one says *retard*, Aurora. Try to join us in this decade."

"So *what?* Cops have suddenly become sensitive to race, religion, and *persons with disabilities?*"

She looked at me like she was going to slug me. I gave her a push, laughing. "You're *so* easy, Janine. Too easy."

We both looked toward the shore again. Lilly and McKenzie were in beach chairs under a big white-and-teal-striped umbrella. Lilly was wearing a cute white one-piece, big belly, big straw hat, her same silly white designer sunglasses. McKenzie had on a ball cap and a baggy granny bathing suit. It was so ugly I was tempted to go buy her a new one, just so I wouldn't have to look at the one she had on. Besides being ridiculous looking, it made it obvious how much weight she had lost. In shorts and a baggy T-shirt, I could ignore it, but here on the beach, it was right in my face.

We were quiet for a minute, then Janine said, "Aurora, I didn't do it."

I didn't have to ask her what she was talking about. I knew. McKenzie had whispered to me earlier that she and Janine had talked about the lawsuit when we were at the market. I didn't look at Janine. "I didn't say you did. *Again*, too touchy."

"McKenzie thinks I did it."

I leaned back, wetting my head, slicking my hair back. I needed sunblock on my nose. I could feel it burning. "She does not."

"She does, too. She thinks just because I lost my shit that one time—"

"McKenzie told you she thought you beat up that pregnant chick?" I didn't usually interrupt people, but what she was saying was too stupid to let slide.

"You're not listening to what I'm saying." Janine lowered her voice. As if someone else in the Atlantic Ocean might hear her. "She thinks I hurt that woman. I could hear it in her voice when she said she knew I didn't do it."

"Are you listening to yourself?" I watched Lilly and McKenzie. Lilly was talking a mile a minute. McKenzie was looking at her romance novel. I couldn't tell if she was listening to Lilly or not. This was good, giving the two of them time together. To talk about being a mom and that kind of crap. It was something Janine and I could never do with them. "Because you're coming off a little nutty. What's your shrink say?"

"About what? Big one."

We both went under the surface of the water to keep from getting slammed by the wave. We popped back up after it went over us. Water streamed off Janine's mirrored sunglasses, which looked cool as the bright sunlight glinted off the drops of water on the metal frames. I tucked the image in place in my brain to recall later, thinking I might be able to use something from it in my work.

"I don't know," I said, running my hands over my head so the water from my hair streamed down my back. "The whole thing. About you feeling like you need to keep telling people you didn't do it."

"I don't need to tell *people*. Just you guys."

"Okay. It's just that the more often someone says they didn't do something, the more likely it is that they *did* do it."

I could feel Janine's gaze boring into me.

"I need your support, Aurora." Her voice was soft. She sounded vulnerable, which didn't happen all that often.

"You've got my support." I draped my arm around her muscular shoulder. Janine worked out at the gym regularly and has always had the most incredible shoulders. "Because I don't give a fuck if you did it or not. If she came at me, I'd sure as—"

"What's this?" Janine caught my wrist. She unwound my arm from her shoulder, but still held on to my hand. "Are those *ligature* marks?"

I wriggled my hand out of her grasp. "Incoming!"

We both went under. When I came up, I lifted my feet so I was floating and paddled backward. Janine swam after me. She was a good swimmer. Strong. If there were one word I would choose for Janine, it would be *strong*. Not just physically, but mentally. Everyone thinks I'm the strong one, but it's all smoke and mirrors. Always has been. Janine is an iron woman.

"Let me see your wrist," she said.

We were over our heads. I treaded water, staying out of her reach. "No. Mind your own business."

"Aurora. Did someone hurt you?"

Lilly and I were laughing this morning about how we loved

the way Janine could get all butchy and overprotective. It was a stereotype: lesbian female cops. But it was true. There was always some truth in stereotypes. I made a face like Janine was an idiot. "Of course no one *hurt* me."

She treaded water with one hand, pushing her sunglasses up on her head with the other. Now I was getting the full-on stare. "Don't lie to me. We don't lie to each other about this kind of shit."

I didn't want to tell Janine anything about the brothers in Venice because she would make a big deal out of it. She would start in again on what she perceived as my suicidal behavior, which was bullshit, of course. She was a five-foot-five female cop, breaking up bar fights, and she thought *I* was suicidal?

We were both quiet for a couple of minutes. We paddled around. I contemplated taking a swim. My goggles were on the beach with my towel.

When Janine broke the silence, it wasn't about the fading marks on my wrists. The subject was equally tender, though. "How's Jude?"

I closed my eyes. "Good."

"Talk to him recently?"

It would have been easier to lie. I wasn't up for this conversation. Not before cocktails. "Not recently."

"When, Aurora?"

I went under. When I came back up, Janine was still there, treading water. Waiting.

"I don't know," I said. "A couple of months ago."

"Aurora. He's your son. You have to make the effort."

I wanted to close my eyes and sink below the surface. Jude. The child of my body, who had never felt like mine. Not even when the nurse first put him in my arms after I spent twenty-one hours in labor and two hours pushing him out of my vag. He'd looked like an alien, red and squalling. When Hannad, my *ex*-boyfriend by then, said it would be better if he took Jude home, I let him. What was I going to do with a *baby?*

"He's good," I told Janine. "He still likes Stanford. He'll graduate next year. He's got some sort of internship in the computer science department for the summer."

"You going out to see him?"

"I don't know. Maybe. He's, you know, busy."

"You should fly out to Palo Alto."

I ignored her. A middle-aged couple on the beach caught my eye. They were standing on the water's edge, looking at something beyond us. The woman, in a flowered muumuu, pointed in our direction. Other people on the beach were looking now, too. I saw McKenzie lay her book on her lap and look up. I could tell that Lilly was still talking, but she was looking, too.

"Dolphins," I said, paddling to turn around. "That or a big ass shark."

"Where?" Janine did the same.

I scanned the water, bobbing up and down. And then I saw them . . . two . . . no, three Atlantic bottlenose dolphins. We watched them as they rose and fell gracefully, their glistening gray bodies throwing off spray as they cut through the water.

"Gorgeous," Janine sighed, the tiny wrinkles around her mouth softening.

I treaded water beside her, watching the three dolphins as they swam south, becoming smaller and smaller until they were just dots in the distance.

"Ready for a drink?" I asked Janine. I swam past her. "I am. Race you."

# ᓚ 9 ᓯ

# Janine

Istared at the digital clock on the nightstand beside my bed. It was almost oh four hundred hours. I had dozed off almost immediately when I went to bed at midnight; the Jack always helped me fall asleep. But I only slept about two hours. A typical night. I fell asleep, exhausted or drunk, slept a few hours, then woke up and couldn't go back to sleep. My shrink said it's PTSD. He was full of shit. I bet he slapped that diagnosis on every soldier he saw. I was an insomniac long before Afghanistan.

I groaned. I was lonely in my single bed in my empty room. I missed Chris.

I rolled over and stared up at the ceiling fan. Light from a street-lamp leaked around the accordion blinds, casting shadows across the end of my bed. I tried to relax, count perps or something, but I felt jumpy in my skin. Like there was something I needed to do. I threw my legs over the side of the bed and sat up.

Fritz, who slept on the floor under the window, lifted his head and looked at me. I could see his brown eyes in the semidark-ness. He was used to me being awake in the middle of the night. He watched me for a minute, then lowered his head and closed his eyes. He knew I'd call him if I needed him.

I listened to the quiet house. I could hear the wind; one of the shutters rattled. I could hear the surf. I could imagine the white foam washing up on the sand.

I stared at the floor. For years, whenever I looked at my bedroom floor, I saw Buddy lying there. His eyes were always closed, which was weird; on TV, people died with their eyes open.

The good thing was, he appeared less and less on my floor, until I rarely saw him. He wasn't there tonight.

I closed my eyes. My mouth was dry. At Lilly's insistence, I'd had most of a bottle of water before I went to bed. Clearly, it hadn't been enough. I had a slight headache. Dehydration. I grabbed the bottle and chugged the last couple of mouthfuls.

I got up. I wore my typical pajamas. Not Lilly's pretty white or pink nightgown: boxers and an army green T-shirt with my last name stenciled on the inside of the collar. Not my whole name. Just part of it.

Fritz half rose.

"Stay, boy."

He dropped to the floor obediently.

I was halfway down the staircase before I heard someone upchucking in the downstairs bathroom. McKenzie was the only one sleeping downstairs. I'd been awake for more than an hour. Neither Lilly nor Aurora had passed my room or even stirred. I stuck my head in McKenzie's bedroom. The light was on. The bed was empty.

I padded barefoot down the hall. The bathroom door was closed. I hesitated, then knocked. "McKenzie?"

She didn't answer right away. Her voice was strange when she did. "Yeah?" She sounded as if she were a million miles away.

I was going to ask her if she was okay, but she clearly wasn't. I pressed my hand to the white door. It was cool to the touch. Lilly had the air conditioner cranked up. Apparently, being pregnant made you hot. "You . . . want some company?"

"While I puke my guts out?"

I smiled, my hand still on the door. "Anything I can get you? Water?"

"Go back to bed, Janine. I'm going to be here a while."

I rested my cheek against the door. I wished it were me in the bathroom instead of McKenzie. I mean, if God wanted to kill one of us off, didn't it make sense for it to be me? (And it wasn't like He didn't have the opportunity: Afghanistan, the Rusty Nut bar on any Saturday night.) McKenzie had her girls. She was a good person. A really good person. So many people would be broken when she died. Maybe too broken to want to live. I'd been thinking about that for months. If it were me dying of cancer, it wouldn't be so bad. No kids. No spouse. No family to speak of. Who would really miss me? Aurora, McKenzie, and Lilly, sure. But wouldn't they be a little relieved, too? Wasn't I always the elephant in the room?

I sat down on the floor. It was dark in the hall, except for the glow from the back deck light shining through the kitchen windows.

McKenzie retched again, and I dropped my head to my hands. It tore me up, hearing her. Not being able to do anything for her. She was just dry heaving now, though. So maybe she'd feel better soon.

I waited. She flushed the toilet. I heard the water in the sink running.

"You sure I can't do something?" I asked through the door.

"You could go to bed." She sounded more like herself now. A little smart-assy. "And not listen to me puke."

"Nah. Can't sleep. Seems only fair I stay. How many times have you listened to me puke? Watched me?" I drew my knees up to my chest. My bare legs were bristly. Chris likes them shaved. The crazy thing is, I like shaving them for Chris. "I think I actually puked *on* you once."

"More than once." Her voice was getting closer. I imagined her crawling across the floor. The floor creaked, and the light coming from under the door changed. She was on the floor on the other side now. Just an inch of pine between us.

"You sick because of some kind of meds?" I asked, wondering if she was on painkillers.

"Yeah."

We were both quiet for a minute. I could hear the surf. I didn't know if she could hear it, too, from behind the door.

"The docs can't change them up? I mean, with modern medicine and all, you'd think they could give you something to help that wouldn't make you puke." I was quiet again. "Of course, you'd think with modern medicine they'd be able to cure cancer, too."

"You'd think."

Again, we were quiet, but it was an okay quiet. I leaned my shoulder, my cheek against the door, and I could feel the heat from her body. Was that even possible? Maybe I was just imagining it.

"You okay, Janine?" McKenzie asked.

"Am *I* okay?" I sat up. "Okay with what? You puking in there? You dying? Hell no, I'm not *okay*."

"I meant are you okay being here," McKenzie said. "Sleeping in your room. You're welcome to sleep with me. I'm lonely down here by myself."

I've tried to explain, over the years, why I need to sleep at night alone, in my room. It's like . . . I have to be there with Buddy. With the ghosts. As crazy as it sounds, it makes me stronger. Not weaker. Lying in my bed at night, here in the house with my girls, I find the courage to get up in the morning. Do what I do.

I didn't answer her.

"You know," McKenzie said after another long silence, "I don't think you did it. The pregnant woman."

Tears burned the backs of my eyes. But I didn't cry. I tried never to cry.

"I know you wouldn't, Janine," McKenzie said. "I know you could never hurt—"

"That's a lie, Mack. You know I *could*." I drew my knees up closer, folding over them. "You guys know. It's always been there. The . . . potential."

"But you *wouldn't*."

I closed my eyes. Suddenly, I was sleepy. "I hope not."

# ❧ 10 ❧

# McKenzie

I was excited that my girls were coming over. I know it sounds crazy. I'm their mother, for heaven's sake. I carried them in my womb, gave birth to them, sans drugs. I've wiped their butts and threatened to wash out their mouths with soap. How many hours have I spent with them over the last seventeen years?

They could be a pain in the ass. Particularly Maura. Mia was sweet-tempered, for the most part. I always felt as if she wanted to please me on some level and sought my approval. Not that she does everything she's told or always takes my advice. But I always felt like she listened to me. Like she valued my opinion. And she tried to be a good girl. She got good grades in school. She never missed curfew. And when she had a boyfriend, he always seemed like a nice boy from a good family.

Maura, on the other hand, had never been so amiable. At least not with me. As a toddler, she was the one who threw temper tantrums and her milk cup. She brought home a steady stream of Cs with teachers' comments like "not working to her potential." Maura fought me on every front: what she wore, what she said (no F-bombs in my house, please), and whom she dated. She wasn't a bad kid. She had a good heart. But she worried me. What was she going to do when I was gone? Who was going to remind her to do her homework . . . and to go to class when she went to college?

If she even got into college. Right now, she was likely looking at living with her dad and going to community college for a year or two. It worked for a lot of kids, but my Maura . . . I just couldn't see her getting motivated enough to get out of bed and drive to class every day. And I certainly couldn't see her dad making her do it. He was all about "I never went to college and I made out fine." And I understood that argument, but Maura hadn't expressed an interest in a trade. Of course, she did have the NBA-star-wife possibility to fall back on.

So, Tuesday afternoon, I sat on the porch, wrapped in a beach towel because I was chilly. It didn't matter that it was a high of ninety-one today. My new drug seemed to be playing havoc with my central nervous system. This morning I discovered a rash on my palms and the bottoms of my feet that made them tender. I had been warned that that was one of the possible side effects (among thousands, including erectile dysfunction). Was there no end to this joy?

I was alone for a few minutes. Lilly and Janine were in the kitchen making dinner. Mia had called an hour ago and said they were on their way, which in her book meant they were *thinking* about heading out. Aurora was supposed to be on "McKenzie watch," I think, but she'd gone for a walk. Clearly, she wasn't taking her duties seriously.

I laid my book in my lap. A historical romance. Another book *not* on the best one hundred books of all-time list. Fritz looked at me. I looked at him. He was lying in front of the door to the living room; maybe he was on McKenzie watch. I could smell ground chicken with chili powder and cumin frying. I was tickled that Lilly remembered that Mia and Maura liked tacos. At home, we made them for dinner at least once a week. We called it Taco Shmaco night.

"Hey," I called to Aurora, and waved. She was walking off the beach, toward the house. Her hair was pulled up in a messy pile on her head the way high schoolers wore theirs. She might not have been carded at a bar, but she could have passed for twenty-eight.

"Hey, yourself," she called. "Girls here yet?"

I liked that Aurora, Janine, and Lilly all had good relationships with Mia and Maura. It would make it easier for my daughters when I died.

Wouldn't it?

I kept coming up with ways I could make the transition from having a mother to being motherless easier for them. It was a way to alleviate some of my guilt. Because I felt so damned guilty about abandoning them. Logically, I could tell myself it wasn't my fault. I hadn't asked for stage four cancer. My hand was definitely down when that question was posed. But I still felt guilty. I wondered if I had done something, somehow, to deserve this. When I was feeling really dark I wondered, had I known this was going to happen, would I have chosen to have children?

Aurora came up and over the dune. She was carrying something in one hand. She bobbed up the steps to the porch. Fritz lifted his head, checked to see who it was, and relaxed again, closing his eyes. He and Aurora (she wasn't into domesticated animals) felt ambiguous toward each other, and both seemed okay with that.

"Should be here any minute," I said. "They both have off today so they don't have to be anywhere."

"Seventeen-year-old girls always have somewhere to be." Aurora dropped a seashell from her hand onto the arm of my green Adirondack chair. "For you."

I picked up the bleached cockleshell and ran my finger over the ribs. "Beautiful," I sighed. We didn't get loads of shells on the Delaware beaches, not like some beaches I'd been to in Florida. Something to do with the tides, I supposed.

"It's got a hole in the top. I've got three more." Aurora sat down in Lilly's chair beside me.

There was sand all over her legs. She didn't seem to notice. I resisted the urge to brush it off. I loved the beach but hated the sand.

"I thought I'd get something and string them for all of us so we can wear them. Maybe something classy like silver thread." She made her living welding huge pieces of metal together, but she could draw and paint and make jewelry.

"I'd wear it." I handed it back to her for safekeeping.

"Girls are here!" Lilly hollered from in the house. I heard the squeaky brakes on the Ford Focus they shared; their father was supposed to have taken the car to the shop two weeks ago.

Fritz rose and trotted into the house; we rarely kept the air-conditioning on during the day. Instead, the doors and windows were left open to welcome the sea breeze. He barked a greeting. Then there were squeals from Lilly and the girls, followed by more squeals from the girls. When they saw her belly, I would bet. I hadn't told them. I wanted to let Lilly surprise them.

I listened to the voices in the kitchen: Janine's, Lilly's, Maura's, and Mia's. It made me smile to hear them talking all at once. Like good friends. But what they really needed was a mother, not a friend. Aurora and Janine didn't have much maternal instinct. Lilly did, but she was about to have her own baby. I wondered if there was any way to cultivate a little maternal instinct in Aurora and Janine. Was it something that could be learned or was it really *instinct?*

Maura walked out onto the porch first: butt-cheek-length, white cotton shorts and a light pink T-shirt. The hem of the shirt didn't quite meet the waistband of the shorts. I could see her hot pink bra through her shirt. I bit my tongue; I didn't want to start a fight. She knew how I felt about some of her wardrobe selections.

She could have been a Victoria's Secret Pink model. She was tall and thin. Her long red hair was lighter than mine and Mia's. A strawberry blonde. A mother never likes to think that one of her daughters is prettier than the other. I think they're both gorgeous, but Maura definitely has the couture look shown on one of their favorite reality TV shows, *America's Next Top Model.*

"Aunt Aurora!" Maura threw out her arms and ran past me to hug Aurora. I saw that the word *Hotty* was printed, in rhinestones, across the back of her shorts.

*How could that even be comfortable?*

"Maura!" Aurora wrapped her arms around my daughter and kissed one cheek and then the other.

"How was Italy?" Maura gushed. "Did you eat a lot of spaghetti and gelato?"

I sat there smiling, trying hard not to be jealous. Why wouldn't Maura hug Aurora first? She'd seen me last week. She hadn't seen her Aunt Aurora in months.

"Drank a lot of wine. Dated some hot Italian guys," Aurora said.

Maura's eyes got big. "You have to tell me everything." She glanced at me with none of the enthusiasm she had for Aurora. She didn't even try to fake it. "Hey, Mom."

"Hey, sweetie."

Maura leaned over me and brushed her lips across my cheek, barely making contact. I closed my eyes and savored the smell of her strawberry shampoo and the more elusive scent of her skin. I once read about a study where mothers were blindfolded and separated from their infants. The subjects were able to find their own babies in a room of babies, just by their scent. A scent others couldn't detect. I could find my girls with my eyes closed in an auditorium full of teens in booty shorts.

"Hi, Mom." Mia walked out onto the porch and leaned over my chair, giving me an awkward teenage-girl-hugging-her-mom-because-she-has-to hug. But she touched her cheek to mine, and for just an instant, I felt the deep connection I'd known when she was a little girl. Before the rules of society and her hormones came between us. Mia had used the same strawberry shampoo as Maura this morning, but her scent was subtly different. I could have picked her out from Maura in a roomful of girls, too.

"How you feeling?" She adjusted my teal head scarf. "You look good. Like you got some sun. Have you been on the beach?"

Before I could answer, Aurora took center stage.

"Mia!" Aurora opened her arms.

Mia was shorter than Maura and a little thicker in the waist and hips. Mia desperately wished she had been an identical twin. She was always talking about going on a diet. And wanting me to let her lighten her hair so it was closer to Maura's shade. She wore her hair piled on top of her head like a bird's nest—just like Maura's and Aurora's. She was the least skimpily clad of the three of them, though, in cute jean shorts and a white volleyball team T-shirt with our last name on the back.

Mia threw herself at Aurora. "I've missed you so much," she murmured, her voice surprisingly emotional.

"Me too." Aurora kissed her on both cheeks, too. The girls loved how she did that. *European-style,* they said.

"So tell me what's going on." Aurora looked from one teen to the other.

Maura had her cell phone out texting. Apparently it had been located.

"Boys? School? Boys?" Aurora asked.

I wondered what Jude would think if he saw his mother interacting with my girls this way. Would he be jealous? Or did he just not care? He'd grown up a privileged kid with his über-wealthy father and stepmother. To my knowledge, Aurora hadn't seen him in at least two years, and that encounter had been unplanned; they ran into each other in Geneva.

So maybe he didn't think of Aurora as his mother at all. I wondered if she was like a cool auntie to him. Or just a nice stranger? I honestly didn't know. Aurora would talk about nearly anything: her sexual escapades, her yeast infection, or how she got her pubes caught in the zipper of her jeans. No subject seemed to be taboo with her, except Jude. Janine was the only one who could bring him up, and even she had to be cautious. Aurora had been known to take an unplanned trip to the Azores, just to avoid a conversation about the boy she gave birth to twenty years ago.

"I'm not going out with anyone. Andy and I broke up before the end of school." Mia lifted her shoulder and let it fall. "He was going to college. I didn't think it was a good idea, dating him when he'd be in Virginia and I'd still be here. But you have to ask Maura about *Viktor*." She sang the name, using the silly pseudo-Russian accent again.

"So you guys are going out?" I asked, looking at Maura.

She didn't glance up from her phone. "We're just talking," she deadpanned. Then she held up her phone in her sister's direction. "Do the kiss thing again, Aunt Aurora. I want a pic."

Aurora complied, kissing Mia on both cheeks.

"Got it." Maura hit the screen of her phone with her thumb.

"Your camera looks different than mine." I leaned toward her to look at the screen.

"It's the same." She sounded annoyed with me. I thought I was pretty technology savvy for a woman my age, but I wasn't in the same league with seventeen-year-old girls.

"I don't have that red button on my camera."

Maura turned the phone so I could see the screen and hit an arrow key in the middle of the photo of Mia and Aurora. The still photo became a video, and I watched Aurora kiss Mia again.

"Wow. My phone will do that, too?" I picked mine up off the armrest.

Maura rolled her eyes, taking my phone from my hand. She scrolled and touched the screen several times, faster than I could keep up, and the red button appeared. "You just hit the button to start and stop the video." She handed it back to me.

I was momentarily fascinated. "Do it again," I told Aurora, gesturing with my free hand.

"Mom," Maura groaned.

"Aurora, kiss her again." I held up the phone.

Aurora and Mia humored me. I watched Aurora kiss Mia on

both cheeks through my screen. "Aww," I sighed. When they were done, I hit the red button. The little light kept blinking; it kept recording. I pressed it again. It stopped. "And I can upload this onto my Facebook page?" I asked. I hit the replay button and watched it, hearing my "Awww" in the background and Maura muttering, "Really, Mom? Facebook is so lame."

"Where does the video go when I close the app?" I ask.

Mia looked at her sister, then me. It was a "be patient" plea. "With your pictures. Pick the photo icon and it will be under *camera roll*. You should have something that says *videos*, too."

"So which does it go in?" I asked, trying to follow her instructions with my two left thumbs.

"Both, I think."

"Ah, there it is." I didn't know why I was so delighted. Actually, I did. Because something had just occurred to me. "Aurora, what would you think of me doing a video diary this month? Instead of the usual written account? Think that would fulfill my obligation?" I looked at her through the lens of the camera in my phone. "This would be way easier."

Aurora shrugged. "I like reading the stuff, but I guess. It might be cool."

Lilly walked onto the porch, with Janine following behind her, carrying a tray of glasses of iced tea and sodas. I hit the record button again.

"Dinner will be ready in fifteen minutes," Lilly announced. "Just waiting on the rice."

I watched them, via my cell phone screen. It gave me an interesting perspective. Janine looked funny carrying the tray, walking behind Lilly like she was her maid: Lilly in her pristine sundress, Janine in her baggy board shorts and a K-Coast T-shirt. What was even funnier was that Fritz was following dutifully behind *her*. Which made it crowded on the front deck. And everyone was talking at once.

"Unsweetened," Janine told Mia, pointing at one of the iced tea glasses. She pointed to another glass. "Coke."

"Nope, just one," Lilly was telling Maura as she rubbed her protruding abdomen.

Aurora grabbed a glass of iced tea and set it down on my armchair, filling my screen with the glass. I'd have to learn to use the focus button.

"Sugar?" Aurora asked.

I hit the red button. The video stopped. "Please."

We sat on the deck and sipped our drinks; Lilly and I in the chairs, Janine standing, Aurora and my girls perched on the rail. Everyone talking, and Lilly was getting loud—to be heard—and it was . . . glorious. I was so happy. The five most important people in the world to me were at arm's length.

I listened to Maura giggle over something Lilly said. I heard snatches of conversation between Janine and Mia; they were talking about where Mia would be applying to college. As I listened, I felt as if I was taking a step back from them. One minute I was in the fray, the next, I was an outsider. Watching, but not participating.

Would it be like this when I was dead? Would I be able to watch my daughters interact with my best friends from the clouds? Would my spirit hover over my daughters? Guide them? Would I ring bells on Christmas trees? Would my face appear in condensation on glasses, to let my daughters know I was with them, in spirit if no longer in the flesh? Or would it be like one of my assistant librarians had said: When you died, you just no longer existed?

One would think that dying would force one to come to some conclusions about death. So far, I hadn't. It wasn't that I hadn't thought about it, because I had. A lot. I was envious of my friends who had strong religious beliefs—who *knew* what was going to happen to them when they died. I wrote "Methodist" on forms when asked of my religious affiliation, but only because when I was a kid we'd gone to a Methodist church on Christmas and Easter. My mother now attended regularly and belonged to a prayer group at her local church. I got the feeling, though, that the women spent as much time drinking tea as they did praying. She said they prayed for me all the time, though exactly what they were praying for, I wasn't sure. For me to be healed. Or at least not die, I suppose. I found it hard to believe old ladies drinking tea could save me when science couldn't. But I wasn't so convinced that I had asked my mother and her friends *not* to pray for me.

Fritz sat down beside my chair, and I glanced at him. We were both outsiders.

He looked at me, at the others, and then at me again. I felt as if he was trying to communicate something to me, but I'm not good at doggie language. We didn't even have a dog anymore. Our border collie had died two years ago. We had planned on getting a puppy, but we'd been waiting for an opportunity to rip up the old carpet in the family room . . . for I don't even remember how long. Then I was diagnosed, and I guess we forgot all about the puppy.

Fritz stared at me with his expressive dark eyes. And I smiled. I smiled at him. At my girls. At my friends, and then at the great wide ocean that was my front yard.

Dinner, served at the table in the living room, was more mass confusion. Everyone was still talking at once. Janine's phone rang twice, Lilly's, too. Fritz, who never barked, went crazy when some kids rolled a stalled scooter in behind my girls' car and started it again. Maura managed to keep up with what was being said at the table while texting to friends. At home, we had a rule about no cell phones at the table, but I knew Jared allowed them. I was learning to pick my fights. And no one else seemed to mind that Maura was with us, but not entirely.

Since we were clearly ignoring the no-phones-at-the-table rule, I recorded with mine: Lilly chattering about a belly band; Janine taking a big bite of taco and it exploding all over her plate; Maura texting madly with one hand, munching a taco with the other; Aurora sitting back, nibbling on a taco shell, and drinking a beer; Mia smiling at me from across the table, salsa on the corner of her mouth.

Lilly's tacos were good, though I dared eat only one and a little rice. Refried beans? No way. My gastrointestinal tract was already a hot mess.

My girls didn't really talk to me. They wanted to know about Lilly's baby; she showed them sonogram pictures on her phone. Janine was telling them about some class she and Fritz were taking; he was learning to open gates and jump over fences. Why, I didn't catch. Aurora, on her third beer of the meal, regaled us with tales of London, Paris, and Geneva.

Jealousy bubbled up as I watched Maura rest her head against Lilly's shoulder while Lilly let her feel the baby moving in her belly. It wasn't so much jealousy over the relationship Janine, Aurora, and Lilly had with my girls, but with the time they would get with them. A part of me thought Maura and Mia should be sitting on each side of me, talking to me, putting their heads on *my* shoulders. Why didn't they want to spend every minute I had left with me?

Of course we'd had long talks about this. I had stressed again and again how important it was to me that they go about their lives. That it would break my heart to see them miss their senior year of high school, moping around, waiting for me to drop. I made it clear to them that the only way I would not crack up, the only way I could do this gracefully, was if they lived their lives as if I *wasn't* dying.

I guess I just hadn't expected them to actually listen to me.

Too soon, dinner was over. And suddenly I was exhausted. Everyone began to carry dirty plates and empty bowls to the kitchen. I just sat in my chair, my chest feeling heavy. It was as if someone had sucked all the oxygen out of the air. And I had thought earlier today that I was breathing a little easier. I'd walked down to the beach this morning and had barely gotten out of breath. Had it been my imagination?

"Why don't you go lie down," Lilly suggested, hovering over my shoulder. "Maybe stretch out on the couch."

I picked up my plate; it was incredibly heavy. She took it from my hand.

"Go on," she urged in a whisper. "You look beat."

Janine watched me from the other side of the table, where she'd been clearing dishes. She had a bowl of shredded cheese in one hand, a water glass in the other.

I glanced at the open windows across the front of the house. The sheer curtains were whipping around. It had clouded up outside. We were expecting rain tonight. But it was supposed to be clear for the Fourth on Thursday, Janine had said.

I heard my girls laughing in the kitchen with Aurora. Then the garbage disposal running. It was clinking. Someone had dropped something down it, a spoon or a bottle cap.

I looked up at Lilly, feeling as if the world were spinning on its axis a little slower than it had been when we sat down for dinner an hour ago. "Maybe I will," I said, my voice breathy.

I didn't see Janine put down the dishes or come around the table, but somehow her arm was around me. "Come on," she murmured.

"I don't know what's . . . wrong with . . . me," I heard myself say.

"Up you go." Janine practically lifted me out of the chair. We walked, arms around each other, across the room to the couch. "You want to lie down for a minute?"

I shook my head and cut my eyes in the direction of the kitchen. I didn't like my girls to see me like this. Weak. "Maybe just . . . the chair."

The ten feet to the chair felt like eight miles. I actually sighed with relief when my butt hit it. I didn't know why I was so tired. Why it had come on me so quickly.

Janine covered my lap with an old patchwork quilt that someone had made for her. I couldn't remember who.

"Need anything?" she asked. "Water? A gin and tonic?" Her dark eyes twinkled.

I tried to breathe deeply. "Maybe some . . . new . . . lungs."

She was squatted in front of me. I could tell she was worried, but she was trying to play it cool. "You think you need a hit of oxygen, sweetie?"

I had let her bring the portable oxygen tank into the house, just because I didn't know if it should be sitting in my hot car. But so far, it had just sat in the corner of the bedroom. I shook my head. "I'll be fine."

"Okay." She stood up. "We'll just get the dishes cleaned up and then come in." She glanced over her shoulder as she headed for the kitchen. "Smells like rain coming."

I closed my eyes for a second. Maybe five minutes.

"Mom."

Startled, I opened my eyes. It was Mia.

"You okay?" she asked.

I forced a smile. "Just tired."

"It's like . . . six thirty, Mom."

A piece of hair had fallen from her updo, and my hand itched to reach out and tuck it behind her ear. She'd had bangs for a while, but she was growing them out.

"You tell her we're leaving?" Maura walked into the room.

I looked up. "I thought you were staying." I looked at Maura, then at Mia again. "You're not staying to play cards?"

Mia cut her eyes at Maura. "We . . . were thinking about going over to Sondra's place. She invited us . . . her parents will be there and stuff. I guess we could—"

"No, go. It's okay."

Maura had her phone out again, texting. Mia's was clutched in her hand. I heard it ding, telling her she'd received a new text message.

"They wanna know if we want to go for ice cream," Maura said.

"Go," I repeated.

That was all Maura needed. "Okay, see you, Mom. Bye. Love you." She threw me a kiss.

"Love you, Mom," Mia murmured. She leaned over me, rested her hands on my shoulders, and kissed my cheek.

"Love you," I said, making my voice steady. I was already feeling better. I wasn't sure what that had been at the table. "Love you, Maura Alexandra," I called after her. "See you for fireworks."

"Traffic is going to be awful," Maura moaned. "I was thinking we could skip it this year. I don't even like fireworks."

"We'll get Dad to drop us off." Mia backed away, looking at her phone. "We'll be here, Mom."

"You could invite your father to join us. Chelsea and Peaches, too," I said cheerfully. "You know we have the best view on the beach."

"Right. Like *that* wouldn't be awkward," Maura mumbled as she left the room.

"Call you tomorrow, Mom," Mia promised.

"Call you tomorrow, Mom," Maura hollered from the kitchen.

I sat back in the chair and listened to their good-byes.

A minute after the back door closed, Aurora walked through the living room, making a beeline for the deck. "You good?" she asked as she went by. She didn't make eye contact.

"I'm good."

"I'm just going to get some air." She slipped through a tangle of sheers. The curtains were whipping around in the wind. Someone needed to close the doors.

"I think it's starting to rain," I called after her.

Lilly walked into the living room, glancing in Aurora's direction. I could hear Janine in the kitchen, water running.

"She okay?" Lilly whispered, pointing in the direction of the deck.

I looked at her. "What did I miss?"

# ❦ 11 ❧

# Janine

I glanced toward the open doors to the front deck. Fritz watched Aurora from just inside the living room.

The wind had picked up. The sheer white floor-to-ceiling drapes Lilly and I had hung two summers ago whipped like eerie dancing ghosts. It had gotten cooler outside. I could hear the first pit-pats of rain on the glass.

When the house is warm and sunny and bright, I'm not afraid, but when it rains, I feel uneasy.

It had been raining that night. The night of Buddy's demise.

"What's wrong with Aurora?" McKenzie asked me. "Did Maura—"

"I don't think Maura said anything wrong," I said. McKenzie looked pale. Except for bright red raised circles on the apples of each cheek. Not good. Did she have a fever? She'd been breathing heavy this afternoon, even though she hadn't exerted any more energy than it took to walk from the deck to the table. I didn't know if I should say anything. She wasn't exactly touchy about being sick, but she'd made it clear that she didn't want us to dwell on it every minute of every day. Of course it was all I could think about.

"Because I know," McKenzie went on, "that Maura can sometimes . . ."

She didn't finish. She didn't have to. I knew what she meant. At some point or another, Maura, since hitting her teenage years, had brushed each of us the wrong way. Most of the time it was McKenzie. Maura could be critical and antagonistic and sometimes downright mean. But I'd been in the kitchen with the girls and Aurora. Aurora had seemed fine until Mia and Maura went out the door. Then she'd suddenly teared up and walked abruptly out of the kitchen, out onto the deck.

Lilly came into the living room, a dish towel in her hands. She took one look at our faces and lowered her voice. "What's going on?" She glanced in the direction of the deck, then back at us. "Aurora?"

I touched my cheek with my fingertip and drew downward.

"Crying?" She made a face like she didn't believe me. Lilly knew she was the crier of the group. McKenzie and I were somewhere in the middle, but Aurora? Aurora never cried.

*Why?* she mouthed. Then she looked at McKenzie and reached out and laid her hand on her forehead. "You okay? You don't feel hot, but you look like you have a fever."

"I'm fine." McKenzie grasped Mother Lilly's wrist and lowered her hand.

Lilly looked at me. "Go see what's wrong." She pointed.

I glanced at the open doors. Rain was coming in, making little round circles on the hardwood in the doorway. Fritz just stood there, muzzle thrust out. Watching Aurora.

I looked back at Lilly. "Me?" I whispered. "I'm not good at this. Maybe . . . maybe Mack should go."

"She's sick," Lilly hissed. "She needs to stay put." She pointed at McKenzie, just to make sure she understood her instructions.

McKenzie looked up at me. She was wrapped up in the quilt. She didn't move a muscle. "I'll go."

"No," I said, sounding like I was headed for the electric chair. "I'll do it."

I wanted to call "dead man walking" as I went slowly to the door. I was so *not* good at this. With tears. With emotion in general. At least any emotion that wasn't anger. Anger I was pretty good with. I could even deal with a little rage on the side.

I stood in the doorway, sharing it with the dog. The lights on the front deck were out, but I could see Aurora on the north end, leaning on the rail. Lamplight from the living room backlit her.

Rain hit me in the face.

Fritz whined.

*Okay, okay, I'm going already. But you know I suck at this.* Some dog owners say they have a telepathic connection with their pets. I looked at him. He looked at me. Whined again. Maybe it was only one way with Fritz and me. Maybe he could read my thoughts, but I sure as hell couldn't read his.

I stepped out onto the deck. The wind caught my hair and blew it back. The rain was cool on my face. It felt good. I walked to the rail and stood beside Aurora. I gazed out over the beach, then at her. Tears ran down her face, wet from the rain. But she didn't make a sound.

I just stood there for a minute, hands stuffed in my pockets. "You okay?" I finally asked.

She didn't answer.

I heard Fritz come outside, his nails clicking on the wood deck. I needed to get out my Dremel and sand them down.

"Aurora?"

She pressed her lips together. She was so pretty, even with her hair wet, beginning to stick to her head.

"You think he thinks about me?" Her voice sounded as if it were coming from far away, ethereal almost.

It took me a minute to realize whom she was talking about. *Jude.*

"You think he ever wonders . . ." She closed her eyes and raindrops hit her eyelids. "You think he wonders what would have happened if I hadn't abandoned him?"

"You didn't a—"

She opened her eyes and glared at me, and I shut up instantly. "No lies," she said.

"No lies," I repeated. It was our code, hers and mine. The other two, we let them tell us untruths sometimes. We told *them* untruths. Little ones at least. Untruths to smooth over hurt feelings or cover for our occasional inadequacies. But never Aurora and me. There was no need for lies. She knew my deepest, darkest place. She'd been there.

So Aurora had a right to call me on the lie I had almost told. Fair was fair. She actually *had* abandoned her son at the hospital less than twelve hours after he was born. She had handed him to her ex-boyfriend and walked out of a private LA hospital. The next time she saw Jude, he was two and a half.

I looked out over the rail. Though the sun hadn't set yet, the clouds covered it. I could hear the waves hitting the beach. I could see the white foam in the wet sand. "You did what you thought was the right thing at the time," I said.

"Right for me. But what about him, Janine? What about Jude?"

I didn't say anything. What was I going to say? If I'd gotten knocked up by my boyfriend (which, of course, wasn't possible because, at the time, I had been with a cute little gal from west Texas named Clementine), I wouldn't have given up my son. Clementine couldn't have pried him out of my arms.

Aurora took a shuddering breath. "Maura and Mia, they love McKenzie so much. They adore her, and she adores them. I could have . . . I could have had that with Jude. I could have had someone of my very own." She looked at me, her lower lip trembling. "He could have loved me the way Maura and Mia love her. I really fucked up, Janine."

My eyes felt scratchy behind my eyelids. I wasn't used to seeing Aurora cry or hearing such devastation in her voice. She never second-guessed herself. She was the tough one. We cried on her shoulder, not the other way around.

"You can't go back," I told her. I leaned my forearms on the wet rail. "You can't change what you did. But you *can* go forward." I glanced at her and then out over the dunes. A rabbit hopped through the swaying sea grass.

Fritz spotted him and made a grumble in his throat, pushing his muzzle between two vertical rails. It wasn't a growl. He was better disciplined than that, but his canine instincts were still there.

"Have a seat, boy," I said, my voice low.

He dropped to his haunches. It was beginning to rain harder, but his thick coat shed the water easily.

Me, on the other hand—my hair was getting wet. It was beginning to stick to my face and the back of my neck.

"I don't know how to move forward," Aurora whispered. "How do you make up for twenty-some years of being a shitty person?"

"You're not a shitty person." I felt like I should put my arm around her or take her hand. Something. But I wasn't good at that. I wasn't like Lilly, who kissed everyone hello and good-bye. Hugged in line at the grocery store. So I just stood there, feeling like an idiot, feeling like my own heart was breaking with hers. "You're not a shitty person," I repeated.

"I'm a shitty mom," she said.

"Okay, so you are that," I agreed.

We both laughed. Which was kind of warped.

She sniffed. "You guys should have told me not to leave him."

"We did. Don't you remember? All of us were in your hospital bed. We stayed all night. Even when the nurse threatened to call security."

"Then you shouldn't have let me do it."

"What?" I looked at her. "I should have handcuffed you to his bassinet?"

"If you had to."

I didn't respond. Even though it sounded like she was trying to blame me for her abandoning her kid, I knew she wasn't. And the thing was, over the years, I did sometimes feel as if I didn't do enough to keep her and Jude together. And that's on me. Always will be.

In a way, Aurora abandoning Jude had been the easy way out, not just for her, but for us, too. I could imagine how messy that would have been, Aurora with a baby, with a toddler, a middle schooler. He would have ended up at our homes more than hers. Especially since she didn't really have a home.

"What I'm trying to say," I told her, "and doing it badly, is that if you want a relationship with Jude, it's not too late."

"It is." Her voice broke again.

"It isn't. I mean, okay, it's too late to be his mom, but maybe . . . maybe you can be something else, Aurora. *Someone* else. Maybe just his friend."

Another silence stretched between us. We just stood there, side by side, looking at the beach, lost in our thoughts. Then it began to rain harder. The temperature started to drop. I was beginning to feel chilled, now that I was soaked through.

"We should go inside," I finally said. "See how McKenzie is feeling."

"She looked sick tonight at the table."

"Yeah. She says it's nothing. I don't know. If she doesn't look better, maybe we should take her home to see her doctor or something."

"I don't think she wants to do that." Aurora turned to me, leaning against the rail. She looked thin, too thin, with her hair and clothes plastered to her skin.

"So maybe we shouldn't give her a choice. She's so weak." I glanced in the direction of the living room. "I could probably pick her up and carry her ass out of here."

"She has a right to do this the way she wants to." Aurora sounded better. More like her usual self. Nothing suited her better than a good argument. "You don't—*we* don't—have the right to make her do anything."

I pushed my hair back, slicking it over my head. Crisis averted, at least temporarily, and I was cold. "I'm going inside. You coming?"

"Race you to the bar."

# ❦ 12 ❧

# Aurora

I'm surprised I heard my cell ring at all. I probably wouldn't have, except that I had plugged it in on the nightstand to charge before I went to sleep/passed out. It was dead: It had been dead two days apparently. When I plugged it in, the screen came up to tell me I'd missed eleven calls. I didn't bother to see who had called: my agent, my manager, my publicist probably. Maybe Fortunato. Time to change my number again.

So anyway. The phone. It rang in the middle of the night. Not that unusual. If I'd realized it was on, I would have shut it off. But the gin had gotten the better of me. What was unusual about the event was that I answered the phone. I wouldn't have picked up if I'd been awake and sober.

"Yeah?" I sat up on the edge of the bed. I was wearing a T-shirt and bikini top. Not sure where the bottoms had gotten to.

"Aunt Aurora?"

I squeezed my eyes shut. Opened them. I felt as if I were on a merry-go-round. Only two people called me that. "Mia or Maura?" I muttered. I could never tell them apart on the phone.

"Mia. Aunt Aurora, we need your help."

The tone of her voice revived me more than what she was saying.
"Okay."

"We need you to come get us. The police are here. I think they're going to arrest Maura."

*Shit*, I thought. Maybe I said it out loud. I fumbled for the light switch on the lamp beside my bed. Knocked over a half-filled bottle of water. I heard it splash on the floor. No lid.

"Aunt Aurora?"

I flipped on the light on the third try. "Yup. I'm here." The brightness of the seventy-five-watt bulb made me wince.

"Can you come? Maura says if you come now, maybe they'll let her go. You know, because of Aunt Janine. Maybe she should come, too. Maybe Aunt Janine can make them not arrest her. Cops do that, right? For each other? Get friends off for minor stuff? She didn't murder anybody or anything."

Mia was talking so fast that it was hard for me to follow. "Slow down, slow down." *And talk a little quieter.* "Where are you?"

"On the beach."

"Where on the beach?" I said, annoyed. "Give me a city. A state."

"Um . . . I don't know. We're in Delaware. Delaware. North of Lewes. You take Route 16 from 1. After you go over that bridge thing. I think they're going to take her to the police troop. The one next to Wawa."

I was having a hard time following. Maura got arrested, and the cops were going to take her to get a slushy? "State police?" I asked, spotting my white bikini bottom on the floor.

"Yeah." Her voice was trembling. I could tell she was trying hard not to cry. "She was smoking, too, I think. Weed. Can they tell if she's been smoking with the Breathalyzer thing?"

I stood up, and the phone got yanked out of my hand and hit the nightstand. It was still attached to the wall. I picked it up, unplugging the charging wire. "Mia, you still there?"

"Maura said you'd come." She was crying now. "She said you'd know what to do. You and Aunt Janine. Maura can't go to jail, Aunt Aurora. Mom can't handle that right now. She shouldn't have to."

Mia's words were all running together again.

I picked up the bikini bottom, thinking I had to get dressed. Then I realized the bikini bottom didn't count as clothing, and I let it fall to the floor again. "I'm coming."

"You are?"

The room spun, and I wobbled on my bare feet. "Yup. Of course."

"Okay, but you won't tell Mom, right? Maybe she doesn't have to know. Maybe she'll die before Maura gets sent to jail and she'll never have to know. It's not like she'll be able to see from heaven, right?" She sniffled.

Mia's sweet, naive words made me smile . . . and sober up a little. I grabbed a pair of jeans off the back of a chair draped with my clothing. "I won't wake your mom. If she has to be told, it doesn't have to be tonight."

"She doesn't," Mia said, panicky again. "Maura says she never has to know. It'll kill her, Aunt Aurora. That's what Maura said to tell you."

I stepped into the jeans, one foot, then the other, steadying myself with the chair, keeping the phone trapped between my chin and my shoulder. My mouth tasted like I had thrown up a little in it. I eyed the water bottle lying on the floor. It looked like there might be a sip left in it. "Exactly where are you?" I asked. When she didn't answer, I asked again, "Mia, where are *you?* The police and Maura won't be hard to find. The flashing lights and all, but I need to be able to find *you*."

"I'm at my car. Parked along the road. I think it's called Bayview or something like that. It runs along the beach. I didn't know what to do or where to go. Maura said—"

"Just stay put, okay?"

"I'm scared, Aunt Aurora. She wasn't even very drunk, only this guy we don't even know got into a fight with some other guy, and they said he pulled a knife and . . . I don't know who called the cops. Maura thought we should run, but then they put the spotlights on us and—"

"Probably just as well you didn't run," I interrupted. Her jabbering was making me nauseated. I slipped my feet into flip-flops and slapped to the door, then, realizing I'd left the light on, I went back to turn it off. "Both of you would be locked up and then who would have called me? Stay where you are, Mia. Stay in your car. No booze and no pot. At least until I get there." I raised my finger threateningly.

"I wasn't drinking," Mia wailed. "I was the DD. I'm always the DD."

I sort of laughed. Except that clearly this wasn't funny. If Maura got arrested for drinking underage and possession, McKenzie would come unglued. "Be there as quick as I can."

I hung up and checked the screen of my cell. It was two eleven. I stepped out into the dark hallway and debated whether or not to pee first or wake Janine first. If I startled her and she pulled a gun or a Bowie knife on me, or some shit like that, I was liable to piss my pants. On the other hand, time was of the essence here, and she needed at least a couple of minutes to get dressed and get her cop face on.

I walked past Lilly's quiet room. At Janine's door, I tapped lightly. I didn't want anyone else in the house to hear me, but I wasn't dumb enough to open the door and get eaten by a dog, either.

"Yeah?" Janine's voice came. It didn't sound like she'd even been asleep.

I opened the door a crack, thinking if Fritz came at me, I could slam it on his snout or something. I've never even seen him behave aggressively, but tonight wasn't the night I wanted to test him.

"I need you to take a little ride with me," I said softly.

"Okay." I heard her get out of bed. "Bring Fritz or leave him?"

"Better leave him." I closed the door. Janine didn't ask where we were going or why.

# 13

# Janine

"Thanks, Aunt Janine. Thanks so much." Mia gave me an awkward side-hug as we walked toward my car, parked along Bayshore Drive. Not Bayview, as she had told Aurora. Luckily, I knew exactly where to go. We arrested kids here all the time.

"Yeah, thanks, Aunt Janine. This whole thing was bogus," Maura said, sounding all righteous and tough.

We had gotten lucky. No one had administered a Breathalyzer test to Maura yet when we arrived. Clearly, she'd been drinking. And smoking marijuana from the smell of her hair.

The troopers had so many underage drinkers rounded up that they were still waiting for backup when Aurora and I arrived. I knew one of the troopers on the scene well. He let me take Maura without much more than the warning to her that if her aunt wasn't such a good cop, if he didn't respect me so much, Maura would be on her way to the troop with the rest of her friends. It wasn't even a big favor really. One less teen to process tonight.

"Should . . . should we just go back to Dad's?" Mia asked as we crossed the road.

I leaned toward her, sniffing. "How much did *you* have to drink?"

"Nothing!"

It was dark. I could hardly see her face, but I didn't need to. "Pants on fire."

"Like one beer," Mia insisted defensively.

I glanced at Maura, walking on the other side of me. She was a little drunk, but I knew she'd only blow a .07 or so. Wouldn't have mattered. She was underage. If the girls hadn't had the good sense to call Aurora right away, Maura would have been looking at an underage drinking charge. And possible possession when they frisked her. I didn't want to know what was in her pockets.

"My sister was the DD," Maura insisted. "If she says she only had *a* beer, she only had *a* beer."

"I could use a beer about now," Aurora muttered, just loud enough for us to hear. She was walking behind us, smoking a cigarette she'd bummed from one of the teens huddled in a group, waiting to be carted off in a paddy wagon.

We didn't have paddy wagons, of course. Well, we did have vans for transporting multiple suspects at a time, but my guess was that they wouldn't even call them to the troop. Too much work. It would take too much time away from real police duties. Their parents would be called, their information would be taken down, and they'd be notified of their court dates. I'd worked this same scenario enough times that I could have worked it drunk. I snickered at my own joke.

"You're not driving home," I told Mia.

"What about my car?"

I pulled my keys out of my pocket and unlocked the doors of my Jeep with the remote. "We're leaving it here."

"How am I going to get it in the morning?" Her voice was getting high-pitched again. "Dad'll want to know where the car is. What am I going to tell him?"

"You'll think of something. My guess is that this won't be the first time you lied to him." I climbed in the driver's side. They all got in: Aurora beside me, the two girls in the back.

Aurora buckled in, then leaned on the seat to talk to the girls as I pulled back onto the road. "Here's what you do. You tell your dad you had a beer and—"

"I can't tell my dad I *had a beer!*" Mia wailed, too loudly, from the backseat.

"No, no, listen to me," Aurora soothed. "You tell him you had a beer, just one, but you knew it wasn't safe to drive home, so—"

"Don't you have a curfew?" I asked. A cruiser, blue lights flashing, passed us going the other way. "Where does your dad think you are right now?"

"I don't know. Probably in bed," Maura said. "He doesn't wait up. Peaches gets up a lot at night still. Dad sleeps like he's dead when he can sleep."

"Mia, you tell him you knew you shouldn't drive, so you just got a ride home," Aurora suggested. "He'll be offering to give you a ride back to get your car."

I frowned.

Aurora looked at me. "What? It'll work. You know it will. Parents eat that shit up, thinking their kids made *good choices.*"

I thought about our conversation the night before. About Jude. Maybe Aurora really had made the right decision, letting his father take him. I couldn't imagine Aurora being a mother to teenagers. She acted like one herself still.

"I'm telling you, he'll totally believe you," Aurora said.

She'd still been half wasted when she woke me up. Right now, I guessed that she and Maura would be blowing the same blood alcohol level. But Aurora knew how to handle her booze. And she was an adult. Free to screw up her life as she saw fit. Maura wasn't old enough to be making those kinds of decisions. At least she wasn't in my book.

"I don't think beer should be in the explanation." I glanced in the rearview mirror at the girls.

Annoyed that I wasn't agreeing with her, Aurora harrumphed and settled back in her seat. "I'm just glad you called, Mia." She glanced over the seat. "You know your sister saved your ass, Maura."

We rode in silence out to Route 1. I made a U-turn and went south.

We were passing through the Five Points intersection when Maura asked, completely out of the blue, "Hey, Aunt Aurora, who's Buddy McCollister? Or should we be asking you that, Aunt Janine?"

I swear to God, I wasn't expecting that question. I mean . . . I was expecting it one day, but . . . not tonight. Not now. Not with their mom being so sick.

I looked at Aurora. She looked at me. We'd talked about this day. About what we would do when they asked. We had hoped that McKenzie would tell them before it ever got to us. She should have told them by now. Even Lilly agreed. But none of us were living in the real world right now. Certainly McKenzie wasn't. We were in some kind of limbo, waiting for her to die. Waiting for our hearts and our lives to shatter.

"Who told you about Buddy?" Aurora threw over the seat. She'd been besties with the girls a minute ago, but now she sounded angry.

"Nobody. We read it on the Internet. Wikipedia," Mia said.

I cut my eyes at Aurora. She stared straight ahead. Suddenly, she was looking completely sober.

"What did it say?" I asked, keeping my voice level. Wikipedia? Fucking *Wikipedia?*

"That Aunt Aurora killed him when she was fourteen years old." Maura. Slightly accusatory. My guess was that this was her way of defusing the situation. I was known to use the same coping mechanism myself, on occasion. "Then I Googled his name. I found the obituary. It said he'd died at home in Albany Beach."

I could have told the girls we'd talk about it later.

I felt light-headed. I wasn't ready for this. Not right now. Not with McKenzie being sick. Lilly with a bun in the oven. Me with . . . Chris and the lawsuit. I gripped the steering wheel until my fingers hurt.

"If we don't tell them," Aurora said, not even making an attempt to keep them from hearing her, "they're just going to find more stuff on the Internet. Better they hear it from us."

We drove past the outlets on the northbound side, then the southbound side. *Tax free shopping!* a sign declared. All shopping in Delaware was sales-tax free. I signaled left to turn onto Rehoboth Avenue. The light was green.

"You don't have to tell us," Mia piped up. "Not if you don't want to, Aunt Aurora."

"I think we have a right to know," Maura said.

I scowled. But I got off on the circle before the exit to Jared's house and continued on Rehoboth Avenue. It was quiet. Bars were closed. There were a few cars parked on the street. The lights were green, one after another.

"Where we going?" Mia asked. She sounded a little uneasy. Like she thought maybe we were going to kidnap her or something.

"We'll sit on the beach for a few minutes," I said. I checked the dashboard. It was three forty a.m. "Then I'll take you home." I made a U-turn and took First Street on the right.

"You don't have to say a word," Aurora told me softly. She slid her hand across the seat, touched my leg, and pulled it away before I had a chance to push her off.

I parked practically on the boardwalk on Olive. The street was empty except for a lime green VW Beetle. New. 2013. 2014. Maryland plates. Purple *Fractured Prune Bakery* bumper sticker. Crooked, on the right side of the rear bumper. Weird that I would notice those details.

I'm good with details. Especially when it comes to vehicles. Tool of the trade.

I got out of the Jeep. Everyone else got out. I locked it with the remote and led the way onto the deserted boardwalk, down the steps, and onto the sand. The last couple years, the landscape of the beach in the whole area had changed. Mother Nature kept pushing with hurricanes and nor'easters and the US Army Corp of Engineers kept pushing back with dredging operations and dune construction.

We sat in a row, in the damp sand, facing the ocean. Me, then Aurora, then Mia. Maura was on the end. The rain had passed hours ago, and I could tell from the barometric pressure that it was going to be a clear day.

"Me or you?" Aurora asked. She was drinking from a water bottle she'd found on the floor of my car. Considering how much gin she'd consumed the previous night, I was pretty impressed that she'd sobered up so quickly.

"You." I drew my bare knees up, hugging them to me. "I can't. Not tonight."

We were all quiet for a minute; there were just the comforting sounds of the waves washing on the shore.

"So it's true? You really killed someone, Aunt Aurora?" Maura asked. "He was your relative, right, Aunt Janine? Oh my God," she murmured then. "He was your father, wasn't he? The obituary said he was forty-one when he died."

I lowered my forehead to my knees, drawing myself into a tight ball. Aurora didn't dare touch me, but her voice was a caress.

"You're okay," she murmured in my ear. "You're going to be fine."

And I was fine. Surprisingly enough.

Aurora told the story. She kept it brief, but she didn't sugarcoat it. What would have been the point of that? What, with Wikipedia out there?

"We were all staying at the beach house. Janine and her family lived there year-round. It was Janine and her mom and dad and us. Her little brother wasn't there," Aurora explained. "My room now—that was Todd's. I was sleeping in his room that night because . . . I don't know. I slept in there sometimes. It was a Friday night in September. Rainy."

I squeezed my eyes shut, trying to concentrate on the sound of the waves and not the sound of my father's footsteps outside my bedroom door.

"I got up to go to the bathroom, and I heard your aunt Janine in her bedroom. She was crying." Aurora's voice broke.

The girls sat motionless in the dark. Neither made a sound.

"She was talking to someone. Begging him . . ." Aurora sat in the sand in her jeans, her legs stretched out in front of her. We'd all left our shoes in the Jeep. She had dark polish on her toenails. Blue.

Aurora glanced at the girls, then at the water again. "I opened the bedroom door to see what was wrong."

I rocked very gently back and forth. The sand was wet under me. Cold. I vaguely wondered if I should go back to the Jeep for towels. Mia and Maura might be cold.

"I opened the door, and there he was. Buddy McCollister." She spoke his name as if he were a plague upon the earth. Which, of course, he was. "He was in Janine's bed."

"Oh my God," Mia breathed, starting to cry softly. "Aunt Janine, I'm sorry. I'm so sorry."

"You mean, like, *in* her bed?" Maura asked, clearly trying to wrap her head around what Aurora was saying. "Like—"

"Yeah," Aurora said. "Come to find out, the fucking bastard had been raping his own daughter for two years."

I listened to the sound of the waves, trying to block out Aurora's voice. People describe it as a crash, but it's not really a crash. A crash is the sound of glass shattering, metal buckling. Like in an automobile accident. The waves are just white noise. There's no violence in their sound.

I tightened my arms around my knees and wondered how it could be twenty-eight years later and Buddy could still bring me into a fetal position.

Aurora went on talking. "He was drunk. Crazy. When he saw me, he got out of her bed. He came after me. He knew I'd tell."

"Where did you get the gun?" Maura breathed.

"He was a cop and a dick. There were guns all over the house.

Loaded. He liked them. A lot. He was always talking about how he hoped someone would break in so he could blow their head off. I guess he had one with him when he went into Janine's room. His way of keeping her quiet. Guys like him, they do that kind of shit," Aurora told the girls.

She was sticking to the story she'd told the cops. Only the four of us knew that Aurora had gone downstairs and gotten the gun out of the kitchen cabinet where Buddy kept it. I sometimes wondered if my mom knew the truth. If she did, she had never voiced it. Not to the investigating officers. Not even to me.

"So how did you get his gun?"

"It was on this table near Janine's bed. We were doing a big puzzle on it that afternoon after school. Because it was raining." Aurora stopped for a minute.

I looked at her. She was staring out at the ocean. Dry-eyed. She was glad she killed Buddy. She'd always been glad. I'd never heard a breath of regret from her. She'd done what I hadn't had the guts to do. She'd saved me.

"We both went for it, and I beat him. He knocked over the table. The puzzle pieces went flying."

That part was true. About the puzzle. He did throw it over. As he went down. It was a *Goonies* puzzle. My brother's. I remember the box. The color of the pieces.

"It all happened so fast," Aurora told the girls. "I don't exactly remember it. It's like a movie in my head. Like I saw it, but not like I did it. He lunged for me. I aimed the gun. He said terrible, awful things. He kept coming. I pulled the trigger."

"Just once?" Maura whispered.

Aurora looked right at her. "All it took."

# ❦ 14 ❧

# McKenzie

Lilly was making tea when I walked into the kitchen the morning of the Fourth of July.

"Hey." She smiled, all bright and sunshiny.

"We the first ones up?" I asked. It was almost nine.

"Yup. I don't know how long they stayed up after we went to bed. How you feeling? You look better." She studied me intently, making me feel self-conscious. "Your color is better."

I adjusted my turban. "Good. I'm good." I was feeling surprisingly good. I'd had one brief bout on the toilet around four a.m., but other than that, I'd slept well.

"You look good."

She was so cute in her short, white, flowered robe over her pink nightgown. She'd tied the robe high, making her belly seem even bigger this morning than it had the previous night. Maybe it *was* bigger. She'd parted her hair down the middle and sported little spiky pigtails behind each ear. Adorable. I, on the other hand, was wearing men's boxer shorts and a ratty T-shirt, and I knew for a fact that my face was blotchy. The lavender terrycloth turban didn't add much to my ensemble.

"You want tea?" Lilly asked.

"Yeah." I came around the counter. "But I can get it myself."

"I'll make it. You sit. Rest."

"I rested all night."

"Let me do this for you. For me, if not for you. I feel bad that there doesn't seem to be anything I can do for you."

"That's ridiculous. You being here. For a whole month. That's for me." I opened my arms wide. "Let's face it. This is all for me."

Lilly flitted around the kitchen like a bee. She poured water from the teakettle into the mugs. She took out a pitcher of orange juice. She popped an English muffin in the toaster. "Butter or strawberry jam?"

"I don't think I want—"

"Sit. I'll get both. You've got to eat something. You're too skinny. You don't want your boobs to get saggy."

I didn't dignify that with an answer. It was already too late to save them. "Coins in a sock" was the phrase that came to mind. I sat on a stool.

"Were you sick last night?" She took a yellow plastic tray from one of the cupboards. She'd brought it from home a summer or two ago. Lilly was into serving trays. She had a bunch of them at her house, themed for holidays and the seasons. "We should eat out on the porch. The rain's passed. It's going to be a beautiful day."

I watched as she set the mugs on the tray, added a plate with an English muffin, and popped another muffin into the toaster. Next, she put the sugar bowl on the tray. She didn't get milk. She never drank milk in her tea, being Asian, I suppose, and she knew I wasn't doing dairy.

"Weird that Janine's not up." I glanced over my shoulder in the general direction of the staircase. "She never sleeps in."

"I heard her early this morning. Like . . . five thirty or six. She was letting Fritz out."

"Doubly weird. He never gets up at night." Surprised that I was actually a little hungry, I reached for a half of the muffin on the plate.

"Jam?" Lilly held up a butter knife. "It's strawberry. From the farmers' market in Lewes, Janine said."

"Dry is perfect." I waved the crispy muffin half at her.

She leaned forward, forearms on the counter, and lowered her voice. On her left hand she wore a platinum wedding band and an enormous marquise diamond. "So what's Janine said to you about the new girlfriend?"

I shook my head. Nibbled. "Not much. She's a psychologist. I think she does work for the state police and that's how Janine met her."

"How long have they been dating?"

"You know how Janine is; she never wants to share the juicy details. A while, I think though. Eight or nine months?"

"They living together?"

I shrugged.

Lilly lifted one of the tea bags out of a yellow mug and, using a spoon, wrapped the tag around it and squeezed the tea from it. She tossed the tea bag in the trash under the sink and came back for the other. "You ask her about her?"

"Tried. She wasn't all that forthcoming."

"So why do you think all the secrecy?" She wound the tag around the second tea bag. "Think it's just an eff-buddy kind of thing."

I laughed.

"What?" Her eyes got big.

"It just sounds so funny. *Eff*-buddy. Coming out of you. Miss Priss."

"I'm not *prissy*. That's not very nice." She tossed the second tea bag in the trash. "I just don't like the F word. It's uncouth."

"*Uncouth*," I repeated. Then laughed again.

Lilly tried to look annoyed and retrieved the second muffin from the toaster. "I think you should ask Janine about Chris." She set the plate on the tray and lifted the tray off the counter. "We need to know what's going on."

"I can carry that." I got off the stool.

"I can do it."

We stood there regarding each other for a second. The pregnant woman versus the woman dying of cancer. I sighed and headed for the deck.

"I told you. I already asked Janine about Chris." I walked through the living room. "She didn't want me to know anything about her."

"Did you tell her to invite her over?"

I unlocked the door and opened it for Lilly. Leaving it open, I followed her out onto the deck. "If she doesn't want to tell us anything about her, obviously she's not going to *invite her over*. You're probably right—she's probably just a fuck buddy."

Lilly waited for me to sit, then set the plate with the English muffin with the bites out of it and the blue mug on the arm of my Adirondack. She put the tray on a little white wrought iron table between her chair and Aurora's and sat down. "I think we should just tell her to invite her over." She held the sugar bowl for me.

I spooned sugar into my tea. "So *you* tell her."

"She'll say to mind my own business. She'll do it if *you* ask."

I sighed and picked up my naked muffin. "I don't like this, you know." I took a bite and looked out at the beautiful blue sky, the pale sand, and the water in the distance. It was the same sliver of earth that I had been looking at since I was in middle school, and it still didn't fail to take my breath away. I liked the idea that the ocean, the dunes, the sea grass, even the rickety red dune fence would go on looking the same when I was gone. "Being the one with cancer," I said.

When Lilly didn't answer, I glanced at her. Her eyes were full of tears.

"Ah, sweetie, don't." I reached with my free hand and gave hers a squeeze.

She pressed her lips together, trying hard not to cry.

I took my hand back and sipped my tea. "Let's talk about something more cheerful. How's the nursery coming along? Did you go with owls or kangaroos?"

"Owls. I got all the bedding and an owl lamp, and the rocking chair has an owl carved into the back." She gestured as she explained, becoming instantly animated. "The walls are pale green, and I had that girl from the art school come in and paint a mural on the south wall. Trees and a big mama owl and a big papa owl and a baby owl. It's gorgeous."

"Sounds like it. I want to see it." I sipped the hot, sweet tea. "I'd like to."

"Of course you should come and see it. You should stay with us for a few nights next month. I know Matt would love to have you come and stay."

"How is Matt?"

"He's good. Great. We hired another optometrist last month. Business is booming."

"I meant how's Matt *with you?* I know you guys had hit a rough patch a few months ago." What I *hadn't* known, at the time, was that she'd been pregnant. She'd been pregnant, and he'd been talking about moving out, which obviously concerned me, now that I knew.

"We're fine. He's good." She began to butter her muffin.

"So he was unhappy in the marriage in March and now he's happy?" I asked suspiciously.

"I think he was bored or something. Or maybe it had just occurred to him that I was the only woman he'd ever sleep with again. I think some salesgirl who comes into our office was batting her eyelashes at him." She rolled her eyes. She was trying to act like she wasn't worried, but I could tell from the look on her face that she was.

I sighed. I was hoping for an easy morning with no serious discussions. They could be so tiring. I just wanted to have a fun Fourth of July. "What's going on, Lilly?"

She took a bite of her neatly buttered muffin.

"I can see it on your face, Lilly. Is it Matt? I swear to God, I'll kick his ass if he's done something stupid. I'll send Janine to kick his ass. You know she'll do it for me."

She set the muffin back on her plate and chewed slowly. "It's not Matt." She looked down at her hands now on her lap. "I mean it *is*, but . . . really, it's me."

I sipped my tea and waited.

Finally, she looked up at me. "I know what you're going to say, but . . . I think I need to tell him."

I instantly knew what she was referring to, even though we probably hadn't discussed it in four or five years. "You don't need to tell him."

"We're *having a baby* together. He's trying so hard to make it work. We're all about honesty and telling each other how we feel. And what am I doing? Basically, I'm lying to him."

"You're not lying to him."

"I'm keeping the truth from him. I never keep anything from him."

"I don't think the same rules apply, not when you're talking about the past. You were a kid. It was twenty-two years ago," I argued. "Long before you met Matt, for heaven's sake." I opened my arms. "Matt probably has a past he doesn't care to share, either."

"He doesn't have the kind of past I have. I can guarantee you." She sat there for a minute in silence. "It seems wrong."

"Eat your muffin," I told her. "It's getting cold."

She spread strawberry jam on her muffin, concentrating way too hard on it. "And it's not just Matt. I feel like I'm lying to Janine and Aurora, too."

"You never lied to them, either. You just never . . . provided full disclosure."

Once, a long time ago, I might have felt guilty about me knowing about this part of Lilly's life and Aurora and Janine not knowing, but at some point, I'd realized it just wasn't that important. I'd only found out by sheer coincidence, and Lilly had been so ashamed that I'd agreed to keep it to myself. As the years passed, I sort of forgot about it. She hadn't hurt anyone. She hadn't stolen anything. It was just sex. Who didn't have sex with someone when they were twenty that they wouldn't care to admit to at forty-two? So she took money from these men. She only did it three times and decided that it didn't matter how much she got paid, she wasn't *escort* material.

Lilly sat there, looking out over the railing.

I exhaled. "I don't want to see you make a mistake like this. A hormonal mistake. If you really want to tell Matt, I think you need to wait another six months. Wait until the baby's been born. When you're yourself again." I shrugged. "Then tell him if you want. Tell everyone. Aurora and Janine, your dad, my girls, hell, tell my mother, if you want. It will give her something to bring up every time I mention one of you besides Aurora flashing the security guard at the football game our junior year in high school."

"You're making fun of me. Trivializing a painful time in my life."

"I'm not. I swear I'm not." I thought about it for a moment. "No, actually, I am because it *is* trivial." I held up my hand, refusing to let her interrupt. "You were young. You made some bad choices. We all did. Remember Billy Locket? My junior year at UD? Basically, I had sex with him so I could go to fraternity parties and get free beer."

"It's not the same thing," she said.

"It is. No one is going to fault you for mistakes you made twenty-two years ago. When you were twenty." I had to hold back to keep from shouting the words at her.

"Then why shouldn't I tell Matt?"

"Because he'll fault you for it" is what I wanted to say. "Because, while I like him, he can be uptight and unforgiving." But I didn't say it. "Let's talk about it with Aurora and Janine, okay?"

She hesitated. "So you think I should tell them?"

"Will it feel enough like a confession to keep you from telling your husband?"

She considered my words. "I don't know. Maybe." She fiddled with a bread crumb on her plate. "I guess I need to think on it a little more. Don't say anything to them, please?"

"I won't," I promised.

She waved her hand. "Let's change the subject. I'm tired of talking about this. I'm tired of thinking about it and worrying about it."

I felt a little bit like I'd dodged a bullet. My initial reaction was to think, considering my circumstances, that this *did* seem trivial. But I knew I couldn't look at it that way. My having cancer didn't cancel out what Lilly had done or the shame she had felt afterward. Still felt, obviously. I had to keep that in mind sometimes. My terminal cancer didn't trump everyone else's problems. I was going to be gone someday, and they were still going to be here. With their problems.

I reached for my mug. "Tell me your plans. How long are you taking off after the baby is born? Going back full time? Part time?"

I could see her trying to shift gears. She did it, though. And I was proud of her for it.

"Part time," she answered. "Definitely. Matt's totally in agreement."

Lilly went on for a half hour and a second cup of tea about her and Matt's plans for the office, for their house, for their lives. I could barely get a word in edgewise, which was fine. I liked listening to her. Watching her. Lilly was so easy to be with that it was a relief to have her to myself for a little while. Not that I didn't love Janine and Aurora as much as I loved Lilly. I did. But both of them took *so much* energy. At one point, while Lilly was talking about having baby-proof latches put on all of her kitchen cabinets, I retrieved my phone and recorded her talking. She was so beautiful, so animated. She glowed with happiness. I was definitely going to include this in the final cut of our video diary.

I was licking strawberry jam off the butter knife when Fritz came down the stairs and out onto the deck. He stopped at the top of the steps to the beach and looked at me. "It's okay, boy," I said. "Go ahead."

He trotted down the stairs. He had a potty spot on one side of the house that Janine had made for him. He was the best behaved dog I'd ever seen. I knew he'd run down, do his business, and come right back. Sure enough, three minutes later, he was loping back up the steps.

Aurora stumbled onto the deck in jeans that looked like they'd been slept in and the bikini top she'd been wearing the day before. "Coffee," she groaned.

Lilly got up. "Coming up." She took the tray and headed for the kitchen.

Aurora walked to the rail and gazed out. "It's bright out here. Damn it's bright out."

I grabbed a pair of my drugstore sunglasses off the table. "Here." She turned, and I tossed them to her.

She caught them and slid them on. "Christ on a crutch. Who the hell can see out of these things?"

"Sorry. Left my Guccis in the car. You two stay up all night?"

She walked over to her white Adirondack chair, sat down, and slumped back. "Something like that."

I shook my head. "Drinking having fun? Or drinking having a breakdown?" She knew I was talking about Janine.

"A little of both." She tipped her head back and rested it on the chair.

I looked down at her bare abdomen. She had a kick-ass body. Amazing abs. I didn't understand how that was possible, the way she abused her body. She didn't eat enough. She drank way too much. I liked to think she'd left her drug days well behind, but I knew for a fact that she still smoked a joint once in a while.

"So what's up with her?" I asked, lowering my voice. If Janine let Fritz out of her room, she couldn't be far behind.

"You know, the usual." Aurora kept her head back. I imagined her eyes were closed behind the dark glasses.

"Anything I can do?" I asked.

"If I could turn back time . . ." she sang. On key.

I chimed in, not on key, "If I could find a way."

"What? We're singing Cher? Really, you guys?" Janine walked out onto the deck. She was in her running clothes, a bottle of water in her hand. She looked tired, but not hungover like Aurora.

"You don't like Cher?" I asked.

Aurora was still thrown back in her chair, glasses on, staring at the sky or the insides of her eyelids. "Who doesn't like *Cher?*"

"Half-breed . . ." Lilly sang, joining us on the deck. "How I learned to hate the word . . ." She did a little dance like she was an Indian maiden circling a campfire, and we all laughed.

Growing up, Lilly had struggled with her parentage. Her mother's family had never accepted her father because he was a black man, and her father's family had never accepted her because of her Japanese *peasant* stock.

"You guys are nuts. I'm going for a run." Janine walked over to Aurora and nudged her with the toe of her running shoe. "You okay?"

"Great," Aurora said, not moving a muscle.

"Maybe cut back on your gin intake," she suggested, walking toward the steps. She ran on the beach in the morning. Every morning.

"Maybe cut back on the sass," Aurora countered.

I laughed and sat back in my chair, thinking I was the luckiest woman on earth.

"How was your run?" I asked Janine, holding up my cell phone, watching her on the screen.

She was stretched out on a striped towel: red sports bra and a pair of bleached-out board shorts. We were all on the beach: Lilly and I in chairs. Janine and Aurora on towels. Aurora, in a tiny lime green bikini, lay on her stomach, sound asleep, I assumed.

"You know, Cancer Girl, you're plucking my last nerve with

that video camera. Put it away," Janine ordered, waving her hand at me, blocking the screen.

"I can't. I'm the recorder. I have to record what's going on. So what's going on, Janine? How's Chris?"

Lilly lowered the book she was reading: *Ina May's Guide to Breastfeeding.* "Cancer Girl. Ouch. I think she means business, McKenzie." She steered my phone until I was looking at her face. "So how is Chris, Janine?" she sang, tilting her head side to side.

I filled the frame with Janine's face. I'd found the zoom on the app this morning.

"Chris is fine." She adjusted her mirrored sunglasses. "What are you two? Fourteen?"

"You haven't said a word about her. Is she cute? Smart? Blond or brunette?"

"Blond."

"You always did like blondes," said Lilly.

Janine raised her hand. "Could you shut that thing off? I'm serious."

I sighed and hit the red button. "There."

"It's off?"

"It's off." I dropped the phone into my lap. I was wearing a cotton cardigan over my bathing suit. When I got warm, I'd take it off. A few minutes later, it would go back on again.

"We're just curious, that's all," Lilly said. "We've been worried about you."

"You don't have to worry about me." Janine sat up. Her abs were as well defined as Aurora's. Maybe more defined. She worked at them. Hard. She ran, she went to the gym, and she ate well.

"We want you to be happy," I said.

She made a face like that was the stupidest thing she'd ever heard. "When have you ever known me to be happy?" she asked. *"Ever?"*

"You know what I mean," I said gently.

She lay back on the towel with a groan. "Chris is good. I . . . I just don't know where it's going. That's why I haven't said much."

"Do you really like her?"

She didn't answer.

I looked at Lilly. She looked at me.

"That a yes?"

"Could we talk about something else, like maybe Lilly's vagina again?" Earlier in the day, much to Janine's distress, we'd talked about Lilly's labor and delivery. Extensively. Aurora had gone for a swim, just to get out of trying to even pretend to be interested.

"No. We can't talk about something else. We're talking about you and your new relationship."

Janine rested her arm across her forehead. "It's too soon to know what's going on."

"We think you should invite her for dinner," I said.

"I'll make something nice. A pork roast," Lilly said. "Does she like pork, Janine?"

"I don't know if Chris likes pork roast."

"Maybe you need a nap, missy. You're cranky." Lilly opened her book again.

Everyone was quiet. I watched a little girl of four or five, in a pink polka-dot bathing suit, run to the water's edge with a plastic bucket. She scooped water and ran back onto the beach where another girl, a little younger, waited. The girl in the polka dots poured the water into the sand to the delight of the little one. They both squealed with laughter, and I smiled. I remembered my girls playing together, hauling buckets of water back and forth. I wish I had appreciated those times more than I did. I knew, at the time, that they were good times. I laughed with them. I took pictures of them. But now that they were older, I longed for those days again. For that laughter that was so pure, so innocent.

"I really like Chris," Janine said.

I glanced at Lilly, who never looked up from her book. "So invite her for dinner. So we can get to know her," she said.

Janine still had her face covered. "I can't imagine anything more awkward."

"Or you could invite her for fireworks tonight," I suggested. "That might work. No pork roast. It'll be dark so we won't see her and she won't hear anything Lilly says because the fireworks will be too loud."

Janine surprised me then. With laughter.

# ✎ 15 ✎

# Lilly

"**S**he asleep?" I asked Janine as she walked into the laundry room carrying a mesh bag of dirty clothes.

McKenzie had decided to take a nap before the festivities began. We planned to grill burgers. I'd made potato salad and had the fixings for baked beans. It would be just us for dinner. Mia and Maura weren't coming until eight, in time to make s'mores on the grill before the fireworks. No fire on the beach for us tonight. The city didn't grant open fire permits on Independence Day. Too many nuts on the beach already, armed with six packs of Bud Light and illegal pyrotechnics.

"Sound asleep." Janine dropped the bag onto the floor on top of a pair of Aurora's flip-flops. "I'll do that."

I was perfectly capable of moving the wet beach towels from the washing machine to the dryer. I was pregnant, not a quadriplegic, but I stepped back. I understood the need to be useful. I'd spent my whole life trying to fulfill the needs of others, striving somehow to fulfill myself in my usefulness.

"She seems better today, don't you think?" I asked. "I was worried about her the other night when the girls were here. She looked really . . . sick."

Janine eyed me as she tossed a Green Turtle Pub towel into the dryer. "She *is* sick, Lilly."

I reached above the open dryer to the shelf lined with laundry detergent, bleach, fabric softener, and assorted items, some that didn't belong there. I had to stand on my tiptoes, and when I did, my baby belly pressed against the cool metal of the dryer. I grabbed a box of dryer sheets. Spotting a second, I pulled that box down, too. "She's better today. Her color's good, and she ate a whole sandwich at lunch. Most of one," I amended.

"She is better today than she was yesterday, but that's the way cancer works." Janine pulled a blue towel out of the washer. "You have good days and bad. But she's going to have fewer good days. You get that, don't you? It's the progression of the disease."

"You're such a cynic." I pulled fabric softener sheets out of the smaller box that was crushed and stacked them on top of the dryer, making a neat pile.

"I'm a pragmatist." She waited for me to step back so she could throw the towel into the dryer. "And the reality, Susie, is that McKenzie has terminal cancer and she's going to die."

*Susie.* Susie Sunshine. That's what she called me sometimes. It wasn't meant as a compliment. She thought I was overly optimistic. Excessively positive. I'd once looked up the name but hadn't been able to find, for sure, the origin of it. As best as I could figure out, it came from a 1930s British film based on a book written by a Hungarian named István Szomaházy.

"Let me put the rest of these in," she said.

I stepped back so she could throw the last two towels into the dryer. I closed the door, started it, and returned to my dryer sheet task.

Janine picked up her laundry bag.

I knew she was going to throw the whole thing into the washing machine. Years ago, I'd given up trying to teach her how to separate her delicates from her lights and darks. She didn't really have delicates, just sports bras and cotton Fruit of the Looms, so it didn't really matter, I supposed.

"I'm thinking about selling this place," she said without looking at me.

I concentrated on the dryer sheets, stacking them neatly.

"I don't know if I can come back here anymore. Not after she's dead."

Realizing that I'd forgotten to put a sheet in the dryer with the towels, I opened the door and tossed one in. "I know. I've been thinking the same thing."

Janine looked at me. "So you think I *should* sell it?"

"I thought you should have sold it the minute your mom deeded it to you. I think it's crazy that we come back here, year after year. A little perverted even. You know?" I met her gaze. "Like we, on some level, want to torture ourselves with the pain. What kind of friends are we to do this to you, year after year?"

"You know I needed to be here. Which makes you the best kind of friends because you've been willing to come here with me and watch me torture myself." She gave a little laugh that was without humor. Her just-washed hair was wispy around her face and so flattering. She was a pretty girl, our Janine. Prettier now than she had been in her twenties.

"You have to do what's right for you, Janine. We can't tell you what that is."

She stared into the washing machine. "I'm just thinking it might be for the best, you know? Because . . . I don't know what we're going to be when McKenzie dies."

I looked at her. "What we're going to *be?*"

"The three of us." She glanced at me, then quickly away. "You *know* we can't be the same, Lilly. Not with her gone."

"But we'll still be best friends," I said, not liking the way she had said that. As if she didn't think we would be. "We'll still love each other and be there for each other. We have to. For McKenzie."

"Right." She nodded. "Anyway. The house."

"The house," I repeated. "Maybe you're right. We're in our forties. Things change. We've changed. Maybe it's finally time."

"Chris says the same thing."

I shut the door and hit start. The dryer buzzed, then hummed as it began to tumble again. "Maybe she's right. She's a psychologist, isn't she?" I felt better with this line of conversation. It had never occurred to me that Janine would think we couldn't still be friends . . . or at least wouldn't be the same to each other without McKenzie. That just didn't make sense.

The new girlfriend was definitely a safer conversation. I kept my tone casual, trying not to sound as interested as I was. If McKenzie wasn't going to get the dirt, I was going to have to get it myself.

"A forensic psychologist."

I only vaguely knew what that meant. I'd Google it later on my iPad. I slid the neat pile of fabric softener sheets into the bigger box and flipped the little box over. Seeing it couldn't be recycled, I tossed it in the garbage can under the utility sink. "I'd like to meet her."

"I know."

I pressed my lips together, thinking I needed to go find a tube of lip balm. My lips were dry. Hopefully not sunburned. "If you sold it . . . would we still come to the beach every summer? You, me, and Aurora? Rent a house maybe? I can't imagine raising a child and not bringing him or her to Albany Beach."

Janine opened her laundry bag and pulled out running shorts, then a T-shirt. "We could do that."

"But we won't, will we?" I tried to control my emotions. Janine hated it when I cried. I know how much she hates it when I cry.

"I don't know, Lilly." She dropped the clothes into the washing machine and reached into the bag again. "I can't imagine what life is going to be without her." She pulled her hand from the bag and pressed the heel to her forehead. Hard. "I try to think about what it will be, but I can't see it." She looked at me, eye to eye. I'm only a little shorter than she is. "I can't imagine anything after she's gone." Her brow creased, and she squeezed her eyes shut. "It's like . . . I wonder if I'll just disappear when she does. You know?" She opened her eyes. "Crazy?"

The crazy thing was that I *did* know what she meant. McKenzie was so much a part of me, of us, that I'd contemplated the same thought. Was it like on *Star Trek: The Next Generation*? (Matt loved *Star Trek*.) Would we just cease to exist when McKenzie was gone? Or would we die slowly, one cell at a time? Which wasn't crazy, because that's kind of true, isn't it? We're born dying?

"Have you talked to Aurora? What does she think?"

Janine took a pair of socks, balled together from the bag, and tossed them into the washing machine. Navy shorts and T-shirt, a forest green T-shirt, and white no-show socks. I wondered if the socks would come out green or blue.

"I haven't broached the subject."

I reached up over the dryer to take a stray liquid fabric softener lid from the shelf. There was another behind it. Two blue bottles of softener. Both already with lids. I threw the extra lids in the trash. "I don't know what she'll say. I can see her going either way. Hell no, we're not selling the place. We're coming back next year and the year after that. Or"—I rubbed my belly thoughtfully—"hell no, we're never coming back."

Janine smiled and reached into the bag again. "Right." She pulled out a lacy demi-cup pink bra.

I glanced at the bra. "Bringing a little something of Chris's with you to remind you of her?" I asked.

She threw the bra up on the dryer. "No."

I picked up the bra. "Yours?"

She snatched it out of my hand and held it over the washtub.

"Don't you dare." I snatched it back. "It's too pretty to ruin with those nasty running clothes. Whoever's it is. It goes in a lingerie bag." I pulled a small white mesh bag from the shelf and tucked the bra inside. "Got matching panties?"

I was just kidding, but Janine proceeded to produce a pair of lace thong undies.

I laughed and held open the lingerie bag for her. She dropped them in.

"We should talk to Aurora about the house," I said.

She nodded, adding board shorts and a black wifebeater to the washer. I hated it when Janine wore those things. They were so ugly, so . . . stereotypical.

"I guess we need to talk to Mack, too," she mused, tossing the laundry bag on the dryer.

"You think?" I zipped up the lingerie bag. "I'll wash these with my things tomorrow," I told her.

She added too much detergent to the washer and closed the lid.

"Did you go out last night?" I asked her.

She punched buttons on the washing machine.

"I just wondered if you went out to meet Chris or something. You know you can bring her here. No one's going to be, like, horrified or anything, if your girlfriend spends the night. You guys can even have my room. I can sleep in yours. If you want two beds," I added.

She pushed the start button, and I heard water pour in.

"Last night I heard a car start in the driveway. Two thirtyish. Later, I got up to check on McKenzie and get a glass of water in the kitchen. When I looked out the window, I saw that your Jeep was gone."

The back door opened, and Aurora walked in, clad in her old red bathing suit, still glistening with water. She'd rinsed off in the shower under the house. She was still wearing her ugly swim cap.

"It's not like you have to sneak around with us. We're big girls."

"Where you sneaking to?" Aurora asked Janine. She walked past us, into the kitchen, leaving wet footprints behind.

"Mom caught me sneaking out last night," Janine said.

Aurora looked at Janine. "You tell her about Maura?"

I grabbed the mop from the corner of the laundry room and followed Aurora into the kitchen, mopping behind her. "What about Maura?" I asked, keeping my voice low, just in case McKenzie woke. The rest of the house was quiet, though. All I could hear was the *click-click* of the ceiling fan in the living room.

"I thought we weren't going to say anything." Janine followed us.

"I said we didn't need to tell *McKenzie*." Aurora went to the kitchen sink. She could plainly see that she was leaving wet footprints on the hardwood. And see me mopping up behind her. She didn't care.

"I was going to tell Lilly," Aurora said. "You thought we weren't going to tell Lilly?"

Janine brought her finger to her lips and cut her eyes in the direction of the front of the house. "She's asleep."

Aurora grabbed a glass from the drain board, flipped on the faucet, and watched it fill.

"What?" I mopped up the last footprint, directly behind Aurora. "What's going on with Maura?" I heard the sound of the downstairs bedroom door open, and I glanced that way. All of us looked that way.

McKenzie walked into the kitchen. "Hey, guys." There was still a groggy sound to her voice. "What's going on?"

"I'm going to grab a shower." As Aurora walked past McKenzie, she leaned over and brushed a quick kiss across her cheek.

I followed Aurora, wiping up four more footprints, then surrendering. Her feet were almost dry.

"Going to get more propane." Janine hooked her thumb in the direction of the back deck. "Fritz! Come, boy."

I heard the dog rise in the other room and his foot pads as he bounded for the kitchen.

"How about a nice glass of iced tea?" I asked McKenzie. "You can keep me company while I make the baked beans."

She glanced at Aurora, who was already out of the kitchen. Then at Janine, in the doorway to the laundry room, then me, standing there with my mop. "What's going on?" she asked, looking concerned.

"I was trying to get some good dirt on Chris, but Janine's not putting out."

"Oh, I bet she's putting out," Aurora hollered from the living room.

Everyone laughed, and I walked toward the laundry room with the mop. I cut my eyes at Janine. Whatever was going on with Maura, they were going to have to tell me. I wasn't going to be left out.

# 16

# McKenzie

"So what names are you thinking about?" I watched Lilly through my iPhone.

She pointed at me. "Is that on?"

"Yes, it's on."

She smiled into the camera shyly. "I shouldn't say. Matt doesn't want us to tell anyone. He wants it to be a surprise."

"How are we going to decide what to name our baby if we don't even know the choices?" I asked.

We were sitting on the steps that lead from the house down to the beach. It was getting dark. Out on the beach, we had already heard firecrackers going off and seen two rockets shoot into the sky, explode, and then fizzle. Still no sign of my girls, who promised, who *swore* to me that they were coming for the town's public fireworks. Other than a text from Mia, I hadn't heard from either of them since dinner the other night.

"Come on, you have to tell us," I told Lilly. "We won't tell Matt," I whispered.

We both giggled. That was one of the things I loved about being with Lilly. I could actually *giggle* with her.

"Come on," I cajoled. "Girl's name."

"You won't tell him I told?"

"He'll never know. It will be our secret."

She leaned close to me, and her exotic features filled the frame. "Brunhilda Chrysanthemum."

I lowered the phone with it still recording. "You're kidding." I know my eyes were huge. (Eyebrows drawn in over the little pricklies, just sprouting.) "Please tell me you're kidding."

She looked at me, her face entirely serious. I didn't know what to say. Surely she was kidding. But . . . what if she wasn't? Could I go to my deathbed letting her name the only child she would ever have Brunhilda Chrysanthemum?

I must have looked horrified because she started to laugh. "You should see the look on your face."

I scowled and raised the phone. "Come on. Tell us your choices so far. The names you really like."

She exhaled and looked up at me, her face so bright with promise. "Let's see: Aster, Olivia, Joy or . . . McKenzie." She smiled.

I hit the button on the phone and stopped recording. I lowered the phone. "Lilly, you can't name your baby after me."

"I can if I want." She stroked her belly. She was wearing capris and a T-shirt that said "Baby On Board" with a surfboard on it. "I can name her anything I want. I can name her McKenzie Janine Aurora if I want."

I couldn't tell if she was serious. Clearly she was joking about giving the baby our three names, but was she really considering calling her McKenzie? I wasn't sure how I felt about her naming her baby after me. On the one hand, I was flattered. On the other hand, I had to think about the child. Who wants to be the kid named after her mother's dead best friend. Or best dead friend. "How about boy names?" I asked.

"Elijah, Roland, or Arthur."

I leaned over her belly, cupping my hands around my mouth to talk to her baby. "You better hope you're a girl."

She pushed me away, laughing. "You don't like my names?"

"Of course I like them." I looked up, meeting her gaze. "I'd like any name you chose, because it will be your baby's name, Lilly."

She clasped my hand and peered into my face. "Would you really mind . . . if I have a girl and I name her McKenzie?"

"I don't know," I said, thinking that I'd have to consider the idea later. When I was alone. "Of course I'll never know it if I take a sudden turn and don't—"

"Don't say it. Don't you dare say it." She squeezed my hand. "I want you there, when this baby is born. I need you. I want all three of you there."

I heard the sound of a car pulling into the gravel drive behind the house. Somewhere inside, Fritz woofed. Lilly stood. "They're here!" She clapped her hands together. "Goody, they're here." (She was the only forty-something-year-old woman I knew who could say "goody" and make it work.) "I'm going to take the drinks down." Janine and Aurora were already on the beach. Almost an hour ago, they'd taken chairs down for all of us.

Lilly reached for the cooler on the top step; she'd already loaded it with sodas and beer. "We'll just do the s'mores after the fireworks."

"Sounds good." As Lilly went down the flight of steps, I looked up toward the bright lights of the house. It was my job to shut out all the lights before I went down to the beach, to see the fireworks better. I could hear Fritz in the kitchen, chuffing at the back door. A minute later, I heard the door open and Mia's and Maura's voices.

Fritz trotted out onto the deck, leading the girls.

"Hey, Mom!"

I stood, stuffing my hands into my UD hoodie front pocket. I was wearing one of Janine's old baseball caps. "Hey, sweetie."

Mia came down the steps toward me. Maura was right behind her. Fritz stopped at the top of the staircase as if there were an invisible barrier. No dogs on the beach, Memorial Day to Labor Day, a law he and Janine both heartily disagreed with.

Mia gave me a quick peck on the cheek and passed me on the steps.

"Hey, Mom." Maura copied her sister.

"JAL on the beach?" Janine, Aurora, and Lilly. They called them *JAL* sometimes.

"Yup. Waiting for you. We've all been waiting for you for a while," I called after them, unable to keep from being a mother for just a second. "I was expecting you an hour ago."

"See you on the beach, Mom." Then Mia threw over her shoulder, "Oh. Dad's here. He wants to say hi."

I looked up the steps, then down. The girls were disappearing into the dark. I looked back up again just in time to see my ex-husband walk into the doorway between the living room and the deck.

"Jared," I managed after a second. I adjusted the ball cap. There was no way in hell I was going to let him see my bald head. I was glad I'd put on some makeup. There was nothing I could do about the stubby eyelashes, but at least my face had a little color. I moved up a step.

"Mack." He was holding the baby on his hip. Peaches. She'd be a year old at Halloween.

"Oh, my gosh, Jared. She's gorgeous." I came up the steps onto the deck and leaned over to get a better look at her. "Hello there, sweetie."

The baby had Jared's bright blue eyes and her Home Depot mother's red-blond hair. (Clearly, Jared has a soft spot for redheads.) She could have been one of my girls. "So beautiful," I crooned, reaching out for her tiny hand.

And, for a minute, I forgot about how angry I was with Jared for cheating on me. For leaving me for a woman with fewer wrinkles and better boobs. For leaving our girls. For not coming back to me when he found out I was dying. After all, it would have been no skin off his back. He could have left his wife for me, then gone back to her after the funeral. And I would never have known the difference, right?

Jared looked down at his daughter and grinned. "Yeah, I think she's pretty cool."

The little girl was dressed in a pale green shirt and white overalls that only came to her knees. Her chubby feet were bare. She looked at me and smiled a perfect baby smile.

I was momentarily mesmerized. I couldn't take my gaze from hers. They were Mia's and Maura's eyes.

I suddenly felt light-headed. Where had the years gone? Where had *my life* gone?

I found my voice. "How are you today, Miss Peaches? Having a good day?" I knew they'd had a picnic at their house with family. Home Depot's family. Jared's new family. "Have fun with your sisters?"

"You want to hold her?"

"I . . . sure." I looked up at him, then at Peaches. "You think she'll come to me?" I held out my hands, then let them fall to my sides.

"Of course." He held her out to me.

I hesitated, then reached for her. Jared lowered her weight into my arms, and for a moment I was caught between the scent of him and the scent of her. I closed my eyes and brought her to my chest, just for a second.

I sometimes wonder, when I lay awake in the middle of the night, trying to decide if I want to cry, what would happen if I met Jared now. At my age. If he asked me out, would I go? If I didn't know him and just met him, wherever it was that women my age met men, would I find him as attractive as I had the night I met him in that bar in Philadelphia after an Eagles game?

He wasn't as good-looking as he had once been. His hair was starting to thin on top and he now wore it short and spiky. His waist had thickened, and he had a little bit of a beer gut. He was aging quicker than a lot of forty-five-year-old men. All the work outside, I supposed. The elements. He definitely wasn't the same man he had been at twenty-six. But when I closed my eyes . . . when I smelled him . . .

When I smelled him, I thought yes, I would go out with him if he asked me. As crazy as it sounded, I would go out with the man. I'd probably sleep with him. That thought made me sad.

I opened my eyes but didn't look at him, realizing how silly it was to think about such things. A waste of time, time I didn't have.

I shifted Peaches to my hip so I could look more closely at her. She had fair skin and long lashes and a pink, pursed mouth. She reached for one of my earrings. "Oops," I murmured, tilting my head so that it was out of reach. "No earring, sweetie, that would hurt."

She made a baby sound and touched my T-shirt with a tiny finger.

I glanced up at Jared. I hadn't seen him since the girls got out of school for the summer. End-of-the-year awards assembly at school. Now that Mia and Maura were driving, when we had to discuss something about our girls, it was on the phone. "How are you?"

He crossed his arms over his chest. He was only a little taller than me, not a tall man. He was wearing khaki shorts, flip-flops, and an Ocean City White Marlin Open T-shirt. He was a big fisherman. Entered the tournament every year. Had for years.

He nodded, clearly feeling awkward. "I'm good. We're good."

"You get the brakes fixed on the girls' car?"

He bobbed his head. "Appointment Monday."

I nodded, deciding there was no point in bitching him out. We'd fought a lot. When he first left. Before he left. I was so angry. So bitter. I felt like such a failure. I felt as if he had made me a failure because he hadn't been willing to stay and fight for his family.

Now . . . I was happy to see that he seemed happy. "Mia's got SATs in two weeks. It's a Saturday. In Dover. Make sure she asks off at work." I bounced Peaches on my hip. "I don't know what to do about Maura. We can't make her take it."

"She likes the new restaurant. Her boss says she can start working a few hours a week in the kitchen." He shrugged.

"Maybe something will come of it. She says maybe she'd like to be a chef."

"There's an associate degree in culinary arts available at Del Tech in Dover. Maybe she should look at that."

"Maybe," he agreed.

We were both quiet then. I showed Peaches my bracelet. Lilly had given it to me for my thirty-fifth birthday. It was a lovely silver cuff, my name and hers engraved on the inside. I wondered if I should give it back to her. She might like to have it . . . later.

"Well, guess . . . I should be going," Jared said. "I just wanted to see how you were doing." He glanced away, then back at me. Hesitated. "How *are* you doing, Mack?"

"How do I look like I'm doing, Jared?" There was a sharpness to my tone that was ugly and mean, and I didn't care.

To my surprise, his eyes got watery. He blinked and looked down at his precious daughter. Instead of feeling good at having gotten the best of him, I felt like a total ass.

"Sorry. I'm okay," I murmured. "Doing okay." I pressed my lips together. Released them. "Hanging in there. Hanging on."

His head bobbed again. "You'll let me know if . . . there's anything I can do." He opened his arms to take his daughter.

*Like erase the last five years? Make us a happy family again, so I can die living that American dream?* "Sure." I was reluctant to give Peaches back to him. She felt so good in my arms.

She went right to him, arms open, and he smiled at her. It was a sweet moment. Jared had always been a good father to Mia and Maura. Even when things got bad between us. Even after he moved out. So many dads left their kids behind when they had kids with the new wife. A young wife. But I had to give Jared credit. He had done right by our girls, not just financially, but emotionally.

"I guess at some point . . . we need to talk about . . . if . . . if you get too sick. Once the girls are back in school." He kept his gaze on his little girl. "When you can't—"

"When I can't take care of them anymore." I stared at him.

Slowly, he raised his gaze to meet mine. "We don't have to talk about this now."

"No. But soon," I agreed. I slipped my hands into my hoodie pocket again. "I'll call you."

He started to back up. "Enjoy the fireworks."

"Thanks."

He took two or three steps backward into the living room before turning for the kitchen. Fritz, who had been watching us from the living room, trotted behind Jared. His escort. I stood there for a minute, alone. Feeling alone. Feeling all the regrets of all the years gone by. Then I thought about the feel of Peaches in my arms. About Lilly's baby. Even though the world was no longer full of hope for me, I didn't feel hopeless. Lilly, Aurora, Janine, my girls, they'd go on to lead long, happy lives. And that seemed enough for me, at that moment.

I turned out all the lights in the house, left Fritz standing guard on the deck, and went down to the beach to join the others.

My trek across the sand was slow, partially because I was tired. Partially because I was enjoying the few minutes alone on the beach. The sand was still warm on my bare feet, from the day's sun. There was a breeze, and the air smelled clean and tangy, not briny like it did sometimes. There were hints of barbecued meats still in the air; our neighbors had smoked a pork butt and sent over pulled pork for sandwiches. I could make out the smell of burned marshmallows.

I found everyone in the same spot where we usually set up during the day. The tide was coming in, but it wouldn't be high tide for hours. Lilly and Janine were sitting in beach chairs. Lilly had a towel wrapped around her. Aurora, Mia, and Maura were all on their knees on towels, facing Janine and Lilly. They'd brought down a propane lantern, which cast a circle of light around them.

When Mia spotted me, she called out to me, and the little conference broke up. Mia had a guilty look on her face. I could see it even in the pale light. Maura was a good liar, but I had always been able to read Mia's face.

"Hey, what's up?"

"Nothing," Mia said quickly.

Clearly it was something. I looked at Lilly, who conveniently decided to check her cell phone. "I was getting ready to call you. Fireworks start in six minutes."

I looked at Janine. She was sitting on her butt now, texting someone. She looked guilty, too.

"Come on. What's going on?"

Aurora glanced at me. "We were just talking. Boy stuff."

"You meet someone, Mia?" I shifted my gaze to Maura. "Or is it *Viktor?*" I added a Russian accent. It wasn't very good, but Lilly laughed.

"Boy talk not intended for mothers," Aurora explained.

"Oh." I sat in the chair next to Lilly, trying not to feel left out. "But I want to hear. Why can't you tell me?"

"Because, Mom." Maura was still on her knees. She drew little swirls with her finger in the sand at my feet. "If we say anything, even just mention a guy's name, you start asking questions. You ask every day, like it's a big deal."

I started to say, "I do not," but I guess I do. It wasn't as if I wanted to push boys and dating on them, just that I'm sometimes desperate to talk to my daughters, about *anything,* just to talk to them. There are days when it seems like there isn't a single subject that isn't taboo. I suppose if they mentioned someone's name, I might grab it and run with it. Not such a great strategy, in retrospect.

"Boys?" I said, pretty sure they were all telling a big fib. More likely they were talking about me. About how I looked, how I was feeling. How I was handling my diagnosis. Handling being here with them for what would be my last summer. "You two better not be keeping something from me," I warned Mia and Maura. I opened the cooler beside Lilly. I reached for a soda but took a beer instead. "And you three better not be protecting them. I'm still their mother." I held the beer with one hand and pointed with the other at my daughters. "I'm still your mother."

"We've got it, Mama Hen." Aurora sounded bored. She bored easily, especially when it came to dull topics such as work or child rearing. "Pass me a beer."

# ☙ 17 ❧

# Aurora

I'm not going to feel guilty. And Lilly can't make me. She ought to know that by now.

I could feel her staring at me. I didn't look at her. Instead, I tipped back the beer bottle and took a swig. It was mediocre beer, but it was local. We always drank local beer when we were here. I can't remember why.

The first fireworks exploded out over the ocean, and everyone oohed and aahed. I'm not into fireworks. Never have been. But even though it doesn't fit my personality, I'm into tradition.

Lilly thought we should tell McKenzie about Maura almost getting arrested. Actually, she thought we should make Maura do it. Hold her down in the sand, maybe, let crabs nibble at her bare toes until she confessed?

Lilly was all "It's a mother's right to know what's going on in her children's lives. I would want to know if *my* daughter had gotten into that kind of trouble."

I think that was easy for Lilly to say when her child is tucked safely beneath her belly button. She has no idea what she's in for. And maybe that's good. But I don't think she's being realistic about how hard it's going to be to be a parent. How no matter how hard she tries, she's going to fall flat sometimes. Probably more times than she doesn't. I don't think she's going to be a bad mom. I think she'll be better than most. But I still think she'll screw up sometimes, and that's going to be hard for her to deal with.

Lilly also doesn't get the reality of the situation here with Maura and Mia and McKenzie. She doesn't get that McKenzie doesn't have enough time left to make a difference. Telling her about Maura's tangle with the law wouldn't do anything but worry McKenzie. McKenzie can't change the path Maura is already on. Maybe that's cold. Maybe I can't think like a mother because while I might have given birth, Christ knew I was never a mother and would never be a mother. But I really think it's better for McKenzie if she doesn't know.

As to whether or not it was better for Maura? I don't know. I don't know how much I care. Maybe I will later. Once McKenzie is dead. But right now, McKenzie is the one I care about.

Lilly is blowing the whole thing out of proportion anyway. It was one little tangle with the po-po. She didn't get arrested. No harm, no foul.

I think Lilly is a drama queen. I think she looks for things to get upset about. She looks for things I do wrong. She's never approved of anything I do. It doesn't matter how many sculptures I sell or how much money I make. It will never be enough for Lilly. I'll never be good enough for her.

I took another pull on my beer. The fireworks were exploding in the sky: reds and blues. They were loud. I looked out at the dark water. I missed it. I already swam this afternoon. No second dip tonight. I have to limit myself. I get too dark in the water sometimes. My head gets too crazy. I swim to relieve tension. At least that's what I tell people, but sometimes I wonder. Clearly I swim to escape, but I wonder why else I do it. What's wrong with me that I need to push myself that way? Lose myself?

I glanced over at McKenzie. She was enjoying the fireworks. Her smile made me smile. Who would make me smile when she was gone? I loved Lilly and Janine. They're my left and my right hand. But McKenzie . . . she's my heart. She's the heart of all of us.

A lump rose in my throat, and I swallowed it with a beer chaser.

I still couldn't quite believe she was dying. I couldn't believe she was going to fucking die on me.

I glanced at Lilly. She was smiling, too. Looking up at the sky, in awe. She was so happy to be here. She knew how to be in the moment. Lilly would be okay when McKenzie died. She had the baby coming. She had her bump-on-a-log husband who loved her.

I tipped the beer, drinking the last of it.

Janine was sitting beside me on the towel. She was watching the fireworks, but she wasn't here with us. She wasn't in the moment. I wondered if she was thinking about the lawsuit. I haven't been able to tell from the things she's said this week if she really thinks something could come of it, or if she's just pissed that someone would have the audacity to make a complaint against her.

Maybe she isn't thinking about the lawsuit, though. Maybe she's thinking about the new girlfriend. Home alone while Janine is here with us. She'd said that she really liked her. I suspect she *really* liked her. That's why she hasn't brought her around and won't talk about her.

It was killing McKenzie and Lilly, not knowing the details. I don't care so much. I want Janine to be happy. I just don't think someone else is ever going to make her happy. Not that she can't *be* happy. I don't believe that Buddy took that away from her. I just think that her happiness has to come from herself.

Guess I should take a lesson from my own book.

"How about another beer?" I called to McKenzie. But she couldn't hear me over the rocket that whistled as it flew into the air, then exploded. I crawled across the towel, behind Janine. She was texting.

"Coming through," I announced, purposely pushing her roughly. Lying on my stomach, half on the towel, half in the sand, I lifted the lid on the cooler at Lilly's feet. I couldn't quite get my hand up and over the top.

"Need a beer?" Lilly asked, looking down at me over her pretty nose.

"Two," I said, holding up two fingers.

She frowned, but she passed me one and then another.

"Thanks." I flashed her my best smile.

She laughed, shook her head at me, "the incorrigible Aurora," and gazed up into the sky again. "Oh," she breathed. "That was beautiful. That might have been my favorite. Which do you like best, Maura?"

"The ones that twinkle," she said over her shoulder from where she sat on a towel.

"Those are mine," McKenzie said.

"See, Mom, we agree on something." Maura again.

"How about you, Mia?"

Mia glanced back at Lilly. "Oh, I couldn't choose. I love them all."

I crawled back to my spot beside Janine. "Beer?" I offered.

She shook her head.

"Who are you sexting?" I didn't try to look over her shoulder. I laid one beer beside me on the towel and opened the other.

"The department of—"

"None of your damned business," I chimed in. It was something we used to say when we were in middle school. We both laughed.

I took a drink of the cold beer and gazed out at the water. I *would* swim tonight. Day swimming didn't count. I could hear the depths calling me. The dark, cold water. Then I heard Maura saying something to me and I came back to the land of the living.

# ❦ 18 ❧

# McKenzie

Friday, my chest felt a little tight and I was slightly nauseated when I woke. The good news was that the rash on my hands and feet looked better and they weren't as sore. Checking out my stubbly eyebrows in the mirror while I brushed my teeth, I tried to assess how I was feeling. Was my breathing better? It certainly wasn't in the middle of the night when I was puking, but this morning . . . I took a deep breath, then spit in the sink. I felt like I could breathe deeper. Maybe. Or maybe it was just wishful thinking. I hadn't needed the oxygen I'd brought with me, so far. That had to be a positive sign, didn't it?

I rinsed out my mouth, dropped my toothbrush into the holder on the sink, and pulled my terry turban off. My head looked red this morning, rather than flesh-colored. A peach fuzz of red over the whole thing—except for a patch over my right eye, which was still cucumber bald. I looked awful. My face was blotchy. I had no eyebrows. Almost no hair.

But I had my daughters. I had my friends. And I was still here. I smiled at myself, pulled the turban over my head, and went to get dressed for the day.

We lay on the beach in the morning, before it got too hot. The Weather Channel had predicted a high of ninety-four degrees, with seventy-three percent humidity. Too hot on the beach for cancer girls and pregnant girls alike. By lunch, we were all ready to go up to the house. In the afternoon, Janine had a mysterious errand to run, which I suspected involved her girlfriend. Lilly and I spent the afternoon watching movies on DVD. (*Thelma & Louise* and *Breakfast at Tiffany's*. Easy to guess who chose which movie.) Aurora went back to the beach to nap; she was impervious to the heat.

That evening, after dinner, we sat in the living room and played spades. My choice. (Lilly had tried to convince us to play Clue; she loves that game. But she would have to wait until it was her turn to choose.) Aurora and I were partners, against Janine and Lilly. Taking a leaf out, we played at the table where we ate in the living room.

"Your bid, Lilly." Aurora sipped a gin and tonic. It was her second since dinner. She'd had at least one while we heated up Fourth of July leftovers. "Today, sweetie."

Lilly, refusing to be hurried along, studied her hand before gazing up at us over the tops of her cards. We were playing with two dog-eared decks advertising Jimmy Buffett's Margaritaville restaurant in New Orleans. I wasn't even sure which one of us had bought the cards; we'd all gone on a girls' weekend when Mia and Maura were in the sixth grade. "Five for me, plus Janine's three. Eight for us." Lilly smiled with triumph.

Aurora looked at me across the table from her. "We're going to lose. Three for us."

I tugged on my ball cap. It was more comfortable to wear than the scarves that constantly needed adjusting. "We're not going to lose." I wrote down our bids. "We're going to set them."

"Not with this hand we're not." Aurora gave her pile of cards, facedown on the table, a tap and reached for her sweaty glass.

Janine played her first card. An ace of hearts. "Dinner was good, Lilly. Thanks."

"Just leftovers." Lilly waited for me to toss down my three before she added a four to the center of the table. "Mr. Greene's pulled pork was delicious, though."

Aurora picked up her cards and tossed a ten in. "Sympathy pork."

"Come again?" Janine scooped up the trick.

"Sympathy pork," Aurora said again. She waited until everyone had put in a card and Janine had picked up her second winning trick. Hearts again. "It's sympathy pork. He sent it over because he feels bad for McKenzie. *The cancer.*" She did the quotations thing with her fingers.

"I'll take sympathy pork anytime." I sipped my one and only glass of pinot of the evening. "If it's *that* good. I mean, if it had just been boring, dry pork chops, maybe I would feel differently. Pulled pork is one of those things that smells as good cooking as it tastes when you eat it. I love it when Mr. Greene smokes meat on his deck."

"I'm surprised there's not some ordinance against it. Some people don't like to smell smoking meat while they're sitting on the deck of their beach house." Lilly. "I think it was nice of them to send it over, though. You make it sound so cold, Aurora. The Greenes were trying to be neighborly. When something like this happens, people want to help and they don't know how." She shrugged. "So they send food."

"If I get cancer," Aurora told us, "I want sympathy gin. Fifths of sympathy gin. And dark chocolate. German if they can find it."

"I'll keep that in mind," Lilly said. "Janine."

Janine played the first card of the next hand.

Someone's cell phone vibrated, and I glanced at mine, lying on the table to the left of my wineglass. I was hoping one of my girls had texted me. I love it when they text me just to tell me something silly that's happened. My favorite is when they send me selfies, where they're making silly faces. The screen on my phone was dark. It was Janine's vibrating. She picked it up, read the text, smiled, and tossed out another card. A club. She texted back.

Clubs went around a second time, Lilly winning both hands. Janine's cell vibrated again. Again, she smiled, texted back, and collected her partner's winning hand.

"Chris?" I asked. I was as curious as Lilly; I was just better at not acting like it.

She nodded. I finally took a trick with my one and only ace, an ace of diamonds.

"Care to share?" Aurora asked Janine.

Janine picked up her beer. She wasn't drinking hard liquor tonight, which was a nice change. "Nope."

"Oh, come on." Aurora slid her hand across the table toward Janine's phone.

"You're aware I have a license to carry a concealed weapon," Janine warned in her cop voice. She didn't move a muscle, just eyed Aurora.

Aurora withdrew her hand. "Well, I'm the only one in the room who's ever killed anyone, so there's that."

I looked up at her, knitting my sketched-in brows. "Aurora," I chastised. What I was selfishly thinking was *Really? You couldn't just let us have a fun, boring evening without having to drag out our dirty laundry?*

"What?" Aurora opened her arms, cards in one hand. "You know you were thinking it. All three of you. Be honest. You think about it all the time. Whenever you cross me."

"That's ridiculous. I was not," Janine said, fanning her cards open. "I do not."

Everyone was quiet as we played the next hand.

"Great," Aurora said as she picked up the cards. "So now you guys are all going to be pissy with me because I mentioned the elephant in the room?" She rocked back in her chair, shifting her gaze from one of us to the next. "The elephant we drag from room to room. Place to place, even when we're not here? When we're not even together?"

"We're not going to do this tonight, are we?" Lilly voiced what I had been thinking. She sounded tired, not angry.

Aurora spun her glass, watching the ice cubes go in a circle. "I told the girls, McKenzie."

It took me a second to realize what she was talking about. Then I just sat there, stunned. "You *told* them?" I finally managed. As the words came out of my mouth, I realized that was what they had been talking about the previous night on the beach, when I interrupted them. My intuition had been right. I *knew* something was going on.

"I'm going to need another beer." Janine got up. "Anyone else?"

I eyed my wineglass, seriously considering telling her to just bring the bottle. I couldn't believe that Aurora had told my girls about what she'd done. About Buddy. I had wanted to tell them myself. When the time came.

That was a lie. At least a half lie. If I'd really wanted to tell them myself, I'd have told them before now, wouldn't I?

"I'll take another bottle of water." Lilly got up, raising her finger to us. "Hold the conversation. I have to pee."

Aurora drained her glass and slid it across the table toward Janine. "Another gin and tonic if you're making them."

"I'm not." Janine leaned over my shoulder. "Need anything?"

I shook my head. I sat there across from Aurora, her looking at me, me looking at her.

"I'm sorry, okay?" Aurora finally said. She opened her hands and let them fall to her lap. "They looked me up on Wikipedia."

"Wikipedia?" I asked, surprised that was how they had found out, then surprised Maura and Mia hadn't thought of it sooner. Or none of us had.

I got up and went to my bedroom, bringing my laptop back and dragging a quilted throw. I was cold. In my chair again, I wrapped the blanket around me and Googled *Aurora Boudreaux*. There were hundreds of results, of course, mostly art sites, but also museums and cities where her work was displayed. Apparently, the Rhode Island School of Design was offering a class featuring Aurora, along with several other modern artists. I clicked the Wikipedia listing.

Janine came back in with her beer and Lilly's water, texting.

"I can't believe you wouldn't make me another drink," Aurora said, sounding genuinely hurt.

"My gift to your liver." Janine took her seat, setting her cell on the table.

I was skimming the Wikipedia entry. There was the usual stuff: what she was known for, how her work had impacted the art world. Down in the personal section there were particulars about where and when she was born, where she went to school, what famous person she studied under. I found a single line there that said, "At age fourteen, Boudreaux shot and killed Officer Buddy McCollister in self-defense. No charges were filed."

I looked up. "So Mia and Maura asked you?"

Aurora nodded.

I felt a twinge of something akin to jealousy that they hadn't asked me, but if they had, I don't know if I would have told them without Aurora present. It wasn't my story to tell. As much as I hated to admit it to myself, I also felt a sense of relief. Now they knew and I didn't have to be the one to tell them. Mia was still mad at me because I was the one who told her there was no Santa. It hadn't mattered that she was ten, an age when kids didn't believe any longer. Or that her sister was making fun of her. Or that I hadn't *killed* Santa, just told her the truth of his nonexistence.

I looked up at Aurora over the screen of the laptop. "How much did you tell them?"

Janine leaned forward, clasping her hands and resting them on the table. "What needed to be told."

"O . . . kay." I drew the word out. "And that was . . ."

Lily waddled out of the bathroom. "I told you guys to *wait*." She took her seat.

"Wikipedia just says that Aurora killed Buddy in self-defense and that she wasn't charged," I told Lilly.

Lilly looked at Aurora. "So you told them why you did it, right? About Buddy and Janine?"

"Kind of hard to leave that part out," Janine deadpanned.

My turn. "Did they ask a lot of questions?"

Aurora shook her head. "Not really. I think they were stunned. They knew their aunt Aurora had had her wild times, but I doubt they imagined me a murderess."

"I wish you wouldn't say that, Aurora," Lilly said. "You know how I feel about it."

"They understood though . . . about Buddy?" I asked.

"They understood." Aurora's tone was as flat as Janine's had been. "Mia cried."

I couldn't resist a sad smile. My Mia. Her heart went out to people. That was good. And bad. She was so easily hurt that I sometimes wished she were a little tougher—like Maura.

I turned to Janine. "You okay with this?"

Janine shrugged. "We should have told them sooner."

"I disagree," Lilly countered. "Incest is a mature subject, and this wasn't about some girl in a newspaper, a girl they didn't know. This was about you, Janine." She turned her attention to me. "I completely understand why you put off telling them."

"I didn't mean to let it go this long." I closed the laptop. I hated to ask, but I needed to know the specific details Aurora had given. I assumed she had told the same story she'd provided the police. The same story we all told. (*Often* when it first happened. I couldn't even remember the last time I'd told someone, though.) Even Janine's mom. It was a story that had been with us so long that I almost believed it. Except that wasn't the way it had happened.

"Exactly what did you tell them?" I asked Aurora, taking care with my tone. As tough as she seemed, I knew that somewhere inside, Aurora still regretted taking a man's life. Even a creepy crawler's like Buddy.

"You told them he had the gun in the room?" Lilly asked.

"No, Lilly." Aurora gave her one of her bored looks. The kind that didn't work with us because no matter how hard she tried to pretend, we knew she wasn't the heartless bitch she appeared to be. Her sarcasm was thick. "I told Maura and Mia that I opened the bedroom door, saw Buddy on top of Janine, and then I closed the door quietly. I told them I tiptoed down to the kitchen, got the handgun from the shelf with the Burger King glasses, and went back upstairs. I said I went into the room, hollered at Buddy, and when he got out of Janine's bed and came at me, I aimed for his chest and shot him."

That was the truth. Buddy hadn't taken the gun in with him. Aurora lied to the police that night. She lied to us all. It had been a good lie because no one questioned her story. Janine's mom would have been the one to speak up if anyone would have, but she'd fully supported Aurora's slightly altered version.

Anyone who knew Buddy—extended family members, friends, coworkers—knew he was nuts. Everyone knew he kept guns all over the house. (And it was the '80s; people weren't as conscious of gun safety as they are now.) When people who knew him found out he was raping his fourteen-year-old daughter, and had been since she was twelve, I don't think anyone cared how Aurora got the gun to shoot him. I think some of those people might have done the same thing, in Aurora's circumstances.

After it first happened, I had bouts of guilt. I actually considered going to my parents and telling them what really happened. The pangs faded over time. Now, I couldn't say for sure if it had been the right thing to do or not. Buddy had been a violent man. Had Aurora just walked into Janine's room that night, I don't know what would have happened, if not then, then the next time he had Janine alone. Or Aurora for that matter. One thing I was sure of, Buddy had been capable of murder.

Lilly's eyes filled with tears, and she reached for Aurora's hand.

Aurora tried to pull away, but Lilly wouldn't let her. Our gentle, sweet Lilly fought to hold on. "You came to Janine's defense. You saved her from Buddy," she said with a fierceness we didn't often hear in her voice. "You made sure Buddy would never do that to her again."

Aurora sat there dry-eyed.

I glanced at Janine. She was staring at the beer in her hand. I reached over and took her free hand. Squeezed it and let it go. She turned her head and half smiled, but didn't make eye contact.

I pressed my hands to the table, ignoring my cards, still lying facedown. "So why didn't the girls tell *me* they knew?" I asked. "When I came down to the beach after I talked to Jared, someone should have said something to me right then." I looked around the table. "One of you should have said something to me."

Lilly opened her water bottle. "We should have. We were going to. But the fireworks started and then the girls left right after."

"You were tired," Janine explained. "You went right to bed."

"And this morning?" I asked.

"We were all having a nice day and you seemed . . . like you were having a good day," Lilly said.

I picked up my cards, annoyed, but understanding. In their position, I'd probably have done the same thing. "Let's play."

"Don't be angry." Janine drew her thumb across the label of the beer bottle, smoothing it. "Maura and Mia needed to be told. They're old enough to know. They've *been* old enough for a while."

I didn't know if Janine meant to criticize me, but I made the conscious decision not to take it that way. "Who won the last trick?"

One by one, they picked up their cards. I waited for Lilly to put down the lead card. "What should I do?" I asked. "Call them to talk about it? Wait for them to call me?"

"Call them tomorrow," Lilly suggested.

Janine waited for her turn, then tossed out a card. "Call them and tell them you're ready to talk about it when they are. Give them some space."

I looked across the table at Aurora. She was going to say, "Let it go." She was going to say that if Mia and Maura wanted to talk about it with me, they would. And if they didn't, I needed to mind my own business. She was going to say that seventeen-year-old girls have the right to some privacy. That they didn't have to discuss every thought that went through their silly little heads.

I waited, watching her.

She picked up her glass, trying to get another drop of gin from it. "I think you should call them and make a lunch date. Tell them you want to talk to them about what happened that night. Have lunch with them and explain to them why you kept it from them. Tell them they can talk to you about it now or later. They can talk to any of us, anytime about it."

I was totally astonished by Aurora's reaction. I think Lilly and Janine were, too. "You think you and I should both go?"

"Nope. Aha! We won another one." Aurora scooped up the cards. She looked at me across the table. "I think you've got to do this one on your own."

Aurora had just thrown down her lead card when Janine's phone began to vibrate. And continued to vibrate. A call, not a text.

She glanced down at the phone at the same time that I did. A name hadn't come up, just a number. I was surprised when she picked it up. None of us picked up calls without a caller ID. She must have known the number.

"Hello?" She paused. Then, "No, no. It's fine. It's cool." Janine got up and walked toward the doors to the deck. Fritz was sitting in the doorway. He raised his head and looked at her.

"Okay. Um, sure," Janine said into the phone. She paused to listen again, glancing back at us. "No. I totally agree. You're absolutely right." She looked at us again. Lilly and I looked at her.

"Chris?" Lilly whispered to me.

I made an *I have no idea* face.

"If no one's going to get me a drink, guess I'll get it myself." Aurora rose from her chair. "Tell your girlfriend we said hi," she called to Janine.

Janine was giving the address of the house. It had to be her girlfriend.

I smiled at Lilly. We were both thinking the same thing. *We're going to meet her!*

Of course, I couldn't believe that Janine would date someone as long as she'd been dating Chris (which of course we didn't know because she wouldn't tell us, but it had to be for some length of time, didn't it? I mean, Janine clearly liked this girl) and not bring her here. Or at least show her where the beach house was. Janine rarely came here to stay without one of us.

"Okay. Sounds good," Janine was saying. "Should I come get you?" She had a weird look on her face. She snapped her fingers. Fritz was on his feet in an instant. Janine walked out onto the deck with the German shepherd. Fritz bounded down the steps into the dark.

Janine remained on the phone out on the deck, but she was talking quietly. She didn't seem excited. I wondered if Chris was insisting it was time she meet us, and Janine was only going along with it because she knew she was going to have to let us all meet her at some point.

Janine ended the call and walked back into the room at the same time as Aurora.

"Chris coming over?" Lilly asked, bubbly with excitement.

Janine slid into her seat. "Would there be any way of avoiding it?"

# ❧ 19 ❧

# Aurora

I stood outside her bedroom door for a long time. The light was on, the door open just a little. The whole house was quiet. The doors and windows were closed; the heat pump was humming, blowing cool air through the ductwork.

Janine and Lilly had gone to bed. We managed to finish the game of cards, but everyone had seemed pretty tired. Subdued.

I rested my forehead on the doorjamb. I feel so sad and I don't know why. It would have been easy to make the assumption that I felt bad because I'd had to tell Mia and Maura what a horrific fuck Buddy had been. Because of the horrendous thing that had happened to Janine. Or I could chalk up the heaviness in my heart to the fact that McKenzie is dying.

But I know that isn't why I'm sad. I mean I *am*, but the reality is that I'm sad because I'm a terrible person and I don't want to be. I'm a liar. I've lied to the people who love me the most. I've lied to them over and over again. To the only people who have ever loved me. *Will* ever love me. They think I'm some kind of hero, but I'm not. I'm a selfish, self-centered bitch. I'm exactly what I seem to be.

I knocked on the door and pushed in.

McKenzie was lying in the bed, looking small and pale. And sick. She'd washed her face, so her eyebrows were gone. Her computer was on her lap, but I suspected she'd been dozing. She was wearing a fleece beanie on her head, one more appropriate for the ski slopes than the beach in July.

"Cold?" I asked.

She looked at me quizzically.

I tapped the top of my head.

She chuckled and patted the bed beside her.

I stretched out beside her, propping my head up with my hand.

"I wish you wouldn't swim at night," she said. I was in my swimsuit. My cap and towel were on the deck.

"I know," I said.

"It's dangerous. Half the time, we don't even know you're gone."

"What's the worst thing that could happen?" I teased. "I could drown? A shark could eat me?"

"There are no sharks big enough to do anything beyond nip at your toes in this water," she argued.

"Okay, so maybe a boat runs over me and cuts me up with the propeller."

"Eww." She gave me a nudge.

I went on. "What good would it do you, knowing I was out there? It's not like you could do anything if I *did* get into trouble."

She looked at me, smiling but looking sad at the same time. "I worry about you."

"Which is why you don't need to know when I go at night."

She dropped her head back on her pillow and closed her eyes for a minute.

"I'm sorry," I said.

She kept her eyes shut. "What have you done now?"

I thought about my sadness. About the big lie. The lie I had allowed them to believe all these years. "About Maura and Mia. I didn't mean to usurp your authority."

She laughed and opened her eyes, turning her head on her pillow to look at me. *"Usurp my authority?"*

"They're your kids," I said. "I totally respect that."

"I know you do."

"And you're a good mom. Janine and I didn't mean to be critical, saying you should have told them before. What do we know? We're not parents. And we all know why."

McKenzie raised her hand over her head and stared at the ceiling fan above the bed. I noticed that her cheeks were red, but not a flushed red. More like a rash.

"Do you think so?" she asked me, sounding lost in her thoughts. "I mean . . . really?"

"Do I think what?"

"That I'm a good mom?" She hesitated, then turned her head to look at me again. "I have so many regrets, Aurora."

"Please. I've sobered up. You can't do this to me. I'm not going to listen to you."

She smiled. Still sad.

"I am serious," I said. And I was. "You've been a good mom. A great mom. What did you do? You loved them. And that's hard. I know how hard it is to love people. To do it right." Emotion crept into my voice. I was going to have to cut this visit short if I couldn't get ahold of myself. "You were selfless." I took her hand. Her nails were short and neat. She's always had nice hands. Feminine hands. "Not many parents can say that."

"I tried to do what was best for them," McKenzie said. "I hope they realize that. After I'm gone."

"Oh, God," I groaned. "Are we really going there? I just came to say good night."

"So you could sneak out of the house and go swimming."

"Something like that," I agreed.

"Fine, go get eaten by a shark." She glanced at her laptop, balanced on her bony hips. "But you have to see this before Jaws gets you. I've been working on our video diary. I'm having so much fun."

She sat up, shifting the computer on her lap, and tapped on the keyboard. "I found this app. Downloaded it myself, without Maura's or Mia's help, thank you very much. I'm taking the videos I've been recording on my phone and downloading them to the computer, then editing them with this app. This is just a little piece, but you have to watch this."

I watched the screen as she hit play. It was a clip of Lilly holding up her finger, then hustling down the hall to disappear into the bathroom, followed by Lilly walking into the bathroom again, in a different outfit. Then Lilly holding up her finger saying, "Wait, I have to pee." And practically running to the bathroom.

"Wait, this is the best part," McKenzie said, cracking up.

I was laughing with her as I watched Lilly run into the bathroom, back up, and run in and back up twice more. McKenzie had rewound the same clip and played it multiple times, but it didn't matter that it had obviously been manipulated. Dubbed over the top was Lilly saying, "Have to pee, have to pee, have to pee."

"Oh, Christ, that's too funny. Play it again," I said.

She played it again, then we played it a third time, laughing so hard, I was afraid we were going to wake them upstairs.

"That's terrible," I said, laughing so hard I was snorting. "Awful. Don't show her. She'll make you delete it. She'll make you delete the whole video diary and possibly destroy your phone."

"I know." McKenzie had to catch her breath. "Isn't it hilarious? I think you guys should play it at my funeral. Anyone who knows her will be rolling in the aisle, laughing."

"She would kill you," I said. Then, realizing what I'd just said, I looked at McKenzie. "Okay, that came out—"

We both burst out laughing.

"Go on," she told me, reaching for a tissue from a box on the other side of the bed. "Go swimming. And let me know when you're back."

I climbed out of bed. "That's really not how I roll."

"Well, that's how you're going to roll tonight," she told me, tapping on the keyboard, not bothering to even look up at me.

"Back in an hour," I whispered, slipping out of her room, into the darkness, and back into my cowardice.

# ꬷ 20 ꬴ

# Lilly

"**I** brought some iced tea," I said to Janine, walking onto the front deck, carrying a tray with a pitcher of freshly brewed tea and four glasses. "Where's everybody else?"

I was just making conversation. I knew McKenzie was taking a shower, getting ready for lunch with her girls, and I had seen Aurora leave a few minutes ago, headed out on one of her walks. She might be gone twenty minutes . . . or twenty days.

Aurora had once left here and called us a week later to tell us she was with a guy named Nandi in New Delhi. We had no idea who she was talking about or how she got there. Janine had been pretty pissed. She had screamed at Aurora on the phone saying she'd put out an APB in the area on her. Which wasn't true, of course, but there had been a lot of drama for a couple of days.

"Mack's inside." Janine set her book on the arm of her chair and took a glass from the tray. "Aurora's gone on a walkabout. Said she'd see me later, but—" She shrugged. "I told her she needed to be home by Monday."

"Monday? Something special happening on Monday? Maybe a special guest coming?"

"I promised I wouldn't say anything."

"You promised Chris?" I asked.

"If I told you, I wouldn't be keeping my promise, now would I?"

"Fair enough. I just want you to know how happy we are that you're ready to have us meet her. We know this is outside your comfort zone." I poured tea into her glass. From the look on her face, I knew it would be a good idea if I changed the subject. Otherwise, it was pretty likely I'd be sitting on the porch alone. "What are you reading?"

She glanced at the paperback open on the arm of her chair. "The usual."

I glanced at the cover as I lowered myself into my chair. Janine's book covers all looked the same to me: outer space, planets, sometimes a star exploding or a stormtrooper running across an unfamiliar planet. Janine is a fan of science fiction, something I didn't care for. McKenzie and I both read Oprah picks, *New York Times* women's fiction, book club kind of stuff. (We were all about women's angst.) Aurora, to my knowledge, doesn't read at all.

I suspected Janine liked getting lost in the worlds inside the books she read. There was usually lots of action and shooting, too, which *did* sound like her. She read mysteries once in a while, too, but she had always been a voracious reader of science fiction back when we were middle schoolers.

I sat down in my chair and moved my cell phone from the tray to the arm. I'd called Matt, but he hadn't answered. He was probably still out mowing the lawn. He mowed on Saturdays after he went to the gym and stopped at the grocery store.

I stretched out my bare feet. The deck felt warm beneath them. Smooth, not gritty anymore. I'd swept the deck this morning. There was at least a bucket of sand on it, even though we tried to shower outside before we came up. Or at least rinse off our feet in the tub at the bottom of the stairs that I kept filled with water for just that purpose.

I gazed out over the rail at the beach and at the ocean that stretched out in front of us and seemed to go on forever. It was another perfect day. I glanced at the porch, satisfied with my tidying. The palm tree I'd brought home from the market looked perfect in the corner of the deck against the house. When I put the chairs back, I switched their order. Now mine was next to Janine's, in the middle, with McKenzie's to my right and Aurora's to Janine's left.

Janine drank her tea unsweetened, which was why I didn't sweeten it when I brewed it, the way I did at home. I added two heaping spoons of sugar to my glass, then stirred it with the long iced tea spoon.

Fritz got up from his sentry position at the top of the steps, walked in front of me, and pressed his head against Janine's hand. She stroked his head for a minute, spoke quietly to him, then pointed to her feet. The dog dropped to his belly at once and closed his eyes.

"You think you could teach me a few of the techniques you use on Fritz?" I asked, stroking my big belly with my free hand. I kept stirring my iced tea. I liked the sound of the spoon against the glass. "Might come in handy with the kid."

She looked over the rim of her glass, skeptical. "I don't think I'm the one to give child-rearing advice."

"So maybe you'll be her life coach."

"Her?" Janine asked. "I thought you didn't know if it was a boy or a girl."

"Or him," I added quickly. "We don't know." From conception in the petri dish, I had suspected our baby was a girl, but I kept that to myself. Just my little secret between baby McKenzie and me. Or Olivia or . . . whatever we decided on.

We were both quiet for a few minutes, enjoying the warmth of the sun, the smell of the water. Even the squawk of the seagulls seemed serene today. I sneaked a glance at Janine. She seemed fine. Well, as fine as Janine ever seemed. I was worried about her. Having to sit and listen to Aurora tell Mia and Maura about Buddy. Then having to listen to Aurora tell McKenzie that she'd told them. Janine was tough. I knew that. How else would she have survived all these years? How else would she have survived nearly two years of Buddy hell? Still, I worried.

"I'm fine. Stop looking at me like that," Janine said.

I glanced at her like I didn't know what she was talking about. "I'm not looking at you like anything. I mean . . . I'm looking at you, but not . . . what are you talking about?"

"I can see it on your face." She brought her finger to her temple and spun it in circles. "You're worrying about how I am after telling Mia and Maura about Buddy. After Aurora telling McKenzie that we told them."

"I know you're fine," I said a little defensively. Was I that easy to read? Guess I was.

"I am," Janine said.

"I know."

"Good."

"Good," I repeated. Then I looked at her. "Are we really fighting about whether or not you're okay?"

"We're not fighting, Lillian. I'm just telling you that you don't have to worry about me."

I was quiet for a minute. I sipped my tea. "Would you tell me?" I asked. I added another spoon of sugar. "If you weren't okay?" My lasts words were almost whispered.

It took her what seemed like a long time to answer me. "I hope so."

I felt a tenderness for Janine then, one I don't know that I could describe if I wanted to. I took another drink of tea, and the baby gave me a poke. "Oh!" I brought my hand to my belly. Then I smiled.

She did it again. It was a little foot or a little hand, just below my rib cage. "She liked the sugar. Probably the caffeine, too," I said. Matt didn't want me drinking caffeine. I'd given up coffee for our son or daughter, but my tea was where I drew the line. "She's getting so strong," I mused. I looked at Janine. "You want to feel? She's really kicking. Right here." I showed her.

Janine looked at me, then at my belly. A little bit like she thought I had an alien inside. "Nah. I'm okay."

I try not to let my feelings be hurt. Janine isn't into babies. I know that. She has less maternal instinct than Aurora, if that's possible. Which put her in the negatives. And some people are funny about feeling a woman's pregnant belly. It isn't a big deal. It doesn't mean she wouldn't love my baby when it's born.

She must have seen the look on my face because she said, "Lilly—"

"It's okay," I said. There were a lot of okays between us. Too many. Was it because of the baby? Because of McKenzie? "I understand."

She sighed. "How's that possible when . . . when I don't?" She took her time before choosing her words. "I'm happy for you, Lilly. I really am. I just . . ." She stopped and started again. Not making eye contact with me anymore. Looking out over the rail, at the beach. "I don't know what to do sometimes. What to say. You know I love you." Now she was looking at me.

And it was okay.

# ❧ 21 ❧

# McKenzie

It was Sunday afternoon, market day. We were all in Janine's Jeep Cherokee; I was riding shotgun. Cancer has its privileges.

We rode north on Route 1, with the air conditioner off and the windows down. Even though we were just going to the market, it felt like a road trip in our days of yore. Clapton was on the radio; we always listened to one of the beach's oldie stations. The warmth of the sun and the breeze the car created felt good. It made me feel alive.

I rested my elbow on the windowsill, leaning out a little. "So how's your mom?" I asked Janine. Kathy had called that morning. I'd only heard a snippet of the conversation, but it had sounded like they were arguing. After hanging up, Janine had busied herself cleaning up under the house; because it was built on pilings, the area always seemed to be a catchall for junk. She pretty much avoided us until Lilly had announced that we were all going to the market.

Janine kept her gaze on the road. Hands on the wheel at ten and two. "She's fine."

Looking into the side-view mirror, I tugged my ball cap down snugly on my head. "She call just to say hi or what?"

"Just to check in, I guess. She said to tell everyone she said hi."

I glanced into the backseat at Aurora, who was sitting behind Janine. She wasn't wearing her sunglasses, so I could see by the look on her face that she wasn't buying it, either.

The traffic light at the intersection ahead turned red, and Janine slowed. Beside us, to my right, we passed a Sailfish on a trailer. Four college-aged girls were in the extended-cab pickup pulling it. They had the windows down, the music up; I didn't recognize the song or the artist, which made me feel old. The young women were in bikinis and hats. The driver was wearing a straw cowboy hat. As we pulled up beside them, the girl in the cowboy hat cranked the music up louder. The four girls were singing together. They looked like they were having so much fun. I could tell by the way they were looking at each other and singing together.

They could have been us twenty-some years ago. I hoped the girls in the truck understood how fleeting moments like the ones they were experiencing right then are. I hoped they were getting every drop of pleasure they could that day from the brightness of the sun and the laughter of the friend sitting next to them.

I had to look away. I stared through the windshield at the Harley in front of us. The traffic light turned green, and we moved ahead of the girls with the boat.

"Todd's new baby doing well?" I asked Janine.

"I guess." She must have realized how that sounded because she added, "You know, she's good. Not sleeping through the night yet, of course. Mom says Christie's exhausted, with the three of them. Kids are on summer break, so no school."

I glanced at Aurora. Before turning to face forward again, I caught a glimpse of Lilly. She had a pair of candy-apple-red reading glasses perched on the end of her nose. She was texting furiously.

I realized she hadn't said anything since we left the beach house. Come to think of it, she'd been quiet all day. Something had to be up. But I could only handle one possible situation at a time. I turned back to Janine. "So what were you arguing about, if she just called to say hi?"

Janine looked at me, making a sound of exasperation.

The traffic was moving slowly. I could see the girls with the sailboat in my side-view mirror. They'd almost caught up with us again.

"Is there such a thing as privacy with you guys, *ever?*" Janine asked.

I shook my head and deadpanned, "Nope."

Only Aurora laughed.

Janine sat stiff, her fingers gripping the steering wheel too hard. "Who said we were arguing?"

"We could hear you." Aurora, from the backseat. "Come on, you might as well tell us. You know Cancer Girl won't let it go."

Cancer Girl. It had been a not-all-that-funny joke on the Fourth of July, but now I was beginning to appreciate it. While it could be used in a derogatory manner, there was also a certain power in it. Let's face it: I did feel like Cancer Girl a lot of the time. Against my wishes, cancer had totally taken over my life. Rarely a minute went by that my life wasn't revolving around this sucky situation. Why couldn't we make fun of it a little?

Janine took her time answering me. "It wasn't a big deal. You know, the usual Kathy bullshit."

"She thinks you should come down and see the baby?" I probed.

Janine glanced in the rearview mirror, signaled, and changed lanes so that she was in front of the Sailfish girls. "No. I mean, yeah, she *does* think I should come, but she was calling because . . ." She exhaled and went on. "Because she's coming up for a friend's birthday party or something in Philadelphia at the end of the month."

"And she wants to stop by?" I asked. Kathy never stayed at the house. She hadn't stayed there, to my knowledge, since Buddy had died. She rented it out for years, then Janine took over its management and let it sit empty when one of us wasn't using it.

"She wants to see you," Janine groaned.

*To say good-bye* came to mind. I shrugged. "And that's a problem because?"

"Because I don't want her here, Mack." Janine changed lanes

again. "You know how she is. How she'll *be*. It'll be all about her. How devastated she is that you've got cancer. How upset she's been. How she wishes she had it instead of you."

"Maybe your moms should get together," Aurora injected.

I cut my eyes at Aurora, then looked back at Janine. "I don't mind. Seeing her. I really don't."

"But I do." Another red light.

"Janine." I sighed, thinking before speaking. I didn't get these kinds of opportunities with Janine. To say things like this. When she was trapped in a moving car and couldn't get away from me. "I understand why you haven't been close. I really do, but . . . it's been a long time. I feel like you need to drop this grudge."

"Grudge? *Grudge?*" she said to me. "Is that what you call it? A *grudge?* Like I'm still angry I didn't get the Barbie camper for my fifth birthday? Or a grudge because she gave my brother more money for college than she gave me and I ended up dropping out because I couldn't pay?" She was becoming angrier by the second. "That's a *grudge*, Mack. Knowing my father was fucking me and pretending he wasn't, that's not a goddamned grudge."

I was quiet then. We'd been through this hundreds of times, maybe thousands. Yet here we were again.

Kathy had sworn, at the time of Buddy's death, to police and her daughter, and anyone who would listen, that she hadn't known what was going on. She'd claimed to have been afraid of Buddy, afraid for her life. Which was a reasonable statement, since from time to time, she had had a black eye from *running into a door* or a fractured wrist from *tripping on the stairs*.

All these years, Kathy had held to her story that she hadn't known Buddy had been sexually abusing their teenage daughter. There was no confession and begging for forgiveness. Kathy insisted on her innocence.

I honestly didn't know the truth because Janine didn't have hard evidence against her mother. She didn't have evidence at all. She'd just maintained that she knew her mother knew. I felt, back then, that I had to side with Janine on this one. I still did.

And I understood why, because of the circumstances, that Janine never had much of a relationship with her mother. But the woman just wanted to stop by to say hello. To me, her daughter's best friend, who was dying.

"If you're uncomfortable having her at the house, I could meet her for lunch somewhere," I said.

"And make me look like an even bigger jerk?" Janine asked.

I looked to Aurora, but she was staring out the window. I twisted farther to see Lilly. "You're awfully quiet. You want to weigh in?"

Lilly lowered her cell and glanced up over the rims of her glasses. "I'm sorry?"

"Who are you texting?" Janine asked.

"Matt." Lilly looked serious despite the silly red glasses.

Janine signaled to make the turn into the market parking lot. "Enough, Lilly. Time to come clean."

"You told them?" Lilly tapped the back of my seat. It was more than a tap. A slap. "McKenzie! How could you?"

Janine looked at me. I looked at her. She pulled into a parking space. "Told us what?"

Lilly sat back in her seat, staring at me. "I can't believe you would say something. We specifically agreed I was going to think on it."

I threw up my hands. She was talking about our conversation on the Fourth of July about her telling Matt and/or Janine and Aurora about being an escort. "I didn't." I undid my seat belt as soon as Janine stopped the vehicle and poked my head into the backseat. "What you and I talked about wasn't what Janine was talking about." I didn't mean to sound cryptic, but there was no way I was going to be the one to tell them anything.

"What wasn't I talking about?" Janine cut off the engine, looking into the backseat.

All three of us were looking at Lilly. She burst into tears.

Janine and Aurora looked at me. "What?" I said.

Lilly yanked off her reading glasses, dropped them into her

enormous handbag, and pulled out her sunglasses. "I think I need some air." She opened the car door.

"Lilly." I opened my door.

We all got out. Lilly took off. She cut across the parking lot, walking fairly fast for a woman seven months pregnant. I followed her. I heard the beep as Janine locked her door with the automatic opener.

"Lilly," I called. "I didn't say anything to them. I swear I didn't."

"I feel like an idiot," she threw over her shoulder. "Matt's acting weird. I feel like an idiot," she repeated.

"So slow down and you won't feel like an idiot, running through a parking lot seven months pregnant in those shoes." Aurora caught up to her first.

Then Janine. Then me.

"Will someone please tell me what's going on?" Janine said. "Lilly, what's wrong?"

We walked past a candle shop in the little strip mall where the market was. It smelled good, but a little nauseating, too. I pressed my hand to my stomach, trying to keep up with Lilly's pace. I started to pant, but I didn't slow down.

"Lilly, let's sit down. McKenzie's going to fall over."

Janine got on Lilly's other side and grabbed her arm. "Come on, it's hot out. Let's get some frozen yogurt." We had stopped in front of a sweets shop.

When my girls had been little, I had bribed them into going to the market with me by promising an ice-cream cone afterward. They hadn't known the difference then between ice cream and frozen yogurt, which had delighted me.

"We could go to a bar," Aurora piped up. "Bars are air-conditioned." But she was already holding the door open to the ice-cream shop.

When we were all inside, my cancery lungs gave a sigh of relief. I was impressed with myself, though. I'd almost kept up with Lilly all the way across the parking lot. Maybe the experimental drug was working. I wasn't sucking wind like I should have been. Or maybe, just maybe, there had been a mistake in my diagnosis. Maybe I wasn't dying of papillary thyroid cancer in my lungs after all.

And maybe this was a shop that sold unicorn rides rather than low-cal frozen yogurt.

I half sat, half fell into a white wrought iron chair at a round table by the window.

"I don't want frozen yogurt," Lilly protested, but she sat down. She took off her sunglasses and rubbed her eyes. They were red from crying, and her mascara had smudged under one eye.

"What does everyone want?" Janine asked.

My stomach was a little upset now. I didn't really want anything, but for the sake of the group . . . "A single scoop of sorbet and some water."

"What kind of sorbet?" Janine asked me. I knew she'd taken notice of my *breathiness*. She was looking at me, asking me "Are you okay?" with her eyes.

I nodded ever so slightly. *I'm okay.* "Any kind of sorbet," I told her. "Whatever is the flavor of the day."

"I know what Lilly wants," Aurora said, going with Janine.

Lilly sat back in her chair, her big belly pressing against the table. "I can't believe Aurora knows what I get. We haven't been here since last fall."

I waited until they were out of earshot. "So what's going on with Matt? I thought things were fine."

"They were." She pulled a tissue from her bag and wiped under both eyes. "When I left he was all lovey-dovey, saying he'd miss me and that he'd have to come visit because there was no way he could go a month without seeing me." She exhaled. "But he's been acting weird all weekend." She looked at Aurora and Janine in line to order.

They were talking quietly. Whether it was about Lilly or Kathy or the kid behind the counter with the bad tattoo on his neck, I couldn't tell.

"Of course Aurora remembers what you like," I told Lilly softly.

"There are a lot people in here for three o'clock in the afternoon," she mused.

I glanced around. It didn't seem any more or less busy than usual. A teenage girl and guy, clearly on a date, watched as one of the employees, wearing a paper hat, scooped frozen yogurt into a waffle cone. To our left, two tables over, were a little girl and her mother, and *her* mother, I guessed. A middle-aged couple, a little older than us, was sharing a sundae and engrossed in conversation.

"I really do feel like an idiot. I thought Janine was asking me about what you and I talked about, about me telling Matt. I know. How paranoid does that make me?" Lilly took lipstick from her bag. Even in her hurry to get out of the car, to get away from us, she remembered to bring her bag. So she could have her lipstick. She put it on her lips, then blotted it with a tissue the way my mother did. "What *was* she asking?"

"I think about Matt. What was going on with you two because you were texting back and forth. She was just joking around."

Janine and Aurora were next in line. I reached across the table. "You don't have to tell them about your stripping days."

She made a face. "They know about the *stripping*. Aurora always thought it was funny. She said I was probably bad at it, which I was *not*." Lilly had gone to the University of Miami for two years, years we didn't see much of her.

"What I mean is that you don't have to tell them *the rest*."

"I do. I was a prostitute, for God's sake."

I scowled. "You were not."

"I took money for *sex*," Lilly whispered, leaning closer.

I rolled my eyes. "We already talked about this. Sweetie, we've all exchanged things for sex. If not money, then favors, or a pretty piece of jewelry, or just some peace and quiet so we could go back to reading a book." I took a breath. "That is old news. Old news that you don't have to tell Aurora or Janine or Matt about."

Lilly squeezed her eyes closed. "What you're saying makes sense. I know it makes perfectly logical sense." She opened her eyes. "It's what I would tell you."

I smiled, hoping Lilly knew how much I loved her.

"You're right." She regarded me from across the table. "You're right, and I'm sorry. I didn't mean to throw a snit. I just—I'm worried about Matt. What if that hussy with the fake boobies and the really white teeth has been into our office? I knew I should have called her company and told them to send us a different rep. I knew it!"

I would have laughed at Lilly using the word *boobies*, except that I wasn't sure I had enough breath, and she was too upset to be laughing at her. "Tell me what's going on. How is Matt being weird?"

She was halfway through her story about playing phone tag with Matt when Aurora and Janine returned with paper cups of iced water for everyone and frozen yogurt for them, watermelon sorbet for me. Aurora had gotten a cone of soft-serve with rainbow sprinkles on it. Janine had a scoop of coffee yogurt with chocolate chips on top, and they'd brought Lilly her Miss Lulu, a fruity version of a hot chocolate sundae.

"Eat some. You'll feel better," Aurora said, putting the big cup of frozen yogurt with its assorted gooey fruit chunks and syrups in front of her. She handed her a long-handled plastic spoon. "Then you have to tell us what the big secret is."

I cut my eyes at Aurora. I was feeling better now that I had caught my breath. The sorbet actually looked good. "She's worried about Matt. He's been preoccupied all week. Not returning her phone calls—"

"He does eventually," Lilly interrupted, "but he's distracted. He's not really listening to me. He just says what he thinks I want to hear. Lots of mmm-hmms."

"Maybe he's just having a bad week at work." Janine took one of the chairs between Lilly and me. "If I'm having a bad week at work, Chris can forget it. I can barely hold up my half of a conversation. I can't," she admitted. "It's not that Chris isn't important, it's just that . . . work is everything. It's how I judge myself, you know?"

Aurora had taken the chair on the other side of me, between Lilly and me. We all scooted up to the cute, round, white wrought iron table. "That's a guy thing," Aurora said. "And a Janine thing," she quickly added.

"Some woman has been flirting with Matt when she comes into the office," I explained so Lilly could get another bite of her pineapple yogurt with blueberry topping. "Matt said he hadn't even noticed her when Lilly brought up the subject, but Lilly knows the woman's got her eye on him."

"So was she there this week?" Aurora licked sprinkles off her ice-cream cone.

"I don't know. She wasn't supposed to be, but . . ." Lilly pushed the spoon into her mouth. "Matt says there's nothing wrong, that he's just preoccupied. He had a heavy patient schedule all week. The bookkeeper messed something up on our unemployment taxes, and I guess his mother has been calling about coming to stay with us after the baby is born."

"His mother wants to *stay* with you?" Janine started to pluck napkins from the little aluminum dispenser on the table next to us and pass them out. "I didn't realize you and his mom had that kind of relationship." She made a face. "I didn't think Matt and his mom had that kind of relationship. Isn't she a professional golfer or something? I thought she lived in Arizona."

"Not a professional golfer. She's on some kind of national senior citizen ladies' team," Lilly explained. She took another bite of her sundae. "Matt's overreacting. She's just trying to be nice. You know. Since my mother's dead. She thought I would want her to come."

"You don't though, right?" Janine gave Lilly a napkin and touched her own chin.

Lilly quickly wiped her mouth. "No, I don't want her there. Of course I want her to come see the baby. But not right after we have her. I want some time for Matt and the baby and me to adjust. But I don't see why Matt can't just tell her that."

"Wait a minute. Did I miss something?" Aurora asked, reaching for the napkin Janine had put in front of her. "Are you having a girl? How did I not know that? No one ever tells me anything."

"We tell you things all the time." Janine. "You don't listen, Aurora."

"I'm not having a girl," Lilly explained. "Well, obviously I might be." She gave a little laugh. "I just call it *she*." She stroked her belly with her free hand. "Because it's easier than he/she. Him/her. But we don't know it's a she for sure."

"Ah." Aurora nodded. "So back to Matt. You think he's hiding something?" She'd worn her hair down rather than in a ponytail, and it shimmered over her shoulders and down her back. "But you don't know what?"

Lilly dropped her spoon into her polka-dot sundae cup. "No . . . I don't know. He just seems . . ." She exhaled and dabbed at the corners of her mouth with her napkin.

"Could he really just be preoccupied with having to tell his mother to get lost and having to pay the government a big penalty because someone screwed up his payroll?" I asked. "Which is what he told you?"

"I don't know." Lilly sat back in her wrought iron chair. "Maybe."

"Boys and their mothers," Janine commiserated.

"Not just boys. My sister is like that," I said, taking a tiny bite of the sorbet and letting it melt on my tongue. "She hates to tell my mother no, no matter how crazy my mother's ideas are."

"And the nonpayment and the penalty is a big deal," Lilly agreed. "It's something Matt really would get upset about. And he didn't even want to tell me about it, to begin with. He didn't want to worry me." She stared into her cup of frozen yogurt that was beginning to melt. "Maybe you're right. Maybe I'm making something out of nothing."

"Which brings us to the next topic, or rather back to the previous one." Aurora took a bite of her cone. "What wasn't McKenzie supposed to tell us? That she *didn't* tell us, but now you have to, because you told on yourself."

I licked sorbet off my spoon. "Let it go."

Janine narrowed her gaze. "Big life-changing secret or just some little thing you should have told us fifteen years ago and now you've blown it up to be something big in your head?" she asked Lilly.

"Big thing," Lilly said.

"Little," I said at exactly the same time.

Aurora and Janine looked at me and then at Lilly.

"You wanna table it?" Aurora asked, taking me totally by surprise.

"Can I?" Lilly asked, almost in a whisper. "Aurora, that's so nice of you."

Aurora shrugged. "Not really. My guess is that it probably isn't as big a deal as you think." She took another bite of her ice-cream cone. "So you think on that." She turned to me. "And in the meantime, tell us how pizza was at Grottos with your girls. They ask you all the gruesome details of Buddy's demise? This guy I once knew wanted to do some kind of crazy calculation with blood volume from the crime photos. Needless to say"—she smiled her "gorgeous blonde" smile—"I didn't go out with him again."

# ⤾ 22 ⤿

# Janine

Monday morning I woke up nervous as hell. I wished I were anywhere but here at the beach house. Waiting. Having everyone watching me, then pretending they aren't when I look at them.

I'd told them all the night before that I didn't want to be grilled about the visit today. I'd promised not to provide details (beyond the fact that it was not my mother coming), so I wouldn't be providing details. Lilly wanted to make some sort of celebratory dinner involving boneless chicken breasts, artichokes, and brie; I warned her not to. I was pretty sure our "guest," as Lilly kept saying, wouldn't be staying for dinner and aperitifs in the conservatory.

But Lilly wouldn't listen to me. She went on a tear, cleaning the house. I told her it wasn't necessary. She did it anyway. There had been no stopping Lilly and her nesting *before* she became pregnant. Now . . . I sure wasn't going to take her on.

So I watched for a while as she buzzed around the house vacuuming and dusting. I shot the breeze with McKenzie on the front deck. Aurora finally graced us with her presence after sleeping in until ten thirty, and she and I got into a serious discussion, bordering on an argument, as to what was the best cheap beer. She insisted it was Lone Star. My vote was for PBR. Pabst Blue Ribbon.

Starting to feel nervous about the lightning that was about to strike, I tried to keep myself busy. I took out the recycling. I fixed the float in the toilet tank downstairs, which Aurora insisted was Lilly's fault because she was using it so much. McKenzie recorded Lilly pulling her maternity shorts down to show us a cute butt cheek and telling Aurora to kiss it. Then McKenzie replayed it for us three times, and we all, including Lilly, laughed so hard that Lilly had to run to the bathroom again.

I was so desperate to keep busy, to keep from being nervous, that I got out the old electric lawn mower and mowed our postage-stamp-sized back lawn. Mr. Greene usually took care of it. He had a riding mower to mow *his* postage stamp. I mowed ours, and then his, just because with the mower running, I couldn't hear Lilly, Aurora, and McKenzie talking about my love life *as if I weren't even there*.

They were scheming. Conjecturing. Even Aurora, which surprised me because she rarely fell into gossipy-female mode the way McKenzie and Lilly could. Someone brought up marriage, and Lilly took that and ran with it; I was pretty sure I heard her planning a reception in the Hotel du Pont's Gold Ballroom.

That was when I decided to take Fritz for a run in Cape Henlopen State Park. I had time before our *guest* arrived. Fritz and I went to the park all the time, year-round. It's a good place for both of us to blow off steam. He's required to be on a leash, but when we got on the trail in the pines, if the place wasn't busy, I let him run off leash.

I ran his legs off and mine.

It felt good to push myself. To clear my mind of a tangle of anxieties. About a year ago, I figured out that I didn't need Zoloft if I ran fifteen miles a week. I'm not sure if it's the physical exercise or the opportunity to be alone with my thoughts that calms me. I don't care. Running makes me feel good. Zoloft doesn't.

After a mile and a half, I slowed my pace and began to systematically tackle my *problems of the day*. Right away, I decided I wasn't going to think about what was going to happen this afternoon. It didn't make sense to worry about all the ways the shit might hit the fan. I'd just wait to see what happened and then stress over it.

McKenzie was, of course, right on the top of my list of things I *needed* to worry about. I'd miscalculated with Mack. I'd had ideas, before we all came to Albany Beach, ideas about how this last time together was going to go. I thought that if we had this time together to prepare ourselves, prepare *myself* for her death, I'd be okay. I had it all wrong. I'd miscalculated, misconstrued, misjudged.

After a week with McKenzie, I felt as if it was going to be *harder* to say good-bye, not easier. Somehow, I'd gotten the idea in my head that if we could all be together, if we could talk about the shit we needed to talk about, that I'd be able to distance myself a little from McKenzie. Maybe *distance* wasn't the right word. I didn't want to *distance* myself so much as *insulate* myself. I didn't *want* to separate myself from her physically or emotionally, but I had to know I could let go, right? I had to know that I could *literally* survive without her.

This morning, watching McKenzie record Aurora plucking her eyebrows on the front porch, I felt like my heart would just shrivel and die. Or maybe explode. It actually physically hurts to watch Mack. People always talk about heart*break*, but because I'd been to Afghanistan, I tend to see life as something that ends with an explosion and the flying apart of body pieces, rather than just a splitting in two.

There was no way I was going to be able to live after McKenzie died. Maybe I'd explode right there at the funeral. The idea, in a freakish way, kind of intrigued me. How would my mother feel then? Would she be relieved I was dead? No longer around to remind her of how she failed her daughter in the greatest way a mother could fail her child? Or would she mourn the loss? Would *her* heart be at risk of shattering into a million raw pieces?

Fritz and I circled a copse of pine trees. There were no rocks, but the area reminded me of northern Afghanistan. The memories flood back every time I run this route. Americans think about Afghanistan as being a big desert, and part of it is. But up north, it's mountainous, rocky, and covered in evergreens and undergrowth.

Breathing hard, I pushed for the next mile marker on the trail. Fritz stayed ahead of me. Encouraging me, staying with me, even when his natural instinct was to run ahead.

As I pumped my arms and legs, I moved on to door/crisis number two: the lawsuit against me. For weeks, I'd been going over the whole thing in my mind, wondering if there was some way that I could have produced a different outcome. When I caught the public nuisance on the beach, I hadn't been adequately forewarned by dispatch. To be fair, a teenage lifeguard had called it in. Dispatch didn't have enough information. How could the lifeguard have predicted when he called 911 how quickly the incident would escalate?

And he wasn't trained in crowd control, but I was. Why hadn't *I* seen the signs the minute I came over the dunes?

The thing was, I *had*. I called for backup *before* my newbie partner and I had walked down to the water to look into the call. In my first interview, after the incident, I'd been asked by my lieutenant why my partner and I didn't wait for backup before going down on the beach. I couldn't have done that because the skinny kid-lifeguard was down there trying keep the incident from escalating. I had a duty to that kid. Before my duty to my partner and me.

The alarm on my cell in my pocket went off, startling me. I turned it off and made a loop around a Frisbee golf goal. "Back to the car," I told Fritz. I was sucking wind.

The subject of Chris was next on my agenda.

Was I in love? Was that even possible, less than a year after Betsy and I broke up the last and final time? Was it rebound love or not love at all? Did I want to be in a relationship so badly that I was willing to fantasize that there was more to Chris and me than just me being scared and lonely? Had McKenzie's devastating diagnosis played a part in my moving so fast in this new relationship with Chris?

I hadn't come to any conclusions by the time Fritz and I made it back to the Jeep. I gave him some water in the bowl we carried in the car and finished off the liter bottle while I walked in circles around my vehicle to cool down. Then I checked the time. I had to get my ass back to the house or I was going to miss all the action. Which was tempting.

Approaching Route 1 in the Jeep ten minutes later, I seriously considered turning right instead left. Going north instead of south to Albany Beach. I wondered what it would be like to pull an Aurora and just take off. As I sat at the traffic light, leaving Lewes, I wondered where I would go if I ran away from home. Mexico? I'd been there once with an old girlfriend and had liked it. Or would I go farther south? South America appealed to me. The slower pace of life and all. I'd once read a John Grisham book where a lawyer had changed his identity and gone to Brazil. Fritz and I could go to Brazil.

I looked at the German shepherd in the rearview mirror. He was perched on the rear seat, looking back at me.

"How do you feel about Brazil?" I asked him.

Fritz whined. I cussed under my breath and headed south.

# ❦ 23 ❧

# Aurora

We were all sitting on the front deck. Janine had just come downstairs from taking a shower after her run. She was wearing one of her dumbass wifebeaters with a white, cotton sports bra underneath. Her long, baggy shorts had enough room in the cargo pockets to carry a six-pack of beer. I'd taken more care to dress to meet her girlfriend than she had. I'd actually put on a skirt and shaved my legs.

"You going to wear that?" I asked, looking at her dubiously.

"Yes, Mom, this is what I'm wearing." Her hair was wet, but at least she'd combed it.

I glared and sipped my first gin and tonic of the afternoon. If I was going to put up with Lilly oohing and aahing over Janine's new squeeze, I wasn't going to do it sober if I didn't have to.

Janine looked at me. "I wish you wouldn't do that," she said.

"Do what?"

She sighed and glanced away like I could read her damned mind. "It's not even five o'clock, Aurora."

"I don't know what we're talking about," I argued.

"You know."

"I don't know!" I practically shouted. I did know, of course. Janine thinks I'm an alcoholic (the beer and gin) and a drug addict (the occasional bowl). The fact that she drinks Jack Daniel's like the distillery is about to close? That she doesn't want to talk about.

"You okay?" McKenzie asked Janine.

McKenzie had tied on a pretty paisley head scarf and put on some makeup. She looked pretty good. At least, pretty good to someone who didn't know her. I hadn't seen her bald head since the day she arrived. I'd caught glimpses of red peach fuzz at the edges of her ball caps and scarves. I was pretty sure her hair was growing, which worried me. If the new drug was working, wouldn't she still be bald? She was still puking her guts out pretty regularly, though. So maybe that was a good sign.

"You don't have to be nervous," McKenzie was telling Janine.

"I'm not nervous," Janine argued. Then, "Well, I am, but it's not why—" She stopped and started again like she was all tongue-tied. She looked like she was sweating even though it wasn't that hot. "I just want to say . . . up front," she stuttered and stammered, "that this isn't the way I would have done this. I only agreed to it because he . . ." She tucked a wet strand of hair behind her ear, something Janine did when she was really nervous.

"Now you're making me nervous." I took another sip of the cool, crisp equalizer. It was an equalizer because once I'd had a couple I didn't care any more about one thing than another.

I wasn't excited about meeting Janine's girlfriend. Not like Lilly, who wants everyone to be happy and in love with red paper hearts hanging over their heads everywhere they go. And not like McKenzie, who was eager to interview the girlfriend before she met the grim reaper and make sure that she was good enough for Janine.

"Wait a minute," Lilly said. She pointed at Janine. "You said *he*."

"What?" Janine asked.

"You just said *he*. You said you wouldn't have done it this way, that you only agreed to it because *he* . . . Who's coming? I thought Chris was coming."

"I didn't say *he*."

Lilly and McKenzie were looking at each other. Then at Janine. Now I was looking at Janine. She looked guilty as hell. Janine isn't a good liar. Or at least I can tell when she's lying. When I'm paying attention. I wasn't totally sure I had been paying attention through this whole "Chris is coming over" thing.

"Janine," I said slowly. "Is Chris—"

There was a crunch on the driveway stones in the back of the house, and Janine bolted for the door. Lilly pushed out of her chair and beat Fritz to the door and into the living room.

McKenzie glanced up at me. She was sitting in her green Adirondack chair. I was at my usual spot on the rail. "You sure you're okay?" I asked McKenzie.

She smiled. She'd spent a little time in the sun earlier in the day, and freckles stood out on her nose and across her cheeks. She really did look okay today. "I'm fine."

Fritz started to bark, and I looked through the windows into the living room. Why the hell was Fritz barking at Chris? If they weren't all three living together, they were sure as hell seeing a lot of each other. He should not have been barking like that. Even I knew that.

McKenzie turned to look over her shoulder, thinking the same thing, I suspect.

I raised my hand to take another sip. My lower lip touched the cool glass, and then I froze, staring through the window. I was sure I was mistaken. But I wasn't. No mother, not even me, doesn't recognize her own son.

# ❧ 24 ❧

# Janine

I saw the look on Aurora's face, through the window, when we walked into the living room. It was a mixture of shock, fear, and . . . longing. I felt like such a shit. I had assumed she was going to be angry that I hadn't told her that Jude was coming. But he'd made me promise. I know he'd made me promise not to tell her because he was afraid that if she had any warning, she would have taken off. And even though I wanted to tell Jude she wasn't that person anymore, I was pretty sure she was.

Aurora's anger I could deal with, but her pain? Totally out of my comfort zone.

"I can't believe you're here," Lilly gushed, genuinely thrilled to see him. "Do you want to stay the night? We'd really like you to stay."

"I can't stay." He was talking to Lilly, but he was looking at his mother out on the deck.

Mother and son were sizing each other up. For a second, I thought Aurora was going to cry. Then she tensed, setting her glass on the rail, and I was afraid she might make a run for the steps.

Instead, she just stood there on the deck, her hands limp at her sides.

"You want a beer?" I asked Jude as we made our way outside.

"No, thank you. I can't stay long."

"What on earth are you doing on the East Coast?" Lilly waddled two steps behind us. "I'm so glad you stopped, even if you can't stay. I know your mom's going to be—" There was an awkward hesitation. "Thrilled."

"Right. She certainly looks thrilled," he said, sounding far more like Aurora than I bet he realized.

Jude was a startlingly handsome young man with his father's dark hair and skin that was a shade left of his Arab father's and right of his Norwegian mother's. He had soulful, hooded black eyes that reflected a maturity far beyond his years.

I stepped aside at the door and let Jude walk out first onto the deck.

"Jude?" Aurora's gaze immediately went to mine. She didn't seem angry so much as hurt.

"Surprise?" he said with an awkward laugh.

She ran the last two steps to him and threw her arms around him, surprising me, and Jude, too, I think.

Her hug was genuine. His was ill at ease and only halfhearted.

She hugged him long enough to make me feel self-conscious. Then she let go of him.

"Jude, oh my God, I can't believe you're here." McKenzie was out of her chair, hugging him. "Why didn't you tell us you were—" She cut herself short, probably realizing that Jude hadn't warned them because he hadn't wanted them—meaning, his mother—to know he was coming.

Lilly bounced up and down in her pretty sandals, then took off for the kitchen. "I'll grab drinks. Some chips. I think we've still got some guac and salsa left."

I moved to the open doorway, my hands stuffed in my pockets. Aurora gazed past McKenzie and Jude in their embrace to look at me. *Sorry,* I mouthed.

She pressed her lips together, nodded, and returned her attention to her handsome son who wasn't really a son to her at all.

"You've gotten so tall," McKenzie was saying.

I never got it when people said that to kids. Of course he had grown. Boys grow until they're in their early twenties. McKenzie, being a mom, had to know that. I guess it was something people said when they didn't know what else to say.

Jude studied McKenzie's face as she backed up and sat down in her chair again. In his eyes, I could see the inventory he was taking: no hair, no eyelashes, thin and pale, even with a little color from the sun. "How are you doing?" he asked her.

I had told him how she was doing, of course.

Jude and I talked once a month or so. We had since he was in high school. Out of the blue he had tracked me down the end of his freshman year after having dinner with all of us while in DC with Hannad. He wasn't getting along with his dad at the time, typical teenage bullshit. The weird thing was, he didn't get my number from Aurora. He found me online, e-mailed me, and when I gave him my phone number, he called. I think he just needed an adult to talk to, someone who would listen. It was a part of my life that I had never shared with Aurora. I told myself I never told her because I didn't want her to be hurt that he wanted to talk to me and not her or guilty if she didn't want to talk to him. I think that, secretly, I liked the fact that he and I had this clandestine relationship. It made me feel, as stupid as it sounds, *special*. Why I never told McKenzie or Lilly, I don't know. They knew I talked to him, just not how often.

"So, you doing okay?" he asked McKenzie, sounding genuinely concerned. Our Jude had a big heart. He was what some might call a "tender soul."

"I'm . . . okay." McKenzie touched her head scarf, feeling self-conscious, I'm sure. "Hanging in there." She offered a brave smile.

His gaze shifted to his mother. McKenzie and I watched the two of them.

"I . . . I just stopped by for a few minutes," he told Aurora, adjusting the Ray-Bans he'd pushed onto his head. "We're flying out of Baltimore tonight."

"You and your dad?"

He shook his head. "Gabrielle and I."

A look crossed Aurora's face. She didn't know about Gabrielle. *Anything* about Gabrielle.

"We'll take a hike," I said. "Give you guys a few minutes alone."

McKenzie started to get out of her chair.

"That's not necessary, Aunt Janine." Jude was looking at his mother. "This won't take long."

McKenzie cut her eyes at me as if to say, *What's going on?*

"You don't have to go," Aurora agreed, not quite in her own voice. This Aurora sounded so . . . passive. "Whatever Jude has to say to me—"

"No, we should definitely go." McKenzie got out of her chair again.

I turned in the doorway to see Lilly carrying a tray of drinks and corn chips. "Back in the kitchen," I told her, pointing.

For once, Lilly didn't argue. She turned and went back inside. I followed McKenzie off the deck, torn between feeling like Jude had the right to have his mother to himself for a few minutes and wanting to stay with Aurora to . . . I don't know . . . protect her?

The last thing I heard was Jude saying to Aurora, "I came to tell you something."

# ❧ 25 ❧

# Aurora

I looked over Jude's shoulder at Janine as she walked away. Wishing she wouldn't leave me here alone with him. It was a man's shoulder, broad and muscular. He looked like his father, but he was taller than Hannad. Built like me; tall and slender.

I shifted my gaze to meet my son's.

I felt a little nauseated. Dizzy. Not dizzy like too many gin and tonics. Dizzy like my world was tilting a little farther than I liked it to. It was the same feeling I got when I thought about McKenzie and her fucking cancer.

I stared into Jude's dark eyes—his father's eyes—for what seemed like a long time before I realized he was waiting for me to acknowledge what he had said. That he had something he wanted to tell me. I couldn't fathom what that was. I wasn't going to try. "O-kay . . ." I drew out the word.

He looked at his feet in leather flip-flops. He had my feet, not Hannad's: long and slender. He had a swimmer's feet. He wasn't a swimmer, but he could have been.

"I only came because Gabrielle thinks it's important. I want to make that clear. I came for her, not you." Hostility.

"Who's Gabrielle?" I asked. I assumed a friend. A college friend. I don't know any of my son's friends' names, of course. I know almost nothing about his life, other than that he's a senior at Stanford and would be graduating with a degree in something like computer engineering. I don't even know what kind of job he'd be looking for or if he would be looking for a job. Maybe grad school was in his future. I didn't know.

"That's why I came. To t-tell you."

He stumbled over the word, just the one, and I felt a sudden rush of emotion. Emotion I couldn't identify. I swallowed against the huge lump in my throat and blinked. Waited.

"I'm getting married." He found his voice again, steady and clear. "Gabrielle and I."

Married? My son is getting married? It seems like only a short time ago that I was walking out of that hospital and leaving a newborn with his father.

"We're engaged, and we're going to be married next June. In Paris. That's where she's from. We're going to *Jad dee*'s and *Jad datee*'s," he said in perfect Arabic. "Tonight. We're meeting *Baba* in Manama."

Haddad's mother and father. I had never met them. And yet, clearly they were close to my son. Close enough for Jude to fly to Bahrain so they could meet his fiancée.

"Gabrielle said you had the right to know." He glanced away, the beach catching his attention for the first time. "It's the only reason I came. Because she asked me to. I'm doing it for her. Not you."

The first words on the tip of my tongue were "No need to put yourself out on my account." But for once, I didn't let loose the first stinging words that came to mind. I didn't want to hurt him. My son. Because I knew this was my doing. All of it. I knew this wasn't his fault. None of it. It was all on me. It always had been and always would be.

I managed a smile. Even though my heart was breaking. Breaking because I knew this was the last time I would ever see Jude. Breaking because I would never know his wife. Or his children. Breaking because I think I *wanted* to see him again. After all these years, I wanted to know Jude now. And not out of a sense of guilt.

"Congratulations," I said.

"Thank you." He didn't smile. He didn't look at me. He just stared out at the sand that stretched to the ocean's edge.

I knew I should say something else, but I didn't know what. I desperately wished that Janine, Aurora, and Lilly hadn't abandoned me. I wasn't equipped to talk alone with my adult son, and they damned well knew it.

"What's she like?" I heard myself say in a voice I didn't recognize. "Your Parisian Gabrielle?"

"She's pretty. Not gorgeous pretty. Not like you. But pretty. Brown hair. Brown eyes."

My gaze strayed to my drink, and I was so tempted to pick it up that I seriously considered, for the first time ever, the possibility that I might really be an alcoholic. "I meant, what's she *like*? What kind of person is she?"

"Smart." At last, he looked at me again. "Geophysics major at Stanford. Funny and artistic and . . . and a really good person. She makes me a better person, you know, when we're together."

"Artistic?" I mused.

"It's just a hobby, but she makes mugs and plates and things. She has her own potter's wheel."

I tried to imagine my Jude and his Gabrielle in a studio, her spinning a potter's wheel, forming the clay, wet between her hands. Him watching. Encouraging her. I could see Jude in that role.

"Has your father met her?"

When I thought about Hannad, I could barely remember him. I didn't like or dislike him. Our relationship had been so long ago; I had been young, emotionally at least. And profoundly stupid. We used only two condoms on a three-condom night. That was how my son had been conceived. "Does he approve?"

"Baba adores her. At Christmas, we all went to Greece. Gabrielle's family and Baba and Mum and my sisters and I. We stayed at a villa on Mykonos."

I knew that Hannad had married when Jude was three. A girl from Atlanta, my age. Hannad is older. I hadn't known they were still together, though. Or that Jude had sisters. How did I not know he had sisters?

"And he doesn't think you're too young?" I was only a little older than him when I got pregnant, certainly too young to be married. "That you should wait?"

"Baba supports me in my decisions. Gabrielle and I love each other." His dark eyes found mine. "He understands that."

We both stood there in silence. The sun suddenly felt hot on my face, and sunlight glared off the ocean. I couldn't remember where I'd left my sunglasses.

"I should get going," Jude finally said. "I borrowed a car. A friend of Gabrielle's is from around here. Her parents' car." He lowered his classic Ray-Ban sunglasses over his eyes.

"I'm . . . glad you came, Jude. I wish you'd brought Gabrielle." I thought about the fact that she had to be nearby. "I would have liked to have met her."

He stood there for a moment, maybe contemplating a response. I wondered if he had refused her request to come or if she had refused to come when he'd asked her.

Who was I kidding? It was, more than likely, a mutual agreement.

"Good-bye," he said. He didn't call me Mom, of course, but he didn't call me Aurora, either. We didn't have enough of a relationship for me to have a name.

He started to turn away, but I stepped toward him and gave him a quick hug. He didn't hug me back, but he didn't push me away, either.

"Good-bye," I said. "Have a safe flight."

And then he was gone.

I heard the rumble of his voice in the kitchen. Saying good-bye to McKenzie and Lilly and Janine. Then the back door closed. An engine started, and there was the sound of gravel under the wheels of the borrowed car as Jude backed out.

Janine was the first one out on the deck. She found me sitting on the edge of my white Adirondack chair, my glass in my hand. I hadn't taken a drink. I was just holding it.

"You okay?" Janine asked. She stood right in front of me.

"Fine," I managed, "except that you're blocking my view of the ocean. You know what people pay for this view?"

She didn't budge. "I'm sorry, Aurora. When he called, he specifically asked me not to tell you he was coming."

"He told you why he was coming?"

"Yes." It was a sigh more than anything else.

I thought about that for a minute, wondering if I should be angry about that, too. That Janine knew before I did that Jude was going to be a married man. But I suspected Janine knew a lot more about my son than I did. Obviously they had some sort of relationship, otherwise how would he have had her number to call her?

"It's fine." I swirled what was left of the ice in my glass. "I get it. We all know I probably wouldn't have been here when he showed up if I'd known."

"I wanted to tell you. I thought about telling you, even after I told Jude I wouldn't."

"I said, I *get* it." I slid back in the chair and sipped the gin and tonic that was too watery now for my liking. "I wouldn't have told me either, okay?"

McKenzie walked out onto the deck, followed by Lilly. We all took our own chairs: me in the white, McKenzie in the green, Lilly in the pink, and Janine in the blue.

No one said anything. We just sat there, lined up across the deck, and stared at the dunes below us and the mesmerizing water that stretched to the horizon. There was a green and yellow kite with a long white tail fluttering high in the sky.

I couldn't be sure if three minutes or three hours had passed. Except that the shadows on the deck had barely moved. "I think I'll go for a swim," I said.

"I wish you wouldn't. Not right now." It was Lilly. Not the pain-in-the-ass hyper Lilly, though. This was the Lilly who had taken the pistol from my hand that night, set it on the nightstand, and walked me out of the room as easy as you please. As if she were walking me to the water fountain at school. The Lilly who believed I killed Buddy to save Janine.

# ❧ 26 ❧

# Lilly

I knocked on Aurora's bedroom door. When she didn't answer, I tapped again. I knew she was in there. I'd heard her come in after her swim. I'd heard the shower running, then her footsteps as she went down the hall.

"Aurora?"

Janine's door clicked open, and she stuck her head out into the hallway. She didn't look like she'd been asleep, even though we'd all turned in early, an hour ago, at nine forty-five. McKenzie had looked whipped. I knew I was. My ankles were swollen, and I was tired from fighting a ridiculous craving all day for chili dogs. And then there was the whole Jude thing. It was good to see him. Sad to see Aurora so upset, trying not to be. Knowing she had no right to be, but brokenhearted anyway.

"You okay?" Janine asked me. She turned and said, "Stay," to Fritz, then came out into the hall. She was wearing boxers with some kind of animal print on them and a white V-neck T-shirt. Barefoot.

I nodded. "Just checking on Aurora."

"I know she came back."

I glanced at her door. "Maybe she's asleep?"

Janine stopped at Aurora's door and stared at it. "Or just needs to be alone? She had a crappy day."

"Right. Her son coming to tell her he was getting married. And she doesn't even know the girl." I looked at Janine. "But you knew."

"I knew they were serious. I didn't know about the engagement until he told me when he called on Friday."

I put one hand on the wall, the other on my belly as I felt a slight tightening.

"Something wrong?" Janine put her hand on the small of my back. "Christ, are you going into labor?" She looked petrified.

I laughed. "Toning contractions. I have them all the time. They're like practice contractions to get ready for the big day."

"Maybe you should lie down." She hadn't let go of me.

"Janine, I'm fine. They don't hurt. Don't you know anything about giving birth?" I made a face as if I were shocked. And maybe a little appalled. Which I was. "I thought cops had to take some kind of class on emergency deliveries in taxis or something."

"Not a lot of taxis around here."

"You've got a—"

"Are you two going to stand out there all night and yap, or are you coming in?" Aurora called from inside her room.

I looked at Janine and grinned. That sounded more like the Aurora we knew. We both went into her room. Janine closed the door behind us. We didn't want to wake McKenzie, making a racket.

"Scoot over," I told Aurora.

She had a double bed. Which wasn't all that roomy when Janine got in on the other side. Not with me taking up a double parking space with my belly.

"What are you two nut jobs doing in the hallway when decent people are trying to get some sleep?" Aurora asked, sandwiched in between us now.

"Your light's still on," I pointed out. "You weren't asleep."

"Good swim?" Janine asked Aurora.

"It was fine."

Aurora's cell phone vibrated on the nightstand. I picked it up and read the screen. "It's Miguel. You want to talk to him?"

She frowned. "Nope."

"Who's Miguel?" I asked.

"None of your business."

"That's good," Janine said, settling down on her back, one knee bent so she could rest her other ankle on it and stare at the ceiling. "Because I'm not interested in hearing about any of your sexual escapades."

"Who says there were any sexual escapades?" Aurora worked at gathering her damp hair on top of her head. "Miguel is an art appraiser. A big deal in those circles. He's going to be in DC next week." She slipped an elastic band around her hair to hold it up. "He's probably calling with finalized plans."

"You dating him?" I asked, setting the phone down as it vibrated and went to voice mail.

Aurora shrugged. "Not much into dating these days. It's hard, traveling the way I do."

"I thought you were dating Fortunato," Janine argued. "The one with the big—"

I stuck my fingers in my ears. "I swear," I interrupted, "if I have to hear about Fortunato's weenie one more time . . ."

They both cracked up, and I smiled. I was never a potty mouth like these two, but I did play up the Goody Two-shoes thing sometimes, just because I knew it amused them. And I liked making Aurora laugh. She made me laugh all the time.

"Okay, so we've got Fortunato and Miguel, and then there's that guy in Philly you were talking to this morning." Janine ticked the names off on her fingers.

Aurora rested her hand on her forehead and closed her eyes. "I don't want to talk about men. I hate men."

"So does Janine." I laughed and stared at the spinning ceiling fan. "Considering my husband's behavior this weekend, I might well consider playing for the other team, too."

Janine groaned, and Aurora laughed.

"Lilly, no one has said 'playing for the other team' since the 1980s." Janine looked at me over Aurora. "Really, where do you get this stuff?"

I rolled my eyes. "Tell us about Miguel, Aurora." I'd come to check on her because I was worried about Jude's visit, but I knew better than to bring it up. Right now, the wound was too raw. She'd flat out refuse to talk about it, or get up and leave. She was like one of the wild ponies on Assateague Island. You couldn't spook her or she'd bolt.

"First question," Janine said. "Miguel. Married?"

"Nope."

Janine cut her eyes at Aurora. "Don't look at me that way, Miss You've-Hurt-My-Feelings. What about that guy from the art league? He was super married."

I frowned. "What do you mean *super* married? Either you're married or you're not. And you don't date married men, Aurora."

Aurora held up her hand. "He's not married."

"How old?" I asked.

"Dark hair, dark eyes," she answered.

I met Janine's gaze and rolled onto my side. "How *old* is he, Aurora?"

She grinned.

I covered my face with my hands. "Oh please. Not another twenty-five-year-old!"

"Miguel isn't twenty-five. You can't be a world-renowned art appraiser and be twenty-five. Unless," she added, "your dad is a world-renowned art appraiser."

I closed my eyes and sank down in the pillow. "I do not want to hear about a twenty-five-year-old's—"

"Weenie," they both chimed in.

Now we were all laughing. And for a few minutes we just lay there, together, enjoying the feeling of lying side by side in the same bed. The way we used to do when we were girls.

Would this be how it would feel after McKenzie passed? Just the three of us, here like this? Because this . . . this I could live with. Maybe. If I had to.

I turned my head to look at Aurora and Janine. The laughter was gone from my voice. "What do you think, Aurora? Should Janine sell this place?"

"I don't know," Aurora answered softly. "It's so much a part of us. Good and bad." She looked at me and then at Janine. "I guess the question is, will we miss McKenzie more if we come back . . . or less? Will coming back here make us feel closer to her or further away?"

"I can't believe she's dying," I whispered, stroking my belly. "What are we going to do without her?" Tears slipped down my cheeks. "How am I going to have this baby without Mack?"

"We'll still be here," Janine said, looking over Aurora to meet my gaze. "You'll always have us. Won't she, Aurora?"

We both looked at Aurora when she didn't answer. Her eyes were closed. Her breathing was slow and even, but I don't think she was asleep.

# ✎ 27 ☙

# McKenzie

"Do you think some of us are born with maternal instincts and others aren't?" Lilly asked me. "Too frilly?" She held up a white and red baby dress, constructed of layers of ruffles.

We were in a children's boutique on Rehoboth Avenue, killing time until we met my girls for lunch. They were running late, of course.

I frowned and shook my head no. "Looks like something a baby who dances to a mariachi song should be wearing. How about this?" I held up a pale green one-piece sleeper with frog appliqués on the feet. "Neutral color. Good for a boy or a girl. Maternal instinct?" I thought about it for a minute. "Since it's *instinct*, yeah, I think every woman has it, to some degree, why?"

Lilly put the mariachi dress back and picked up another ruffled one, which was almost as ugly. "I was thinking about Aurora." She ran her hand over her belly. She was wearing peach capris and a white and peach hibiscus-patterned maternity top. Her suitcase seemed to be an endless pit of cute preggo outfits. "How did she not feel anything for Jude when he was born?"

I hung the frog one-piece on my finger and began to look through the next rack of sale items, leaving the full-priced items for Lilly to peruse. "Who says she didn't feel anything?"

Lilly propped her hand and the ruffled dress on her hip. "She gave birth and she left him."

"She gave him to *his father*," I corrected. "Not the same thing."

Lilly held up the ruffled dress to look at it again. "I shouldn't be buying dresses, should I? I'm going to jinx myself, buying girl clothes."

"I don't think the sex of the baby is determined by what you buy or don't buy in your seventh month of pregnancy."

She returned the dress to the rack and pulled out a pair of yellow overalls.

I took a moment to catch my breath. I was feeling pretty good today, but I needed to pace myself. I didn't want to be worn out by the time we met Maura and Mia. I wanted to give them the best of me, whenever I could.

"Aurora was in no way equipped to deal with a baby when Jude was born," I went on. "We all agreed, at the time, that it was better if Haddad took him. Don't you remember that night when we all sat on her hospital bed all night long? Aurora cried and cried. She didn't want to give him up, but she knew Jude would be better off with his father. Those were her struggling artist days, before her work was recognized. She was living in that awful room in that roach motel," I reminded her.

"Okay, so she didn't have it together when Jude was born. I understand why Haddad took him then." Lilly switched her monster purse from one arm to the other. "But in all these years, why has she had no desire to have a relationship with him? She's rich and famous now. She can go where she wants, *when* she wants. Money is no object." Lilly was getting worked up now. "Yet, she never flew to Chicago to see him play soccer, get his Eagle Scout badge, or graduate high school. She's only been to Palo Alto once in the three years Jude has been there, and that was because of an art exhibition and some guy named Donut."

I laughed. "I think it was *Donat*. I met him at one of Aurora's shows in Boston. He was Hungarian. He did these crazy paintings with sheet metal and a blowtorch."

"My point is, what kind of mother does that, Mack? Remains removed from her child's life?"

"Seems like a fairly selfless act to me." I continued to thumb through the clothes on the rack, eyeing a cute little boy in a stroller one aisle over. He was drinking from an Elmo sippy cup. I had always wondered what it would be like to have a boy instead of just girls. I smiled and returned my attention to Lilly. "You ever think about it that way? That maybe it was harder for Aurora to stay out of his life than to have been a part of it? Haddad's been a good father. And his wife has been a good mother to Jude. Jude's going to graduate from Stanford, for heaven's sake. Clearly, he's thrived."

Lilly shook her head, then reached up to resituate her white sunglasses, perched on her head. "I could never have done it . . . no matter how *logical* or *selfless* it might have been." She hung the overalls she had in her hand back on the rack. "I haven't even given birth yet, and I'm so attached to this baby. I just can't imagine. I just can't imagine," she repeated.

We moved to a display of exorbitantly priced crib sheets and receiving blankets on a table.

"Look, how to swaddle a baby." Lilly picked up a pink linen blanket and studied the instructions on the back of the package for a minute. Then she looked up. "Okay, so let's pretend that Aurora has mothering instincts, and her instincts told her that Jude would have a better life with his father. But what about your girls? My baby?" She shrugged. "Aurora couldn't care less about them."

I looked at her across the table of pastel-colored linens, surprised by what she was saying. "Aurora *loves* my girls," I defended. "What are you talking about?"

Lilly leaned across the table. "I'm not saying she doesn't *love* them. Of course she loves them. But she doesn't . . . she doesn't have that need to protect them. She wants to be their friend. She always wants to be the cool auntie. The one who offers them a beer and gets them—" Lilly shook the baby blanket at me. "Aurora couldn't care less about my baby. Janine either, for that matter." She squeaked out the last word.

"Oh, sweetie." I came around the table and put my arm around her, giving her a side hug. "Of course they care about your baby."

"They don't understand." Her eyes were teary. "I don't just want them to *love* my baby; I want them to swear to me that they'll defend her, protect her. Keep her safe from harm, always. If you die"—fat tears ran down her cheeks—"who's going to do that? Who's going to be her champion?"

I wrapped both my arms around her. "You and Matt are going to protect her. *And* Janine. *And* Aurora. And Mia and Maura, too. It's going to be all right," I soothed. "Trust me. You're going to be okay," I promised, my own eyes filling up with tears, even though I was fighting them.

This dying, it was becoming a teary business. Before I got here, I thought I'd cried all the tears I had left, but in the last week and a half, it seemed as if I'd found a new well. I couldn't hold back all the emotion welling up inside me. And it was guilt again, bitter in my mouth, stinging in my tears.

How could I be doing this to Lilly? She would never leave me. Not even for cancer.

"I'm not going to be fine," Lilly sobbed. "I know. I know. Please don't cry, Mack."

A salesclerk approached us, carrying a box of tissues. "Everything okay?" she asked cheerfully, not in the least bit flustered by Lilly's gush of tears.

"Fine." I plucked two tissues from the box she offered. Then took two more, just to be on the safe side. "We're a little emotional. First baby." I dabbed at my eyes. Now I was going to have to buy the playsuit. I'd cried in the woman's store and then used her tissues.

"Not a problem," the young woman said. "Happens all the time. We've got some nursing bras on sale in the back, if you're interested. Buy two, get one free." She pointed in that general direction as she walked away.

I looked at Lilly and she looked at me, and we both started to laugh. I don't even know why. I guess because it seemed like a silly response on the part of the salesclerk. How did tears equal nursing bras in her head? I handed Lilly a tissue. "You're going to have raccoon eyes when we meet the girls. They'll be worried something's wrong."

She sniffed and rubbed under her eyes. "More likely they'd be worried if I hadn't been crying." She looked up at me and blinked. "Okay now?" she asked.

"You're perfect and beautiful, as always." I gave her my best smile. "You want to check out the nursing bras?"

"Mom," Mia called from the sidewalk.

We'd taken a table outside on the deck of my girls' favorite organic restaurant, just a block west of the Rehoboth boardwalk.

"Hey," I called over the rail.

She came up the steps. She was wearing denim shorts and her pizzeria work T-shirt. Dark blue Toms on her feet.

When she leaned over to kiss me hello, I smelled tomato paste and garlic. "Where's Maura?"

"Coming. Hey, Aunt Lilly." Mia leaned over the back of Lilly's chair to kiss her.

"Hey, sweetie." She offered her cheek. "Sit next to me." She patted the chair beside her.

Mia slid into the chair across from me and picked up one of the menus from the center of the table.

"Have you seen your sister?" I asked. "About so tall." I held up my hand. "Girl who looks a little bit like you?"

"She's coming." Mia lowered her gaze to the menu.

"But you were the one who had to work. I thought she was off."

"She was, but she came into work anyway. She was in the kitchen doing something for Little Tony. Cutting up peppers or something. I don't know. Green tea?" she asked Lilly, looking at her frosty glass.

"With mint. Want to try it?" Lilly slid the glass toward Mia.

Mia took a sip. "That's good. I'll think I'll have that, too."

"The antioxidants are so good for you," Lilly explained, sounding like a cross between a kindergarten teacher and green tea spokeswoman on TV. "Even at your age."

"Catechins." Mia passed the glass back. "Learned about it in my nutrition class."

I was impressed she knew about antioxidants but too wrapped up in Maura's tardiness to switch gears. "But she *is* coming, right?"

"I *guess*, Mom. She said she was." Mia gave me a quick, exasperated look over the top of the menu in her hand and then spoke to Lilly again. "Are there any specials today? Last week I had this crazy bean soup. They served it cold. It sounds gross, but it was so good."

"On the board." Lilly pointed to a chalkboard mounted on the wall next to the door.

The restaurant was tiny inside, just a couple of tables and a counter where one could order food to go. The deck, built right off the sidewalk, wasn't much bigger; it sat maybe fifteen people. The place was packed; we'd been lucky to get a table. The food was expensive but organic, fresh, farm to table fare. So I sucked it up and agreed to meet here when my girls suggested it. Who was I kidding? I'd have agreed to meet them on the moon if they'd asked me.

"Why don't you call Maura?" I asked Mia. "We'll wait for her if she's coming, but if she's not coming—"

"Can't call her." She was staring at the menu, her brows knitted. "What's buffalo mozzarella?"

"It's an Italian mozzarella made from the milk of domestic buffalo," Lilly explained.

"Ewwww."

"Mia, why can't you call Maura?" When she didn't answer me, I raised my voice an octave. *"Mia?"*

She groaned. "Her phone wouldn't come on, so I gave her mine."

"You gave her *yours?*" I asked. Teen girls did that to a mother,

I'd learned. Caused them to continually repeat phrases, like complete idiots.

Mia slowly lowered her menu to meet my gaze. "I gave her my phone to call *you*. She said she'd call and tell you she was on her way. I was already on my way here, so I didn't need it."

"I can't believe she broke another phone." I glanced at the menu, making no effort to hide my annoyance with my oldest daughter. I wasn't that hungry, but I'd been looking forward all morning to lunch with Mia and Maura and Lilly. It was just like Maura to ruin it for me.

"Her phone's not broken, Mom. It's fine. This sounds good." Mia pointed at something on the menu, showing it to Lilly. "Bacon here doesn't have nitrates," she explained.

"So if it's not broken, why—"

"Mom, it got a little wet. She's drying it in a bag of rice." Mia set down the menu to look at me across the table. "Please, let's not get into it when she gets here."

"Do you know how much one of those phones costs?" I asked. "I—"

"Mom," Mia interrupted. "I know. Phones are expensive. But I didn't do anything to my phone, and I've only got one hour before I have to be back at work, and I don't want to spend it talking about how Maura dropped her phone in the toilet. Or how irresponsible she is or how it's time she started paying the consequences of her actions."

"In the toilet?" Lilly asked, sounding horrified. "She dropped it in the *toilet?*"

"Happens all the time," Mia told her. "You stick it in your back pocket." She pretended to push a phone into the rear pocket of her jean shorts. "And when you go to pull up your shorts—"

"I got it." Lilly pulled her reading glasses from her bag.

Mia returned her attention to me, softening her tone. "I'm not trying to be mean or anything, Mom, but all you two do is argue."

I wanted to disagree, but she was right.

"It hurts my feelings," Mia said softly, looking right at me.

"Everything is always about Maura." Her voice wavered. "Just once in a while it would be nice if we talked about me. About my SATs or my college applications, or"—a tear ran down her cheek, and she brushed it away with the back of her hand—"or how much I really liked Sam and he never even called me after I gave him my *stupid* phone number."

"Mia," I whispered, totally blindsided by what she was saying. I could hear Lilly sniffing on the other side of the table.

"Mia, I . . . I'm so sorry." I was so choked up that I could barely speak. I reached across the table to take her hand.

"It's okay, Mom." Mia exhaled. "Don't make a big deal."

"Mia, why didn't you tell me you felt this way?" I managed.

"Because I—" She let me hold her hand for a minute and then pulled away. "I don't want to argue with you."

"That's not arguing," I said gently. "That's telling me how you feel. So tell me. Tell me now how you feel when your sister and I get into it."

"It's not a big deal." She hesitated, looking down at the table. "But I get tired of it, you know. Because she gets all the attention and pretty soon—" She stopped and started again. I could tell this was hard for her to say. "You know. *I won't have you.*"

"Mom, pick up. Mom, pick up," came a voice from inside my bag.

For a second I didn't move.

"Mom, pick up. Mom, pick up," my handbag repeated.

Mia reached for the menu again. "That's *really* obnoxious."

I slipped my hand into my bag, wrapped my fingers around the cell phone, and pulled it out. "Tell me about it," I said to Mia. Then to Maura, "You on your way?"

"Be there in a minute. I borrowed Viktor's bike," Maura told me cheerfully. "You think you could get me a bike? This is way easier than trying to find a place to park the car."

"See you in a minute." I hung up and looked at my daughter across the table. "I'm sorry, Mia. I never meant to make you feel as if you mattered less. I'm always telling other people how great you are, your good grades, how responsible you've been since I got sick."

She just sat there for a minute, then stole a glance in my direction. "I don't want to talk about this anymore."

I opened my mouth to say something, but the look Lilly gave me made me bite back my words. We all sat there silent for a minute, then I got to my feet. "Be right back."

As I went by, Lilly grabbed my hand. "You want me to come with you?" she asked quietly.

"It's one of those teeny-tiny bathrooms." Mia was studying the menu again. "You know, the kind you have to back into. I know this girl Theresa, and she's so big, I don't know how she fits in there."

I met Lilly's gaze, sunglasses to sunglasses. "I'm fine," I told her, adjusting my head scarf. "I'll be right back."

Lilly let go of my hand, and I ducked inside, past the counter where our waiter was picking up plates of sandwiches. There was no one in the teeny-tiny bathroom. I backed in, as Mia had instructed.

I closed the lid on the toilet and sat down and had a good cry. I never, ever intended to neglect Mia. It was just that Maura . . . Maura took up so much damned time. And here I'd been, feeling like I'd done a pretty good job raising my girls, feeling like they were going to be okay when I died. And now . . . now the guilt, piled on all the other guilt I already had, was almost overwhelming. I had totally screwed things up and hadn't even known it. How could I die now? How could I leave Mia, thinking for one second that she was somehow less to me, that I loved her less?

# 28

# Lilly

"What does buffalo mozzarella *taste* like?" Mia asked me, nose in the paper menu again.

There was emotion in her voice, not related to cheese. Her mother had just excused herself for the bathroom. To have a good cry I was sure.

"Not like . . . buffalo . . . right?" Mia asked.

I had to laugh. "Not like buffalo. It's a cheese made from milk that just happens to come from buffalo. They raise them in Italy to specifically make this kind of cheese. It's supposed to be really creamy, and it has a robust flavor." I was quiet for a minute, and then I laid down my menu. "Mia, are you okay?"

"Sure." She continued to study the lunch selections, or at least pretend to.

"You know your mom loves you."

"Of course."

"Very much. And moms don't have favorites. It's just that Maura—"

"Is a pain in the ass." Mia finally put down the menu. "I know. You think I don't know that? But did it ever occur to any of you that maybe that's *why* she's a pain in the ass?"

"To get your mom's attention?" I asked.

Mia folded her arms over her chest. "To get more of it than me."

I thought about that for a moment. "I don't know if that's true or not, but I do know that your mom has always tried to be fair. You're the one she depends on. I think she worries about Maura because . . ." I tried to search for the right words. This was so hard for me—to talk with Mia about McKenzie dying. I couldn't imagine how hard it had to be for McKenzie. "Because she knows you're going to be okay when she passes. But Maura—"

"I'll take care of her. Mom knows I will."

Hearing a seventeen-year-old say such a thing hurt me so much that I almost felt a physical pain. "She does know that." I brushed my hand over her head, smoothing her pretty ponytail. Her hair was exactly the color McKenzie's had been. I remembered McKenzie's ponytail looking identical when we were Mia's age. Which seems so crazy—that I knew McKenzie when she was the age Mia is now.

"How are you doing?" I asked. "With your mom being sick?"

Mia reached out and took my glass of iced tea and stirred it with the straw. "Good. I mean . . . okay."

"Nobody is *okay* with their mom dying, Mia."

"I bet Aunt Janine was okay with her dad dying. With Aunt Aurora blowing him away."

"Different circumstances," I said, seeing through her ploy. Redirection. I'd been reading all about it in a parenting book. I wasn't going to let her get away with it. "We're not talking about Buddy right now, so no changing the subject. I'm serious. You seem to be handling your mom's cancer very well. Maybe too well."

Mia leaned forward and sipped my tea from the straw. "I guess I'm dealing fine. What's my choice?" She looked at me. "She's going to die whether I deal with it or not. Right?"

I pressed my lips together, not sure if I wanted to laugh or cry. Mia was so her mother's child. Logical. Practical. Tough. But not afraid of her own emotions. "Do you talk with your mom much?" I asked. "About her dying?"

"Not really. Some." She took another sip of my tea and pushed it away from her. "When we do, I try to keep it about dumb stuff. Stuff that's not that important, like staying in Newark until we graduate next year. Which pieces of her jewelry we want. Stuff like that."

"You don't talk to her about how sad you are?"

Mia chewed on her lower lip. "Not really, because"—her voice caught in her throat—"because I don't want her to worry." She nibbled on her lower lip. "You know, about us."

I didn't know what to say, what to do, so I just listened.

"I don't want her to know how scared I am," Mia continued, "about what's going to happen. What it's going to be like not to"—she stopped and started again—"have her. I mean, what right do I have to be scared, Aunt Lilly? I get to stay here." She turned to look at me, her eyes full of tears. "Mom's the one who's going to die and get put in the ground."

Mia's last words came out in a sob, and I pulled her to me. She wrapped her arms around me and rested her cheek somewhere between my breast and my baby belly.

"Oh, Mia. Mia," I soothed, stroking her gorgeous red hair. "I'm so sorry, sweetheart. I'm so sorry. If there was any way I could take this from you, I would. Any one of us would."

Mia didn't say anything else and neither did I. Instead, I just held her until we heard a bicycle bell dinging and Maura went flying by us on the sidewalk below. "Check this out," she hollered, lifting her hands off the handlebars and managing to swerve around a large trash receptacle.

"You're going to feel stupid if you crash Viktor's bike," Mia hollered after her, wiping her eyes.

Maura brought the bike to a halt, whipping it around to nose into a bike rack at the end of the building. "You order yet?" She got off the bike and left it without a lock, coming down the sidewalk and up the steps. "I'm starving." She slid into her mother's chair and looked at her sister. "What's going on?" She looked at me, then back at Mia. "We're not having a cry fest, are we?"

Mia sniffed and picked up the menu, ignoring her sister's comment. "I think I'm getting this grilled panini made with buffalo cheese. What are you going to get, Aunt Lilly?"

Just then, McKenzie came out of the restaurant. "What did I miss?" she asked, leaning over to kiss Mia on the top of the head before she pointed to Maura and directed, "Slide in."

"It's too sunny in that spot. You can slide in." She stood up to let her by.

There was a moment of palpable tension when McKenzie didn't do what all three of us expected her to do—which was slide in.

"Slide in, Maura. The medication I'm taking doesn't allow me to sit in direct sun."

"Well, you're at the beach," she muttered under her breath. And slid over to the other chair.

I could have sworn I saw Mia smile behind her menu.

"And give your sister back her phone," McKenzie said.

"Yeah, did Mia tell you? Mine got wet. I don't think it's going to work again. I went to the phone store this morning. I can definitely get the upgrade. It's only like a hundred dollars."

"Sorry it took me so long to get back." The waiter walked up to the end of our table. He was a college-aged boy: clean-cut, with a goofy smile. "What drinks can I get for you ladies?"

McKenzie waited until the waiter took her girls' drink orders and went back into the restaurant. "Give your sister back her phone," she repeated calmly.

"Okay, okay." Maura pulled it out of her pocket and pushed it across the table to Mia. "But I'm expecting a call. Answer if it's a 222, but not if it's 234," she told her sister. She glanced at her mother. "I was thinking that after lunch Mia could ride the bike back to work and we could go to the phone store and get my new phone. My numbers are uploaded onto iCloud, so I won't lose anything."

McKenzie placed her menu on the edge of the table. "I'm not buying you another phone, Maura. I told you that last time."

"Mom, I have to have a phone."

"I'm not buying you another. You'll have to buy the replacement yourself or get your father's spare."

"He's got a nice flip phone you can use," Mia put in.

I would have laughed, but I could tell Maura was getting angry. It was nice to see McKenzie stand up to her daughter and not allow herself to be taken advantage of or bullied.

"Mom, I have to have a phone. What if you need us? What if you have to go to the hospital or something?" Maura was obviously flabbergasted.

"I can call a flip phone," McKenzie said. She looked at Mia. "I was thinking I'd get the sandwich with the buffalo mozzarella. If you're on the fence, you could get something else and we'll share."

"Mom, I can't use a *flip phone*." Maura said it as if her mother had suggested she communicate by ham radio. "I need a smartphone for . . . for school and stuff."

"Then I suggest that you take better care of the phone you buy yourself."

I looked up to see Mia's and McKenzie's gazes meet and caught a hint of identical smiles.

# ∞ 29 ∞

# Janine

"Who's got the Goldfish crackers?" Lilly leaned forward, eyeing me on the end.

We were lined up side by side in beach chairs in the sand. The tide was coming in fast. It would be high tide in less than two hours. It was time to go in and shower and let Aurora decide whether she was having Mexican or Chinese food delivered. (Her turn to make dinner.) But none of us were in a hurry to go.

I took another handful of cheese crackers and passed the bag to McKenzie, who passed it to Aurora, who passed it to Lilly.

Lilly thrust her hand into the bag. "These things are addictive. I should have never opened the bag."

It was nice this time of evening. The beach always cleared after the lifeguards went home, especially after a hot day like today had been. The thermometer outside the kitchen window had hit ninety-six at lunchtime. By this time of day, families had packed up their coolers and sand toys and umbrellas and dragged their sunburned, whining kids off the beach.

We hadn't come down today until four. McKenzie had needed to rest. She'd slept a lot of the day or read in her room, which wasn't something she'd been doing.

I had suspected, from day one, that maybe she was pretending to feel better than she did, to keep things upbeat. I'd been suspicious enough that yesterday, when she and Lilly were shopping, I had gone into her room to see if she was using the oxygen tank. It had been full, though, and seemed to be in the same place where I'd left it when I carried it in the house almost two weeks ago.

I glanced at McKenzie as I tossed a cracker into the air and caught it with my mouth. She looked fine to me. She looked pretty good, in fact. She was wearing shorts and a T-shirt so she didn't look so bony. And a canvas bucket hat and new wraparound sunglasses.

"I need to talk to you guys about something," McKenzie said. "It's kind of serious."

I groaned out loud and glanced at her. I tossed another cracker into my mouth. "Can it wait?"

Chris had said the same thing to me last night. I hate these kinds of conversations, the kind that people feel the need to introduce. We'd gotten into it on the phone. One of the only real arguments we've had since we moved in together. It was stupid. It wasn't that I didn't want Chris to meet McKenzie and Aurora and Lilly, it was just that . . . I didn't know if I was ready. It seemed like such a big step. Bigger than moving in together. Everyone had liked Betsy so much. (Including me.) I knew they were disappointed when I screwed things up; I guess I didn't want to disappoint them again.

"Can it wait until after cocktail hour?" Aurora asked. She was drinking a beer, covered by a neoprene Koozie, advertising the Dogfish Head brewery. Not exactly subtle—alcohol wasn't permitted on the beach. We didn't pay much attention to the rule.

"Looks like you started an hour ago," McKenzie teased, eyeing the open cooler of empties.

"Beer doesn't count."

"I'm going to need more munchies if we're going to have a serious conversation," I put in, trying to continue to keep things light.

"I've got licorice." Lilly produced a two-pound bag of red licorice from her canvas beach bag. She opened the package, took two pieces, and passed it down.

Aurora took a piece. (Beer and red licorice?) McKenzie took two. I was afraid this was going to be a three-piece chat. My eating habits were slipping fast; I was drinking too much. Eating too much sugar, too much fat. I don't like how it makes me feel, which was out of control.

"I want to talk to you about my funeral."

I knew this was coming. Honestly, I'm surprised she hasn't brought the subject up sooner. McKenzie has always been the one who likes to organize things. Why would her death be any different?

I began to peel off strips of licorice. "Do we have to?" I asked.

"You promised, no more morbid talk today," Lilly pouted, sticking the piece of licorice in her mouth as she folded up the top of the cracker bag. "We already talked about where you wanted us to take Mia and Maura out for dinner after their high school graduation. I don't think I can stand any more of this today."

"This is important," McKenzie said, taking a bite of licorice. "It's important to me that you know what I want. I can't ask my parents; they're going to be a mess. And obviously, I don't want Jared doing it." She pulled off her sunglasses, looking at me on one side of her, then at Aurora and Lilly on the other. "Which leaves you guys."

A big wave washed onto the shore, and the water almost reached our feet. We'd have to pull our chairs back or go up to the house soon.

None of us said anything.

"Come on," McKenzie begged. "I have to know you'll take care of the details. I've written out instructions. They're on my laptop in a folder called *Fini Opus*. I need one of you to be the contact person. I've already chosen the funeral home. I'm going to be cremated. I don't want my girls looking at my dead body. I wrote down what songs I wanted for the memorial service, the contact person for Mom's church, everything you need to know." She paused. "I'd do it for you."

Knife in the gut. I looked past McKenzie to Aurora.

Lilly was looking at her, too. "Aurora can do it," she said. "I'll be too big of a mess. You know I won't be able to do it."

I wanted to be able to tell McKenzie not to worry about it. I really did. That I'll make sure everything is done to her specifications. It makes sense that it would be me; I live the closest to her and I don't have a baby and I'm not famous. Who knows what country Aurora will be in when McKenzie passes? I mean, I hope we'll all be together when it's really . . . time. But that's one thing not even McKenzie can plan. Her exact time of death.

I just can't imagine myself making those phone calls: the funeral home, the fucking florist. I don't know anything about grave blankets. Lilly is right. Aurora is the best choice. She's the strong one. She was the only one of us we can depend on when the time comes.

McKenzie looked at Aurora.

Aurora stared straight out at the water rolling in. "Fine." She took a gulp of beer. "Thanks, guys," she said, resentment in her voice. Which surprised me.

McKenzie rubbed Aurora's bare arm. "I knew I could count on you. I'll send you the file. You don't even have to open it until . . . you have to."

Aurora just sat there, staring out at the water, drinking her beer, and I just sat there looking at her. We all did. No one said it, but I knew what the three of us were thinking. It was certainly what I thought of every day of my life. How thankful I was to have Aurora. She's my hero. Our hero.

# ❦ 30 ❦

# Aurora

Saturday morning I walked out onto the front deck, coffee in hand, to find McKenzie sitting alone. "Morning."

She smiled up at me. She was wrapped up in a beach towel. It had to be eighty-five degrees already. How the hell could she be cold?

"Good morning." She cradled a mug of tea between her hands. "You sleep well?"

"Sure." Which was a lie. How could I have possibly slept? I'd laid in bed the first half of the night thinking about making funeral arrangements for her. The second half, thinking about Jude.

Last night, we'd hashed out, ad nauseam, the whole Jude situation over Thai takeout. Janine had said she thought his reaching out was important to the next step in our relationship. His and mine. I think she's full of shit. She was just saying that because she thought it was what I wanted to hear. Lilly thought that maybe the fiancée would encourage Jude to see more of me. That was just Lilly and her rainbows and unicorns. I know very well that I'll never see my son again, and all of us sitting around discussing it for hours isn't going to change that.

I looked at McKenzie. "You know," I said, "you don't have to wear a hat all the time. It's starting to bug me." I sat down in the chair beside her.

She tugged on the brim of her ball cap like she was afraid I might reach over and snatch it off. An impromptu game of keep-away.

"I can see your hair's growing back. You've got cute little side-burns." I touched my jawline.

"I do not." She made a face at me and sipped her tea.

"I can *see* the red. I can't believe it's coming in red. You wouldn't believe how many gray hairs I have."

"I look like someone colored my head with a red marker."

"Better than bald." I looked out over the dunes below. Some-one must have cut through under the house last night. There was a Coors Light can lying in the dune grass. "How long have you been on the new drug?" I asked, trying to remember if she'd told me when she started it. We hadn't talked about the drug trial since the first night here.

She glanced in the direction of the open door.

"Where's everyone else?" I asked.

"Lilly went back to bed. Janine is running." She picked up her cell phone and checked the time. "Long run. She's been gone an hour."

"So it's no one but us." I studied her green eyes, maybe the prettiest green eyes I've ever seen. "How long have you been on the drug?"

She held on to the mug like it was a life vest and glanced away. "Eleven weeks."

"Maybe it's working."

"It's *not* working. There's a beer can in the dunes." She pointed. "Two. Someone should pick them up."

I ignored the cans and her ploy to distract me. "Your hair's growing back. That has to mean something."

"Yeah, that my body is getting used to the drug."

I thought about that for a minute. "You're still puking," I pointed out. I heard her last night. I sat on the stairs and listened, but I didn't have the guts to come down. What help could I have been? I would have just made her feel shittier than she already felt. "So you've got that," I said, purposefully sounding fakey cheerful.

"I've got that." She set her mug on the arm of her Adirondack chair. "Aurora, I'm going to tell you the same the thing I've told my girls . . . and my mom . . . and Janine . . . and Lilly." She turned to look at me. She had a solemn look on her face. Too solemn for this time of morning.

"I've given up hope that I'm going to beat this cancer, and it's time for you to give up hope, too." She didn't sound all doomsday. She sounded like herself: calm, confident.

I shook my head, looking away from her. I can't stand her looking that way at me. I guess maybe a part of me still *doesn't* believe it, which is ironic because I'm the one who always thinks everything is hopeless. "I never thought you were that kind of person, Mack. The kind that gives up."

"Well, in this case, I am. You've seen the statistics. There's a zero percent survival rate at this stage." She was quiet for a second. "I don't know exactly how to explain this, but . . . Aurora, in a way, this is a relief to me."

I don't want to be here. Not here at the beach house. Certainly not here having this conversation. I think about the ocean and its cold, its darkness. "I don't understand."

"It's a relief to know I've done everything I could, so it's okay. You know . . . to die. I fought the good fight and now . . ." She shrugged under the beach towel. "I don't have to fight anymore."

I didn't say anything. I just sat there looking at the sand and the sky and the blue deep. I could feel the tide pulling me. Calling me.

"You understand, don't you?" she asked.

I nodded because I did. I didn't want to, but I did.

She picked up her mug and took another sip. "I need to go to UPenn in Philadelphia on Thursday for scans and an appointment. For the drug trial. I agreed to it, so I feel like I should. It's the only way they're going to beat this kind of cancer. Someday." She sat back and lifted her bare feet to rest them on the chair, her knees to her chest. "I could probably just drive myself up, but the drive alone—"

"Not a problem. I need to go to an art galley in Philadelphia, anyway," I interrupted. It was half-lie, half-truth. "My manager says I need to have lunch with this chick from this art gallery. I'll make it for Thursday. We can ride up together. You do your thing. I'll do mine."

"That would be great."

I was glad she didn't ask me to actually go to the appointment, and I didn't offer. It was one thing to let her out the door at the hospital; it was another to go in with her and listen to the death sentence.

"Janine will be at work, and Lilly said something yesterday about meeting Matt for lunch in Salisbury one day this week. I'll tell her she should do it Thursday so I can tell them I'm going with you to your lunch," McKenzie plotted. "Matt bought huge life insurance policies for both of them, and he needs her signature or something."

I leaned back in my chair. "Hope he's not planning on killing her for the money."

That made McKenzie laugh. "I don't know what you have against him. I really don't. They're practically perfect together. Way better suited than Jared and I ever were."

I didn't remind her that I warned her not to marry Jared.

I looked up as Lilly walked onto the deck from the living room.

She was on her cell phone. "Okay, talk to you later. Love you."

"What the hell are you wearing?" I asked her as she lowered herself into her pink chair on the end. She'd been moving them around again. I never understood why she did that.

"A housecoat," McKenzie explained.

I made a face like I was horrified, which I was. It was a hideous white knee-length cotton robe that zipped all the way from the hem to the neckline, and was totally without shape, except for her basketball belly under it.

"Go ahead, make fun of my housecoat," Lilly warned, not in the least bit offended. "I'm getting both of you one for Christmas. Matching." She pointed at me and then at McKenzie. "And I'm going to make you wear them."

That evening, we all sat around the table, setting up the Clue game board after having leftovers for dinner. I didn't care for the game, but it was Lilly's turn to choose. Had it been me, I'd have gone for something more fun, like Truth or Dare. Janine was tipsy enough that I might have gotten her to do a little striptease. Better yet, Lilly. She wasn't drinking, of course, but our sometimes-uptight Lilly could be amazingly *not* uptight when she was in the mood.

I had a fun day on the beach, and everyone was in a good humor. Lilly and McKenzie had both taken naps, so neither of them was falling asleep on us. Somehow, we'd gotten on the subject of getting caught naked in public places.

McKenzie had told us about one of Maura's boyfriends walking into the bathroom as she was stepping out of the shower and how when she reached for the towel on the rack, she came up with an itty-bitty teenage girl's T-shirt instead. Lilly's story involved a gym locker room at a health club and wasn't that funny. Janine refused to contribute. I had the best story, of course. I always do.

"Wait!" Lilly was laughing so hard that she was pressing one hand to her big belly.

It's taken me a while to get used to that belly, but I've decided (maybe because I was a little drunk) that I like it. It makes me feel . . . good. Like life really is going on. That kind of bullshit.

"You're making that up, Aurora. You were *naked* on the balcony of the Park Hyatt in Paris? Those balconies are right on *Rue de la Paix!*" Lilly set stacks of cards in the appropriate places on the game board: one for suspects, one for weapons, and one for the rooms. "I've been there. Matt and I stayed there on our fifth anniversary."

"It was broad daylight?" McKenzie was setting the pawns in the appropriate starting places, laughing so hard that her eyes were watering.

"I'm not surprised. Why would anyone be surprised?" Janine took one card from each pile and slipped it in the solution envelope. "If I saw a naked woman locked out on the balcony of a ritzy hotel, I'd expect it to be Aurora."

She and I had started on the gin and Jack before dinner. Even McKenzie was indulging in her allotted glass of pinot grigio.

She looks good. Her cheeks are a little pink from being out in the sun today. And she looks so happy. It's why I keep telling these stupid stories. Because they make McKenzie laugh.

Tonight, she doesn't even look sick. I don't care what bullshit she was feeding me this morning about accepting her death. Maybe she doesn't look like herself, but she doesn't look like she's dying, either.

"So what did you do?" Lilly started to laugh again and then held up her finger as she got out of her chair. "Wait."

Out of the corner of my eye, I saw McKenzie raise her phone. I realized what she was doing and started to laugh. Everyone was laughing, though not all for the same reason.

Lilly was going to be sooo pissed when she saw this segment of the video. Then she'd cry, of course.

We had talked over dinner about the video diary. McKenzie refuses to let us see it. She wants it to be *a surprise*. That's all she'll say. I wonder if she'll send it to us once we all go back to our lives in two weeks or if she'll save it until she dies.

I wonder if she wants us to play clips at her funeral. Will that be in the funeral instructions she's going to e-mail me?

We could, I guess. People do that. Play videos of the deceased. McKenzie has even joked about it. But I know we won't. Not even if she tells us she wants us to. We won't because none of us will want to share what has passed between us, here. Not even with the people who love McKenzie, like her mom and dad. This is going to be for us and only us. Maybe always. Maybe whoever of us dies last will have it buried with her.

"I have to pee," Lilly said. "Stop right there. Don't you dare say a word. *Anyone.* Until I get back."

The three of us watched her waddle down the hall and disappear through the bathroom doorway.

"She's going to kill you when she sees that," I told McKenzie as I reached for my gin and tonic.

We'd run out of limes, and I'd had to do with a slice of lemon, which is fairly foul. One of us would have to hit the market tomorrow. Or maybe we would all go. Lilly wanted to make a big dinner before Janine had to go back to work on Monday. Janine would still be staying with us, but she would be on the day shift; she'd be gone eight to four, Monday to Friday.

And that would be the beginning of the end. Once Janine went back to work, even though we'd be here together for another two weeks, it wouldn't be the same. I knew it. We all knew it. Janine would reconnect with her girlfriend, her coworkers, her perps, and she wouldn't be wholly ours anymore. After tomorrow night, the four of us would no longer be to each other what we have always been. And when McKenzie died, I wasn't sure we would be anything at all. How could we be? How could *I* be?

I took a drink of gin. Another. I could feel myself turn toward melancholy. It happens that way to me sometimes. Quick. One minute I would be laughing and the next . . . I was jumping over the side of a yacht into the Adriatic Sea.

McKenzie passed out the cards, dividing them between the four of us.

I tipped my glass back, finishing it. "You want another drink, Colonel Mustard?"

We played with a game board that has been here as long as we've been coming to Janine's. Since we were twelve. No updated version for us. And we always played the same game pieces:

Janine was Colonel Mustard, Lilly was Mrs. White, McKenzie was Mrs. Peacock, and I was, of course, Miss Scarlet. Interesting that we had known our places at the fairly innocent age of twelve.

"I'll get it."

I could tell that Janine was pretty tipsy, too. She was setting the little silver-colored weapons in the different rooms on the board: the wrench, the dagger, the lead pipe, the revolver, and the candlestick. We'd lost the plastic rope years ago and used a piece of string for it.

Janine took my glass and hers and headed for the kitchen. Fritz, who'd been sleeping on the floor next to her chair, got up to escort her, but she ordered him to stay. When everyone was back in their chairs and the detective sheets and pencils were passed out, Lilly rolled the die first. Some people played with two dice to speed up the game, but not us. We were old school. Sitting here wasn't about the game.

"What happened?" Janine asked as we each took our turn rolling the die. "How'd you get off the balcony?"

"Was it cold?" Lilly asked. "Were your nips cold?"

McKenzie was cracking up. "Lillian, sweetie. You're forty-two and about to become a mother. I think you can say *nipples* in front of us."

"What do you think? I was fucking freezing," I said, an edge in my voice I didn't like. All of a sudden, I was annoyed with Lilly. Maybe with all of them.

It was Lilly's turn again, and she went into the ballroom. "Let's see," she said, eyeing each of us, the sound of suspense in her voice as she picked up the green game piece and a weapon and dropped them on the ballroom square. "Mr. Green did it in the ballroom with a . . . rope." She looked at McKenzie who was sitting next to her. "Can you disprove that?"

McKenzie showed her a card from her hand. Lilly made a face and marked a box off on her clue sheet.

McKenzie took up the die. "What *did* you do, Aurora? Shimmy down a drain pipe, cold *nips* and all?"

"No. I hollered down to people on the street." I leaned back in my chair, wishing I had a cigarette, or better yet, a joint.

"Did you stand behind a potted plant?" Lilly asked.

"Of course not. I was trying to get someone's attention, three stories below. A nice French gentleman was happy to go to the front desk and let them know that there was an issue with my balcony door." I took my turn with the die, headed for the hall. "I met him for drinks later."

# ❦ 31 ❧

# McKenzie

I glanced at Aurora. I didn't like the tone in her voice. She'd had too much to drink. Not for the first time since we'd gotten here, but there was something different about her overindulgence tonight. Something I couldn't quite put my finger on.

I knew she was upset about Jude. I'd tried to talk to her about him, with Janine and Lilly, and alone. Her response had been to pretend she was okay with his visit, with his engagement, with all of it. She wasn't ready to talk yet, I guess.

I took my turn and ended up in the billiard room. I scooped up Aurora's game piece, put it in the billiard room with mine, and guessed Miss Scarlett in the billiard room with a wrench. Janine took a moment from texting Chris to show me the wrench card.

"I hate this game," Aurora complained. "Now I'm stuck in the fucking billiard room."

"Aurora, could you please pick a different word?" Lilly asked.

Janine looked up from her cell phone. Aurora wasn't the only one with tone now.

"I know it's just a word," Lilly said, "and maybe around your artsy friends it's cool, but—"

"*Cool?*" Aurora asked, her voice thick with anger and sarcasm. "What? Are we in middle school again, Lillian?"

Lilly exhaled with irritation. "You know what I'm saying. I don't like it, and you know it. I never have." She was getting on her high horse now, the way only Lilly could with Aurora. "And I'm going to have a child soon, and I'm going to tell you now that I don't want you talking like that in front of her."

Aurora didn't say anything back. Which worried me more than if she had just gone off on Lilly.

We each took another turn, now in silence, and Aurora had the die again. She had exited the billiard room on her last turn, as per our rules, but now she was back inside it. She picked up the little revolver and tossed it into the room with her red plastic playing piece. "Miss Scarlet did it in the conservatory with a .38." She looked up but not really *at* us. "I guess she actually did it in the *bedroom*, didn't she?"

Janine had been texting Chris again. Her thumb froze over her phone, and she looked over at Aurora.

"If she'd had her way, it would have been Miss Scarlet in the *bathroom* with a .38." Aurora's voice sounded strange. Not like herself at all. Not even like herself after too much gin.

Lilly looked at me, then at Aurora. We were all looking at Aurora now. She had the oddest look on her face. Like she was about to cry or . . . dissolve. No one said anything. I think we were all trying to figure out just what was going on. Because something was *definitely* going on.

Aurora's mouth tightened. She went from looking hurt or lost or something, to looking like she could have hurt one of us. "Because I would have, you know that? If I'd had the gun that afternoon. When I got out of the shower to see Buddy standing there, looking at me the way he was looking at me." She paused to sip from her glass.

Buddy had walked in on Aurora in the bathroom? This was the first we had heard of it—in twenty-eight years.

We all seemed to be frozen. I wanted to say something, but I didn't know what. Lilly looked shocked. Janine . . . devastated.

"He came into the bathroom while you were in there?" Janine whispered.

"Yup. Same day. That last day." Aurora sounded as if she could have been talking about taking the garbage out. "Remember, the lock didn't work? Your mom was always asking him to fix it, but he never did." The momentary silence was deafening. We were all waiting, unable to imagine what Aurora would say next.

"You guys were all downstairs in the kitchen. Kathy too. Your brother had already left for his friend's house. Everyone was laughing and talking. I could hear you from the shower upstairs. Your mom had made spaghetti, Janine, and burned the garlic bread. I smelled it when I stepped out of the shower. You know something? I smell that burned garlic bread every time I step out of the shower," she said.

I noticed that Aurora's hand around the glass trembled ever so slightly as she went on.

"I reached for the towel, but he got to it first. He held it out in front of me. Taunted me with it. I tried to cover myself with my hands." Aurora gave a little laugh that was without humor. "I know it's hard to imagine me being shy, but I barely had tits." She shook her head stiffly. Like she couldn't believe what she was saying. Or what had happened . . . "I knew he was a creep, but I didn't know grown men could—not until I saw it in his eyes."

Janine's tears were spilling onto her cheeks. "He didn't—"

"Oh my God," Lilly breathed, staring at Aurora.

"No, he *didn't*," Aurora spit. "But he was going to." She was angry now. With us for some reason. But with Buddy, too. I knew that. Even if she didn't realize it right now.

"Don't you get it? You guys had the story wrong." She set her glass down hard on the table, so hard that the game pieces on the board rattled. She drew a deep breath. Closed her eyes. "And I let you believe it." She turned her head and looked directly at Janine. "I wasn't your *hero*, Janine. I didn't *save* you that night. I saved *my fucking self*." She practically shouted those last words.

Janine drew back from her, more in response to Aurora's volume than what she was saying.

"I don't understand." Lilly leaned over the table. "You're saying that Buddy came into the bathroom and saw you naked while we were downstairs making dinner that day? But you didn't go into Janine's room until—" She stopped and started again. "Did you know? Did you know he was in Janine's room that night?"

"I didn't know until I opened her door." Aurora glanced in the direction of the beach. The doors were closed, the light reflecting off the glass; we couldn't see the dunes or the ocean beyond them, but I knew she was thinking about the water. About swimming.

Aurora's voice took on an ethereal quality. "When I walked in, I saw what he was doing to Janine. I knew I was next. I knew he would be in my room soon. It was only a matter of time. So I closed the door very quietly. I went downstairs. I got the gun, and I went back upstairs. I probably would have shot him right in the bed with you, Janine. But when I walked in your room, he saw me. He came toward me, and I . . . I pulled the trigger."

Janine was crying quietly. Lilly loudly. I was, surprisingly, dry-eyed.

Aurora stood up. Swayed and steadied herself against the table.

"Aurora," I said.

She didn't seem to hear me. "So I've been lying to you all these years. Making you think I . . . I did something *noble*. I didn't." She hesitated. "I'm sorry, Janine. It wasn't about you. It was about me." She didn't look at her. "I'm going to go for a walk."

The three of us were quiet long enough for her to get halfway to the doors. Still stunned I guess.

"You want me to go with you?" I asked, getting out of my chair. I felt like I was moving in slow motion. Thinking in slow motion. What Aurora had said didn't make sense. How could she not have told us, all these years? She had to be lying. But the look on her face . . . I knew she was telling the truth. A truth she'd been hiding twenty-eight years.

"No offense, but you're not much of a walking buddy, Mack." Aurora reached the doors.

"Aurora, wait," Janine called after her.

Aurora opened the door, stepped out onto the deck, and was lost in the darkness.

I turned to look at Janine. She was crying, but she wasn't falling apart. Lilly was falling apart. I put my arm around Lilly, but I was still looking at Janine.

"I don't even know what to say," she managed. "I can't believe he—"

"Janine," I interrupted. "Look at me."

Slowly, Janine lifted her gaze until she met mine.

"He was a sick fuck," I said. "That's already been determined. What your father did to anyone, including you, is not your fault." I was surprised by how strong my voice was. By the fact that I wasn't crying. "And whatever happened to Aurora doesn't change the facts of what happened to you. You've spent enough money in therapy to know that, right?"

Janine seemed to mull that over in her head for a minute. Like me, I guess she felt as if she were processing in slow motion.

"Right," she said finally. She squinted, trying to get her thoughts wrapped around what had just transpired. What had transpired all those years ago. "Aurora thinks I care *why* she did it? She did what I didn't have the guts to do." She blinked. "It never occurred to me to kill him. She saved me." She stared at the floor. "Christ, she was fourteen." She looked at me again. "Does she really think I care *why* she did it?"

"I know it doesn't make sense, Janine. I don't know what's going on with her. I don't know why she would tell us this tonight. Too much to drink. Jude. Me." I gave Lilly a squeeze and let go of her. I went around the table and put my arms around Janine. For once, she didn't fight me.

"I should go after her," she said into my shoulder.

"Let her be for a little while. Let her sober up."

"You don't think she'll go swimming, do you?" Lilly asked. "She's too drunk to be swimming."

I exhaled. It was certainly a possibility that she would. But one of us being with her wasn't going to stop her. "She said she was going for a walk. I think she probably needs to go for a walk and decompress." I let go of Janine.

She stared at the phone on the table. "I want to call Chris," she said. "I'm going to go out on the deck and call Chris."

"Good idea." I handed her her phone. "I'll get Lilly some tissues." I searched Janine's gaze for a moment, checking to make sure she wasn't about to lose it, I guess. She wasn't. Our Janine is tough. We all know that. This was just further proof.

"Come on," I told Lilly, going back around the table to put one arm around her and steer her down the hall toward the kitchen. "Let's get you a glass of water."

Sniffling, Lilly looked to Janine. "McKenzie's right, you know that, right?" she asked. "You know what Buddy did to Aurora isn't any more your fault than what he did to you. You understand that."

Janine managed a little smile and a slight nod. "I'm just going to go out and call Chris."

# ✒ 32 ✑

# Janine

"**Y**ou want me to go with you?" McKenzie asked me. She was standing in the doorway of her bedroom. "Help you look for her?"

Lilly was lying down on McKenzie's bed. She was having those damned fake contractions again, which would have been worrying me if I wasn't so worried about Aurora out on the beach alone right now. Possibly in the water, swimming for who-the-hell-knew where.

At lunch Aurora had been telling us about a woman in her sixties who had swum from Cuba to Florida. Maybe Aurora was attempting the Delaware to Cuba swim right this minute. It wasn't as far-fetched as it might sound. Not for Aurora, who we all knew was just a little nutty . . . and getting nuttier by the year, apparently.

"No, I'll find her. You stay here with Lilly." I pointed. "She okay?"

McKenzie nodded.

"You?" I asked.

She smiled at me from under the brim of the ball cap she was wearing. Her girls had given her the hat advertising a local brewery. "Peachy."

"Good. Well, hopefully I'll be back . . . *we'll* be back shortly." I turned away.

"Hey, Janine?"

I turned back.

"Chris coming tomorrow?" McKenzie hesitated. "I kind of overheard."

"Yeah," I said. "Tomorrow morning."

"Lilly will want to make a big celebratory breakfast."

"Waffles and bacon," Lilly called from McKenzie's bed, lying on her back, stroking her bare belly in big circular motions. "But someone will have to go out for OJ!"

I smiled to myself. I wasn't sure *celebratory* was the right word, but it was sure as hell going to be interesting. "Be back as soon as I can," I told them. "I've got my phone if you need me." I patted my shorts' pocket. I'd put on a hoodie. It was after eleven and probably a little cool on the beach. "I'm going to take Fritz with me."

"Call if you need us," McKenzie told me.

Fritz waited for me on the deck. He was watching through the salt-treated rungs of the rail. Maybe there was a rabbit in the dune grass. Or maybe he was already trying to pick up Aurora's scent.

"Come on, boy," I called. I grabbed a towel someone had left to dry on the rail and threw it over my shoulder.

He trotted down the steps behind me. We crossed the dunes and headed straight for the water. There was no sign of Aurora there. I looked up and down the beach. Not many people out. A few voices drifted in the darkness, but none that were distinguishable . . . or recognizable.

"North or south?" I asked the dog. Like he had any more idea than I did.

He lifted his nose and sniffed, then trotted north. Downwind. Made sense. Lost kids on the beach usually did the same thing. I fell in behind him.

I was glad to be out of the house for a few minutes. Just to be alone. I used to go to great lengths to *not* be alone, but I was finding it easier. Sometimes even pleasant.

So Buddy had gone into the bathroom and seen Aurora naked. *Looked* at Aurora naked. I guess I should have been more shocked about her revelation than I was. I guess I'm not because there's nothing that anyone could say about him that would shock me. Well, if someone said something *good* about him, *that* would have floored me. I'm glad, of course, that he didn't touch Aurora. And that she took away his opportunity to try.

The thought crossed my mind that she could have told someone at the time, an adult, but it didn't linger. I know what kind of person Aurora is. That wouldn't have been her style. To rely on someone else. Certainly not an adult. And she knows me. God knows I would have been too scared to speak up if anyone had questioned me about my relationship with my father. I'd have lied to hide my shame.

That thought was like a trip wire. Trip wires triggered explosions in the field. In this case, inside my head.

*God damn it!* I pressed the heels of my hands to my temples.

I tried not to think about the first time Buddy came into my room.

I had gotten really good at blocking the memories, but sometimes they seeped through the cracks . . . or just exploded in my head.

My mother had gone away overnight to see her sick aunt or something and taken my brother with her. I was twelve. Twelve fucking years old. He'd just walked into my bedroom in the dark and climbed into bed with me . . . climbed on top of me. He didn't say a word. I didn't even realize what was going on until it was too late. Then I only struggled for a second before he wrapped his hand around my throat and told me if I made a sound, if I *ever* made a sound, to anyone, first he would kill my dog Scooter, then he would kill my brother, then my mother, and then me. He told me that because he was a cop, he knew how to get away with it.

At the time, I remember being the most afraid for my dog, of all things.

That intimidation worked for a while. Then, when I got older, he started in on the whole idea that it was all my fault, what he did to me. How I had *tempted* him. How I *made* him do it. How nasty I was. How ashamed my mother, my friends would be if they found out.

I believed him. I believed it was my fault, and I was *so* afraid someone would find out. When I started becoming friends with Lilly, McKenzie, and Aurora, I remember being petrified they would, somehow, know what my father did to me in my bedroom at night.

I thought it was my fault, but not Aurora. Not Aurora who was able to recognize Buddy for the monster that he was, and was willing to protect herself.

Like sand shifting under my feet, I moved back to the present. Aurora. Aurora was out here somewhere. I gazed north, up along the waterline.

I felt bad that Aurora thought I would care why she went downstairs and got the pistol that night. That I would think any less of her, knowing her *true* motivation. She stopped him when I couldn't. End of story.

I felt bad for Aurora, but it also ticked me off a little that she thought I would care. All these years she's known me and she didn't know me any better than that? I'd always suspected Aurora was screwed up in the head, but this . . . guess I shouldn't have been surprised.

I found her T-shirt and shorts about three blocks north of the house. I recognized the artsy graphic shirt she'd been wearing. At least she hadn't gone in naked.

I stood at the edge of the water, my bare feet wet, trying to spot her in the water. "Come on, Aurora," I murmured. "Don't be an idiot." It had crossed my mind back at the house, and again when I was walking, that she could drown, as drunk as she was, as upset as she was. But Aurora was stronger than that. Better than that. I knew she wouldn't do that to us.

Fritz stared out into the dark water. Whined.

"I don't know," I told the dog. We stood there for a long time, then I sat down, next to her clothes, willing to wait until she came back for them. Even if it meant sitting there all night.

Maybe another twenty minutes passed before I thought I spotted someone in the water, north, swimming south, beyond the breakers. I stood up, and Fritz and I walked to the edge of the water. It was dark, and the moon hadn't come up yet so I couldn't see much. As the swimmer got closer, I recognized the stroke. It was Aurora, all right.

I called her name. She didn't answer, but the swimmer headed in for the beach.

When she walked out of the ocean, water streaming off her hair, I was waiting with the towel. Neither of us said a word as I picked her clothes up off the sand. We just started walking south, her in her bra and panties, me with my dog and her clothes.

We walked all the way back to the house in silence. An oddly comforting silence. I could tell Aurora was spent, physically and emotionally. And mostly sober. I found another towel hanging from a hook next to the outside shower, and I offered it to her after she rinsed off and wrung out her long blond hair. She dropped her bra and underwear and wrapped one towel around her head and the other around her naked body. I scooped up her clothes and followed her up the steps to the deck and into the house.

"Janine?" McKenzie called from the bedroom. Then, hesitantly, "Aurora?"

Aurora walked into Mack's room, and I went in behind her. McKenzie was lying in the bed, in a sleep tee and boxers. Lilly was in one of her silly, white, little girl nightgowns. Curled up asleep beside McKenzie.

I was halfway in the room when I realized that McKenzie wasn't wearing a scarf or one of her nighttime terrycloth turbans. She was bald, except for the slightest cast of red peach fuzz on her head. I didn't say anything about it.

McKenzie pushed up on her elbow and put out her hand to Aurora. In just the towels, she climbed into the bed and stretched out, sandwiching the sleeping Lilly between her and McKenzie. McKenzie laid her head on the pillow, but she was watching me.

"There's not enough room," I argued, knowing exactly what she wanted, without her having to say it.

She tilted her fuzzy head ever so slightly, beckoning me. I glanced over my shoulder at Fritz, who had settled down in the doorway between the dark house and the pale light of the bedroom.

I hesitated. Then gave in and climbed into bed. It was a close fit with the four of us. I didn't have a lot of room, especially since I tried to lie there for a minute without touching Aurora. But then she rolled onto her side, throwing her arm around Lilly's belly. McKenzie met my gaze over the two of them and then shut out the light and lay down.

I rolled over and put my arm over Aurora to touch Lilly's belly . . . and to feel the warmth of McKenzie's hand. I closed my eyes against the tears that stung them. We had done this when we were in middle school, all slept together. And in high school, and occasionally in college. But I couldn't remember ever having slept like this in our adult lives. All lying together in the same bed, and feeling the rise and fall of each other's chests with each breath.

I drifted off to sleep.

# ✇ 33 ✇

# McKenzie

When I woke in the morning, I found myself alone in my big
bed. I could smell coffee brewing; the scent of Lilly's perfume was still on my pillow. When I rolled over, I was surprised
to see that the digital clock displayed nine forty. I couldn't believe I'd slept in so late on such an important morning.

I dressed and stood in front of the full-length mirror in the corner of the room, trying on a paisley scarf, discarding it, and then
putting on a ball cap. I had a collection now. I tugged on the
brim, then yanked off the hat and tossed it.

I studied myself in the mirror for a minute and found I was
caught between feeling self-conscious about my fuzzy head and
the sentiment of liberation. Why was I bothering with the hats?
They'd all seen me without it last night. No one had even com-
mented on it. And Chris wouldn't know that I'd once had long
red hair. And she already knew I had terminal cancer.

Looking at myself, I suddenly saw a correlation. All these
years, Aurora had assumed we would think less of her if we knew
she had killed Buddy to save herself. It hurt me; it hurt all of us
to think we would judge her. Was I doing the same thing to them,
underestimating my friends, on a smaller scale? Why did I think
any of them cared what my head looked like? It certainly wouldn't

be an issue for me if it were one of them who was sick. Weren't we beyond such trivial things?

I left the hats and scarves on the dresser, put on my silver starfish earrings, and went out into the living room. I stopped at the bathroom, then followed the smell of the coffee, wondering if I dared try a cup. Maybe just a half cup, black or with a little sugar? It smelled so good.

In the kitchen, Lilly was busy arranging bacon on crumpled foil on a cookie sheet. She was dressed in her signature capris and a cute top with an apron tied around her waist. Lilly is the only person I have ever known, other than my grandmother, who has ever worn an apron. Janine and Aurora sat on stools at the island, sipping from mugs.

"McKenzie!" Lilly waved both hands. "She's on her way. She'll be here any minute. I'll get you a cup of tea. I found a teapot. I knew it was here somewhere," she chattered. "No loose tea, but I still think it's nice, brewing it in a teapot. Don't you?" She poured water from the teakettle into a white-and-yellow primrose teapot. It had to have been something she'd brought from home, sometime in the past. It was too cutesy to be anything the three of us would have brought.

I looked from Aurora to Janine. Neither looked worse for wear after last night. Aurora didn't look like she even had a hangover. Janine was freshly showered, and if I didn't know better, I would have thought she was wearing tinted lip balm.

Aurora nudged a stool in my direction with her bare foot. She was in a tank top and white shorts, her hair pulled back in a sleek ponytail. No makeup, no earrings. Still, a perfect face.

"Should we carry the table out onto the deck?" Lilly asked. She put the tray of bacon in the oven and set the timer. "I love to eat outside, but I know it's a pain to stack the Adirondacks and carry the table out and back in."

"I should have made the deck bigger when I had it rebuilt. You told me to make it bigger," Janine told Lilly.

"Right." Lilly considered that for a moment. "But the permits were going to be a pain in the butt. And I don't know if you would have gotten the variance. I was talking to Lori, two houses down. She had a heck of a time with her driveway permit. The town really cracked down on the rules." She went back to the teapot, lifted it, swirled the hot water inside, and poured tea into my favorite blue mug.

"I think making the deck bigger would have made the house look weird from the shore," Aurora put it. "It would have ruined the lines, architecturally. You did the right thing."

"We don't have to move the table, Lilly. We'll push back all the curtains. You see the ocean from the table." Janine sipped her coffee. "It'll be fine. It's not the president of the United States coming to breakfast. I really don't want this to be a big deal."

I added sugar to my tea. "Speaking of big deals . . ." I looked from one of them to the next. "Are we going to talk about last night?"

Aurora raised her eyebrows as if I had said the most ridiculous thing. "You want to talk about that?" She pointed to my fuzzy head.

I refrained from stroking it. Instead, I stirred my tea, liking the sound the spoon made against the mug. "Nothing to talk about," I said.

Janine made eye contact with Aurora. "Works for me."

"I'm not apologizing for getting drunk, if that's what you're waiting for." Aurora held up her hand. "If I can't drink too much and make an ass out of myself in front you guys, where can I?"

"You didn't make an ass of yourself, Aurora," Lilly said sympathetically. "I think McKenzie's right. I think we should talk about it. See how everyone is feeling this morning. Don't you, Janine?"

Janine shook her head once. "Nope. I'm tired of rehashing the rehash. Aurora's shocking revelation wasn't that shocking. She's probably disappointed," she joked.

"So . . ." Aurora clapped her hands together. "Let's talk about what we all *really* want to talk about." She spun on the stool to face Janine. "What do we need to know about Chris?"

Janine closed her eyes, her fingers wrapped around her mug. "This is a bad idea. I *knew* it was a bad idea."

"No, no, it's a wonderful idea." Lilly plugged in the waffle maker. "I hope Chris likes waffles. I decided against eggs. You think bacon and waffles is enough? We've still got fresh fruit I cut up yesterday. And Greek yogurt. I could make eggs. Scrambled or fried. I don't like fried eggs, but—"

"Lilly!" Janine interrupted.

We all started laughing.

"Please," Janine said. "Let's just have a nice breakfast and pretend like this is not a big deal. Please?" She put her hands together, begging.

Lilly sighed loudly and dramatically. She knew the role she played with us, and she played it well. "I'm not making a big deal." She poured a carton of orange juice into a glass pitcher. "It's just breakfast." She carried the pitcher and five glasses on a tray out of the kitchen.

Janine rolled her eyes and reached for her coffee. I wished I'd had my phone to catch the eye roll on video. Realizing I'd left my phone plugged in to the wall in the bedroom, I took a sip of tea and went to go get it. I was brushing some blush on and was checking out my eyelash stubble when I heard Fritz bark.

"She's here!" Lilly squealed in the other room. "I'm so excited. She's here!"

I heard Fritz run through the living room into the kitchen. I threw on some peach-colored lipstick. I wasn't sure why I wanted to look nice for Janine's girlfriend. It wasn't like she and I were going to have a long-term relationship.

As I came out of my bedroom, I heard the back door open. Janine's voice.

I walked into the kitchen, phone in hand, as Fritz shot into the kitchen from the laundry room. I was really tempted to hit the record button on my phone, for posterity's sake. But if I did, I knew there was a possibility Janine might drop my phone into my mug of tea.

Janine walked into the kitchen, followed by a blond man. A man. She stopped inside the doorway, and he stopped. He was in his late thirties, possibly early forties, nice build. He was wearing board shorts almost identical to Janine's, a faded surf-shop T-shirt, and dark, wraparound sunglasses.

For a second, none of us said anything. Even Lilly was at a loss for words.

Janine pointed at the man beside her. "Chris," she introduced. Then she pointed at each of us. "McKenzie, Aurora, and Lilly."

He took off his sunglasses. He was average looking, with brown eyes, but he had the *nicest* smile. "Great to finally meet you all. I had to practically beg Janine to get an invite."

"Chris?" Lilly breathed. "Chris!" She rushed over, wiping her hands on her apron. "We are so glad to finally meet you. We've been threatening Janine to come find you on our own if she didn't invite you over." She grabbed his hand and shook it with both of hers.

Aurora was looking at Janine and then she burst out laughing.

I was grinning, ear to ear.

Chris looked up. "What?" He smiled and laughed because all of us were smiling, I'm sure.

"Nothing." I came forward, offering my hand. "It's just so nice to finally meet you, Chris."

At noon, Lilly, Aurora, and I headed down to the beach, walking single file over the dunes. We'd left Janine on the back deck, talking with Chris. Lilly had tried to convince him to come back for dinner, but Janine said she'd had enough big happy family for one day. We'd made arrangements, instead, for him to come back Wednesday night. We'd gotten a highly sought after permit for a bonfire on the beach, and he was invited to come then instead.

"Holy Christ," Aurora said, carrying a striped canvas beach chair in each hand. On her back, she wore a woven textile backpack with her towel and suntan lotion in it. The chairs were for Lilly and me.

"Holy Christ," she repeated. Then she looked over her shoulder to Lilly, who was walking between us. "You notice I didn't say holy fu—"

"And I appreciate that," Lilly interrupted. "As does my unborn child."

I trooped behind Lilly, in flip-flops because the sand is always hot. I was only carrying my small canvas beach bag. I was wearing my dumpy blue swimsuit with a cover-up and a big straw hat. There was no way I was taking my bald head on the beach, even in light of my big *reveal*. It would sunburn.

"Did either of you suspect *for a minute* that Chris was a guy?" Aurora asked, still sounding truly stunned.

We all were. I certainly was.

"I had no idea," Lilly said. "Did she ever say *he*, referring to him? I feel like I would have noticed. On the other hand, I guess I just assumed Chris was a she because—you know—"

"Because she's a lesbian?" Aurora asked.

"I know I had to lift my jaw up off the kitchen floor." Lilly adjusted her big straw hat. "I texted Matt. He thinks it's hilarious. Like the joke is on us."

"I hate to agree with Matt." Aurora led us toward our usual spot in the sand, just behind and to the left of the lifeguard stand. "But it *is* kind of funny. That at forty-two years old, Janine's coming out of the closet," she threw over her shoulder. "And she's *straight?*"

"I can't imagine why she didn't tell us," Lilly mused. She was wearing a white cover-up over a pink swimsuit that was amazingly cute for being in a toddler color.

"Janine and a guy." Aurora slipped one chair and then the other off her shoulders. She opened mine first. "You think this means she's bi?"

"Well, *clearly*." Lilly took her chair from Aurora and opened it, setting it next to mine. "I mean, she was definitely in love with Betsy."

"Weren't we all?" Aurora asked.

Lilly propped her hands on her hips. "But Janine's never even dated a guy."

"That we know of." I dropped my bag in the sand and sat down to catch my breath. It wasn't that hot out today, so I wasn't that out of breath.

"What's the world coming to?" Aurora took her towel from her backpack and flapped it in the air before laying it in the sand. "There are certain things you're supposed to be able to depend on in life. The sun rises in the east." She gestured toward the ocean. "And Janine only dates girls."

I reached for my sunblock spray. "You sound disappointed."

Aurora stretched out on her stomach on her towel. Today, her teeny bikini was tie-dyed. "I do, don't I?"

# ✌ 34 ✍

# Janine

I dawdled around the house for at least twenty minutes after Chris left, putting off the inevitable. I took out the garbage. I rinsed out Fritz's water bowl. I even checked my e-mail.

I knew Aurora, Lilly, and McKenzie were going to have the same question Chris had posed the minute he and I were alone. The same question I'd been turning over in my head for days, weeks . . . months.

I know why, in the beginning, I didn't tell them Chris was a guy. Why I didn't tell *Chris* I hadn't told them he was a guy. I was uncertain of the relationship. Uncertain of myself. All I'd ever been is a lesbian. It was the way I identified myself. This was a big deal for more reasons than anatomy.

At first, when we started dating, I was plain scared. He was the first guy I'd ever dated. I mean *ever*. I'd never even kissed a guy before I kissed him at the bar the night we met. I was sure, that first time, that it was just too much Jack and some sort of midlife crisis thing. Even after we saw each other a couple times, I was still sure it was a fluke or a phase, or something. It was weeks before it occurred to me that I might be falling in love with him.

Today, standing next to Chris's car with him, we'd both laughed about it. He had a couple of psychobabble terms to label me, but basically, it was his personal opinion that we can't help who we love. And sometimes, for some of us, that meant male or female.

As I stood on the deck, looking over the dunes at two figures in big straw hats in chairs and a leggy blonde lying on one of my towels, the truth of that statement really hit me. You can't help who you love.

Who would have ever thought that our friendship—Aurora's, Lilly's, McKenzie's, and mine—would survive Buddy? Would survive high school and college and ex-husbands and ex-boyfriends and ex-girlfriends and estranged children? We were so mismatched in so many ways and yet we fit together so well. We complemented each other. They make me a better person.

I groaned, realizing my eyes were getting misty. Lilly was wearing off on me. I grabbed a towel from a basket inside next to the door. "Stay, boy," I told Fritz.

The sand was hot on my bare feet as I hurried over the dunes. Approaching the group, I debated where to lay my towel. Did I lie down next to Lilly? Aurora? Lilly would phrase her questions delicately. Aurora would come right out and ask me about Chris's *wang*. Of course, the disadvantages could be the advantages. Aurora was good at ripping the Band-Aid right off. Lilly picked at it, fussing at the edges, prolonging the discomfort.

I walked past Lilly's chair and spread my towel out right in the middle of them, at McKenzie's feet. I lay down on my back, pushed my sunglasses up on my head, and closed my eyes. The sun felt hot and good on my skin. I waited.

"Anyone want a bottle of water?" Lilly asked after a few minutes. "I brought the minis."

"I'll take one," Aurora said.

"Me too." McKenzie.

I heard Lilly pass out the water bottles.

"Are we inviting the neighbors to the bonfire?" Lilly asked, sipping her water.

I kept my eyes closed.

"We might as well," Aurora put in. "They're going to come anyway."

"And if you invite them," McKenzie said, "you can ask them to bring food to share and their own drinks."

"Right," Lilly agreed. "Otherwise, we're feeding everyone on the block. Anyone want pretzels? I know I had that huge breakfast, but I want something to munch."

I heard her rattle a snack bag. Her beach bag was this bottomless pit of snacks and beverages and lip balm and suntan lotion and baby wipes and anything a person could want on the beach.

"Mia and Maura coming?" Aurora.

"They wouldn't miss it. I told them they could bring a couple of friends, but I expected everyone to be on their good behavior," McKenzie said. "I'll have a pretzel. I told them no drinking and nothing else illegal."

"Here," Lilly said. The pretzel bag crackled again. "Pass them to Aurora."

"You have any Pringles?" Aurora asked. "I always feel like pretzels are a waste of carbs. If you're going to eat crap, it might as well be greasy crap."

I heard what sounded distinctly like potato chips being shaken in a cardboard can.

"Just a few left. Catch."

I propped myself up on my elbows, unable to stand it another second. "The three of you are funny. Hilarious."

"What?" Aurora pulled the top off the Pringles can Lilly had tossed her and looked inside. "Want a chip? Just crumbs." She held out the canister.

I looked at her, then McKenzie, then Lilly. "Go ahead. Ask."

"Ask what?" McKenzie took a loud bite of a pretzel.

Aurora tipped the can, dumping chip crumbs into her mouth.

"I was going to get hot dogs for the bonfire, because you can't have a bonfire without roasting weenies on a stick," Lilly directed to me, "but I was thinking about getting Italian sausages, too. What do you think?"

"Personally, I like weenies," McKenzie said.

"I prefer Italian sausages," Aurora replied.

They were both snickering.

"I'm sorry," I said loudly. "I didn't *mean* to keep it from you. It just . . . kind of happened and then I didn't know what to say."

"*What* are we talking about?" Aurora asked.

"Never mind. Never mind." I dropped back down on my towel.

"Wait, Janine, are we talking about you dating a dude?" Aurora asked.

"I'm sorry," I repeated.

"You're sorry you're dating a *dude?*" Lilly asked. She sounded so funny saying *dude*. "Or you're sorry you didn't tell your best friends in the whole wide world that suddenly you're playing . . . for the . . . original . . . team," she said, obviously struggling to make the analogy fit.

McKenzie and Aurora started laughing. Then Lilly.

I closed my eyes, shaking my head. "I thought you guys were going to be mad at me."

"Because you kept something this important from us?" McKenzie asked. "Because we are."

I pushed up on my elbows again. They had stopped laughing. "You are?"

"We're angry because you didn't tell us you're *in love*."

I know I must have gotten the silliest look on my face. "I guess I am," I said.

# ᦞ 35 ᦞ

# McKenzie

Monday, things felt different at the beach house. I couldn't tell if it was because Janine had had to return to work and the real world, because our month was more than half over, or just because things in life always change. Especially when you don't want them to.

Monday, I lay around and rested, as per Mother Lilly. My girls stopped by to say hi, to clean the refrigerator of leftovers, and to tell me a story about an employee getting locked in to the walk-in refrigerator at work. Lilly spent the whole day fussing over menus and plans for the bonfire, which included three calls to a local seafood shop to make sure the clams we had ordered would be available for pickup. Aurora lay low, talking on her cell phone, walking on the beach, and taking my car and disappearing for a few hours.

Tuesday was more of the same, minus my girls, which made it duller. I read and napped and sat on the deck and listened to Lilly chatter on the phone with neighbors. Everyone got a personal invite from Lilly. Again, Aurora was absent for several hours. Neither Lilly nor I asked her where she had been, and she didn't offer to tell us.

Wednesday was a beautiful, sunny day. Hot, but not unbearable. Late in the afternoon, a friend of Janine's, Bernie, arrived with a truckload of wood. The way Bernie told it, when she wasn't running her furnishings store in Rehoboth Beach, she was acting as a professional bonfire . . . person.

The four of us had learned years ago that while we were all pretty bright, building a beach bonfire was not in any of our skill sets. I was pleased to see that Janine had hired someone to do it, so we didn't have to rely on our neighbors for help (which often led to heated discussions), but it felt weird to have someone out on *our* beach building *our* bonfire. It crossed my mind several times, as I watched Bernie tote wood across the beach, that this would likely be my last bonfire. Which made me sad. I guess I wouldn't know what I was missing, though. Would I?

That evening, I was still mulling over the question of whether or not we know we're dead when we're dead when Lilly started rounding up the troops. "Janine! Aurora! Mack!" she called from the living room. "Let's go! Everyone will be arriving soon. Mia and Maura and their friends are already down there."

A few minutes later, Lilly and I walked over the dunes and across the beach, arm in arm. The sun was setting behind us, and the moment seemed dreamlike. How many times had I come over these dunes to this very spot on the beach, this very place at the edge of the Atlantic Ocean? Where had all the years gone? I wanted them back.

"It's my turn to light it, isn't it? Mom?" Maura came bounding toward me with Mia an arm's length behind her. They were both in tank tops and shorts; I could see bikini straps on both of them. "Tell her it's my turn."

"I got an A in chemistry," Mia argued, out of breath.

They kicked sand up as they came to a halt in front of us.

"I think it's only fair," Mia said.

I did the Mom-eyebrow-lift with my nicely drawn on eyebrows. "You think you should have your sister's turn lighting the annual bonfire because you got an A in chemistry?"

"Mom!" Maura protested.

Mia crossed her arms over her chest. "I do. She got a C."

I looked at Maura. "You're lighting the bonfire. Lilly's got the lighter. Mia lights it next year."

"I'm writing it on the calendar," Mia said, walking away. "And I'm sending everyone an e-mail, so there's no question," she called over her shoulder. "Next year I don't want her trying to say I lit it this year when I didn't."

"When have I ever done that?" Maura started after her sister, then turned back to us. "Can I have the lighter, Aunt Lilly?"

"Not until Aurora and Janine get here."

"Aunt Janine! Aunt Aurora!" Maura shouted up to the beach house.

I cringed. "A little loud," I said, holding up my hand.

"Oh, gosh!" Lilly let go of my arm to put both of her hands on her belly. "She heard that. Mack, she knows your voices." She took my hand. "Feel."

"Does the baby know our voices or does she just think we're loud?" I asked, resting my hand on Lilly's belly.

For a minute there was nothing, and then . . . I felt the motion beneath my hand. It's a sensation unlike any, and it immediately brought a smile to my face. It felt like a roll more than a kick.

"Feel it?" Lilly asked, tears springing in her eyes. "Feel that!"

I don't know what it was about standing there in the sand with my girls and Lilly, feeling the life inside her, but I had this sudden, overwhelming sense that everything was going to be okay. I mean, I knew everything is not going to be okay. I know there's so much sadness yet to come: tears and pain and . . . I don't even want to think about what it would be like in the end to say goodbye to Mia and Maura. To Lilly and Aurora and Janine. So maybe I was kidding myself because that was what we humans did to get through the moment, through the day, the week, the month, the years. But I was okay with that, at least tonight.

"I think you're right," I whispered to Lilly. "I think it's a girl."

She covered her hand with mine.

"We set your chair up, Mom," Mia said. "Come on." She held out her hand for me, something my girls didn't do often.

"Is this like being queen of Mardi Gras?" I asked.

"I have no idea what that means." Mia clasped my hand. "Go get them," she called to her sister. "Tell them to come on or we're lighting it without them and we're drinking all their beer."

I cut my eyes at Mia. That was something I expected Maura to say, but not her.

"Kidding!"

Later, I sat in my chair, snuggled in a sweatshirt, a towel around my shoulders, watching the fire lick up the side of an enormous piece of wood. It was a perfect bonfire night. The sky was clear, and it wasn't too windy, so the smoke drifted upward instead of into our faces. A paper plate sat balanced on my knees: a half-eaten hot dog on a potato roll, steamed clams, Lilly's vinegar coleslaw, and pretzel salad. All the things I loved.

I could see Maura and Mia on the far side of the blaze, sitting in the sand, drinking soda, goofing around with their friends. They'd all been in the ocean for a dip, and Mia's and Maura's hair was wet and stuck to their heads, making them look, in the un-steady light, younger and more innocent than their years.

Janine was sitting in her chair, a few feet to my right, just out-side the brightest circle of firelight. Chris was standing behind her chair, leaning over, talking to her. She tipped her head back and laughed; the dancing light was kind to her, too. She looked young, happier than I could remember seeing her in a long time. Maybe ever.

Next, I searched the crowd of twenty-five or thirty for Lilly. She was walking around with a cardboard box, passing out gra-ham crackers, chocolate bars, and marshmallows, directing peo-ple where to find the sticks to roast their marshmallows. In her element.

I didn't see Aurora for a second, then realized she was standing behind me. She wore shorts and a Dewey Beach sweatshirt, her hair down and falling over one shoulder. I looked back and smiled at her, and she moved closer. She didn't touch me; she just stood there behind me, staring into the fire.

"What is it about man and fire?" I tucked my half-eaten plate under my chair and snuggled under the beach towel. "Why can we sit here for hours and stare and continue to be fascinated?"

"I don't know," she mused. "Some psychologists say it's only Westerners who are enthralled by fire. Those of us who didn't learn to control it or conquer it as children. There are studies that show that in cultures where fire is still used as a tool, where children learn to control it at an early age, they have no more fascination with it than we would a screwdriver or a hairbrush."

"What do you think?" I asked, enjoying a moment with a side of Aurora I didn't see often. The contemplative, not so cynical Aurora. "You use fire as a tool, a tool to create art."

I half expected a smart-ass reply. Aurora often made fun of what she did, of what people *thought* she did, and how much money they paid her to do it. She joked about the ignorance of those who displayed her work and called it brilliant. Or called it art at all.

But she just stood there for a long time. "I used to think," she said, her voice barely above a whisper, "that I *did* control my torch. That I was the master, and my torch was my brush, but sometimes . . ."

She was quiet so long that I thought maybe she had lost her train of thought. "Sometimes," she murmured finally, "I think it controls me. You know what I mean?"

I didn't. I have no artistic talent. I don't even know how to fully appreciate what Aurora creates. I rely on art critics and other artists to tell me how amazing Aurora is. But there was something in her voice that made me think we weren't talking about her torch, or art . . . but about our lives. What I thought she was saying was that sometimes we control our lives, but sometimes we're just washed along, controlled by the tide of people and events around us.

I reached over my shoulder for her hand and felt her take it.

"You ready for tomorrow?" she asked. She leaned closer to keep our conversation private. "The ruse is in place. Janine will be at work. Lilly's got a hot lunch date."

"I'm ready." My voice sounded funny in my ears. "Not a big deal. It's not like this is the first time I'm going to hear it. See it."

"Eww." She let go of my hand and sat down in the sand next to me, facing the bonfire. She drew up her knees and wrapped her arms around them. "They show you pictures of your tumors?"

"Yup," I said. "I've got a big one in my throat." I touched the scar on my neck. "And all these little ones in my lungs. They look like little starbursts on the scans." I opened and closed my hand to demonstrate. "I could tell them I don't want to see the scan results, I guess. Just go, have the scans so they can use them for their research, but just say I don't want to see them."

"Or you could skip the whole appointment," Aurora suggested. "Just not show up. Why do you need to be reminded that the cancer is going to kill you? That doesn't sound like fun. You could go to lunch with me instead. It's at some ritzy place that's supposed to take weeks to get a reservation. Better yet, we could blow off lunch with the art director and do something fun."

"Something fun in Philadelphia in *July?*" I asked, realizing she was serious. "Do you know how hot it is in the city?"

"Where's your sense of adventure, Mack? We could go see the Liberty Bell or . . . or take one of those tours in one of those buses that looks like a duck and turns into a boat once you get to the river."

I laughed because that didn't sound like something I would have ever guessed Aurora would want to do. "Sounds tempting," I said. "But I feel like I should go. You know, play my part in the cure for cancer."

She leaned back against my legs. "I wouldn't go."

"I know," I mused.

# ✺ 36 ✺

# Aurora

I sat at a traffic light in downtown Philly trying to ignore the ass behind me who practically had his BMW in the backseat of McKenzie's Toyota. When the light turned green, I hesitated before hitting the gas to give him enough time to lay on the horn. I thought about giving him the finger. Instead, I looked up into the rearview mirror and gave him the biggest, prettiest smile I could muster, Lilly-style.

He slammed on the horn again. I laughed and ambled through the intersection. It had been a boring day. I'd met with the art director and had a lunch of three martinis and a salmon steak. I wasn't even entirely sure what the point of the meeting had been; I just let her talk while I sipped my gin and twirled the toothpick shaped like a sword with olives on the end. My manager had called twice in the last two hours, wanting to know how the meeting went, I'm sure. I wasn't in the mood to talk about my career.

After lunch, I excused myself, telling the woman I had to meet my friend at the UPenn cancer center. Which was a lie. I just didn't want to talk anymore about my work or what she and the art community thought about it.

I was waiting for McKenzie to text me to pick her up, so I

went to the Museum of Art. There were bigger museums in other cities in the US and in the world, *better* museums, but it had always been one of my favorites. Maybe because I had gone there as a child, on school field trips. Or maybe I liked it there because so many of the pieces were so familiar that they were like old friends. Alone there, without anyone from the art community watching me, I could enjoy a secret pleasure. I liked the American art gallery and had a thing for Charles Willson Peale portraits. I'd totally have hooked up with him, had I met him in the eighteenth century.

McKenzie texted me just before four o'clock. I made two wrong turns and had to go around the block once before I arrived at the Perelman Center. There was a circular drive for the pickup and drop-off of patients.

I spotted McKenzie before she spotted me. She was sitting on a metal bench. She'd worn a blue and green maxi dress, which looked pretty on her, and no scarf. Big earrings. She'd looked nice. Right now, she looked petrified, though. And like she was about to cry.

I stared straight ahead for a minute, gripping the steering wheel. Trying to get ahold of myself. I *knew* she shouldn't have come today. What the hell was the point? Wasn't positive energy supposed to help you live longer? What kind of positive energy could there be in a place like this? A place of death. To hell with helping science.

I looked over to see McKenzie walking toward the car. She was carrying a canvas tote bag that seemed too heavy for her. She got in and fastened her seat belt.

I was glad I was wearing my sunglasses. I didn't want to upset her more, letting her know I was upset.

When she got in, the heat and humidity came with her. I waited until she had fastened her seat belt, and then I pulled away from the curb.

She dug around in her bag and came out with her sunglasses and slid them on. I pulled out when there was a break in traffic. I stole a quick glance in her direction. She was looking straight ahead. Did I ask about the scans and the follow-up appointment with the doctor? Did I comment on how freakin' hot it was in this city and how I couldn't wait to get back to the beach? Did I tell her about Charles Willson Peale and how he'd been a saddle-maker before he became a portrait artist?

"I need to make phone calls," McKenzie said. "Mia and Maura. Lilly and Janine." She sounded short of breath, like she did sometimes when we walked back up from the beach in the loose sand. "My mom and dad. My mom is going to lose it." She pressed both hands to her face, sliding her fingers up under her sunglasses.

I was gripping the steering wheel so tightly that my knuckles were white. I shouldn't have brought McKenzie here today. It should have been Lilly or Janine. Anyone would have been better than me. I'm no good in these kinds of situations. Everyone knew that.

Obviously the news was bad. But what kind of bad news could you get when you'd already been told you were terminal? Only that you were going to be terminated sooner rather than later, I thought. "It can wait," I said, trying to sound casual.

We pulled up to a traffic light, and I looked at McKenzie. She was looking at me. Staring at me.

"You're not going to believe this," she said. Her voice was shaky.

"Okay."

There was a long pause, or what seemed long, before she spoke. "The tumors . . . they're shrinking."

I knew what McKenzie had said. I knew exactly what she had meant, but for a second, I couldn't react. I didn't know how.

She reached out and rested her hand on my thigh. Squeezed it. "Aurora, the medicine. It's working." Suddenly there was joy in her voice. "The stuff that made my hair fall out and then made me puke for two months, it's shrinking the tumors in my lungs." She went on faster. "It's not a cure, of course. There is no cure.

And we don't know how long the tumors will continue to shrink or how much they'll shrink. The drug is just in the testing stage, but—"

Someone blew her horn behind us. The light had turned green. I sat there for another beat of my heart before I pressed on the accelerator. "Holy shit," I said.

She laughed. "Yeah. Holy shit."

I looked at her, then back at the road. The traffic was heavy. I needed to get over to make my exit or we'd be headed back into the city. "And . . . they're sure?"

"I made them show me the scans."

I signaled, checked the mirror, and moved over. "And they were yours?" I asked, still not believing what she was saying. There had been no hope. No hope for months. Every doctor she saw *said* there was no hope. McKenzie was dying. I had seen it in her eyes.

She laughed. "I said the same thing." She turned toward me in her seat. "I'm not out of the woods. Anything could happen. But *this month* I'm better than I was last month. It's not my imagination. I thought it was wishful thinking. I really am breathing better. I saw it. The tumors in my lungs are definitely smaller. The doctor showed me with an electronic ruler thingy how they're measured. She put one scan up next to the other."

"Holy shit."

She laughed. I could tell she was crying. "You said that already!"

It was suddenly hot in the car, and I turned up the air-conditioning, full blast. "I can't believe it. You're not going to die," I said.

She sat back on the seat and laughed. "Not this week."

# ✆ 37 ✇

# Lilly

"Stand back, ladies, and see how this is done." I took an exaggerated practice swing with the mini golf club. We've been coming to this pirate-themed miniature golf course for years. Since Mia and Maura were in grade school. There were better, newer places in town, but this was my favorite course; it was *our* course.

"Careful, Aurora." McKenzie backed away from me, hands up in the air. "You better not get too close to her. Lilly's dangerous with that thing."

"Hey! I'm a pretty good golfer. I'll have you know I'm a ten handicap without this passenger." I indicated my belly.

Janine, standing next to the hole in front of a waterfall that was the most bizarre color blue, cracked up and waved for me to putt the ball. "Come on, Lilly. The next group is catching up with us. We're going to have to wave them through."

"Which will make, what? The fifth group?" Aurora waited, arms crossed.

It was after eleven, way past my bedtime, but somehow McKenzie had convinced us that we needed to play miniature golf. Talk about a new lease on life. I don't know where she's finding her energy, but she was still going strong, even after a late dinner at Arena's. Now she was talking about stopping for frozen yogurt on the way home.

I eyed the hole in the middle of the strip of green indoor-outdoor carpet, then glanced up to catch McKenzie's eye. I'm so happy about the news she came home from Philadelphia with that I'm not even upset that she hadn't told Janine or me about the drug trial, but she *had* told Aurora. More than two weeks ago. I probably *am* upset . . . or at least I will be, once the euphoria wears off.

I understand McKenzie's explanation as to why she didn't tell us—because she was afraid to get our hopes up when she'd been told so many times that there was no hope. But that doesn't let her off the hook. Not completely. And there was going to be hell to pay. Just not tonight.

I tapped my pink golf ball with the club. It banked left and rolled right into the hole. McKenzie clapped and laughed. "You're not going to catch up with her, Janine. She's going to win."

"She hasn't won yet. I'll beat her on the next hole." Janine scooped up her ball. "Even if I have to cheat."

"Right, like you would ever cheat on anything." Aurora led the way out of the fake cave, up a ramp toward the hole on the next level. "I couldn't even get you to give me the answers on an eighth-grade social studies test, so don't tell me what a lying, cheating badass you are."

McKenzie took my golf club from me and looped her arm through mine so we could walk together. "If you're getting tired, we can wrap it up and head home," she said.

"And concede," Janine threw over her shoulder.

"I'm fine. I'm good," I told McKenzie. "And I'm going to beat you fair and square," I called to Janine. I turned my attention back to McKenzie. "I'm so happy that the new drug is working," I told her, squeezing her arm.

She smiled. "Me too." She laughed. "Obviously."

"So how do you feel?" I looked into her eyes. "Is it real yet?"

"No, not really. One minute I'm giddy, the next, I'm afraid I might wake up. When I went into the restaurant to talk to the girls, I almost chickened out. I kept thinking, *What if the hospital got my scans confused with someone else's?*"

I laughed. "With another McKenzie Arnold? With the same social security number as yours?"

"I know." She laughed with me. "I'm just . . . I'm stunned." She thought for a moment. "And trying to keep my excitement tempered. There's still no telling what will happen down the road. I could still die from this. I probably *will*, eventually."

"The heck with tempering. We're all going to die someday." I rested my cheek against her arm. "I'm just so glad it's not going to be any time soon."

"Which means"—she let go of me to switch the golf clubs into her other hand and rub my belly—"I'm going to be there when this little girl is born."

We walked past a speaker that was playing "Yo Ho, A Pirate's Life for Me." Loudly. Janine was already squaring up to take her turn at the next hole.

Aurora was waiting for us at the top of the ramp. "I say we let Janine win and go for a drink at Irish Eyes."

I groaned and took my golf club from McKenzie. "The place will be packed."

"Come on. It's not every night we celebrate our best friend getting a reprieve from the grim reaper."

"A *reprieve from the grim reaper?*" I laughed. I'd laughed so much tonight that my sides hurt. "It's a good thing you're an artist and not a writer, Aurora." I took a practice swing. "Now step aside and watch me finish Janine off."

"I'll give you five bucks if you make a hole in one here," Aurora dared. "Better yet, I'll buy you one of those big froufrou drinks you like. With extra umbrellas."

I frowned. Janine had a two on the hole. It was a par two. I knew I could make it in one long putt. "Can you not see that I'm pregnant, Aurora?"

"So I'll get you a virgin froufrou, and Mack can drink your alcohol."

McKenzie laughed, and I saw her meet Aurora's gaze. We were all so happy, but there was something about the light I saw in Aurora's eyes that made me think that this somehow meant even more to her than it did to Janine and me. Maybe because of Jude? I couldn't tell. And tonight wasn't the night to ask.

# ✺ 38 ✺

# Janine

I walked out onto the deck. The light was out, but I could see Aurora leaning on the rail at the far end.

"Is that weed I smell?" I asked.

"Nope." I heard her inhale and hold her breath. Then I saw her pinch out a glowing ember between her fingers. She exhaled heavily.

I leaned on the rail next to the steps. "Okay, boy," I told Fritz. He ran down into the darkness to do his business. I glanced in Aurora's direction. "Do I have to remind you I'm a state police officer?"

I could hear the frown in her voice. "*Please.* You guys have better things to do than chase down half a joint." She lifted her chin in the direction of the neighbors' house. "Besides, if you're going to arrest me, you have to arrest the Greenes, too."

I glanced at the dark house; they were always in bed by nine, and it was almost one. "The Greenes?" I laughed, knowing she was joking. She *had* to be. "They're in their *seventies.*"

"You've never smelled it?" She didn't sound like she was joking. She sounded like she knew something I didn't.

I thought about it for a second. I thought about it so hard that I knew my forehead creased. "I smell . . . the smoker. He's always smoking meat."

"Ever wonder why he smokes so much meat? What smells he's trying to cover?" Now I could hear her smiling.

I shook my head. The whole possibility was just too much to think about tonight. There was no way the sweet old Greenes were potheads. He was a retired CPA, for God's sake. She was the head of some women's circle at her church. "You're crazy, Aurora. Certifiable." I stared out over the grassy dunes. I could hear Fritz under the house, snooping around.

Aurora climbed up to sit on the rail, swinging her feet over to let them dangle.

I listened to the sound of the waves. It was so soothing . . . soul soothing. I thought about the last week, how crazy things had gotten. Spinning out of control, but for once, not in a bad way. I was still trying to sift through it all, trying to figure out how McKenzie's new prognosis would impact me . . . our lives. Thoughts of Chris, Jude, and Aurora's big revelation kept bubbling up, too.

I glanced at Aurora, then back out over the dunes. For a couple of days, I'd had the nagging sense that Aurora was watching me when she thought I wouldn't notice. That she was waiting for me to *say* something. I had a pretty good idea what it was about. I thought about how to ease into the conversation, but this was Aurora. It was better to just plunge. "You and I haven't talked about what you told us," I said. "About killing Buddy because he walked in on you."

She was quiet.

"You know that doesn't really matter to me, right? It doesn't change anything between us." I waited. Fritz came up the steps, crossed the deck, and trotted into the house.

Still, Aurora was silent.

I sighed. Sometimes I wondered if Aurora truly believed the things she wanted us to think she believed, or if it was all a game with her to get attention. "You were a kid, Aurora. No one could blame you for saving yourself." I hesitated, and then went on. "I guess what I'm trying to say is that it doesn't matter to me why you did it. You still saved my life."

The crash of the waves and the click and whir of the insects in the sea grass below filled the air for a few long moments before she spoke. "I let you believe I was someone I wasn't," she said so softly that I had to concentrate to hear her. "You thought I was a hero."

I gazed at her; I couldn't make out her face now lost in shadows, but I could imagine its stoniness. "You *were* a hero, Aurora. You were *my* hero. The motivation of a scared fourteen-year-old doesn't matter. Buddy would have killed me one day. I truly believe that."

She didn't look at me; she just kept staring into the darkness, toward the ocean. "You mean that, don't you?" Her voice was small, almost like a little girl's.

"Of course I mean it. When have you ever heard me say something I didn't mean, Aurora?"

She looked at me and smiled. "Thank you."

"For what?" I asked.

"I don't know." She lifted a slender shoulder and let it fall. "Just thanks."

Silence stretched between us then, and I knew she was done talking about it, at least for tonight. We'd talk about it again, maybe not tomorrow, but soon.

I closed my eyes, suddenly realizing how exhausted I was. "I think I'm going to bed. You coming?"

"In a few minutes," she answered.

"Okay." I glanced toward the door; I could see Fritz waiting patiently for me. "See you in the morning."

"See you in the morning," Aurora repeated.

The next morning, Lilly and McKenzie greeted me almost in unison. "Good morning!"

I walked into the kitchen from the laundry room; the dryer and the washer were both running. I'd decided to take a personal day; it just didn't seem right to celebrate McKenzie's good news by spending the day making traffic stops and hauling in teenagers shoplifting at the outlet stores. I wanted to be here. With her and Aurora and Lilly.

Fritz went right for his water bowl on the floor at the end of the counter.

"How was your run?" McKenzie was perched on a stool, drinking a cup of tea. She was already dressed for the beach, a pair of shorts over the blue bathing suit we all hated so much.

"Coffee?" Lilly asked. She was still in her white *housecoat*, her dark hair up in a samurai topknot.

"Not yet." I went to the sink and got a glass of water. "Run was good. A little hot. I should have gone earlier. I guess we all slept in." I leaned against the sink to drink my water.

Fritz meandered out of the kitchen.

"No sign of Aurora?"

"Still asleep." Lilly took a mug from the cabinet and set it next to the coffeepot. "Coffee's ready when you want it. It's going to be a nice day on the beach. It cooled down overnight. Only expecting a high of eighty-nine today. I thought we could all go down for a while."

"Mia and Maura are trying to switch shifts with friends." McKenzie reached for the local newspaper lying on the counter. "Either to get today or tomorrow off. They want to go to the waterslides. You up for it?"

As I opened my arms, I heard Fritz bark from the front deck. "Bring it on."

"Any chance Chris might like to join us?" Lilly tilted her head to one side.

"I'm not asking Chris if he wants to go *watersliding* with a bunch of women." I drained my glass and set it in the sink.

"Why not? It'll be fun."

I glanced at Lilly's belly. "You're going on the waterslides? With that?"

She frowned. "Of course not." She dropped English muffins

into the toaster and pressed the lever. "I can sit at the bottom on one of those benches and take videos and hold towels and such. I'll pack snacks."

Fritz barked again.

"Of *course* you're going to bring snacks." I tugged on my little ponytail that was held up more by bobby pins than the elastic band. I wouldn't have admitted it to anyone, but I was kind of proud of my ponytail. I hadn't had once since I was fourteen. "Did I tell you I got on the scale at the gym yesterday morning? I've put on three pounds since we got here. Thanks to *your* cooking and snacks, Lillian."

McKenzie flipped a page in the newspaper. "I've lost another four since my doctor's appointment last month. I'm down to my college weight. *I* don't seem to be having an issue with Lilly's snacks."

I cut my eyes at her. "Taking cancer drugs doesn't count. If I was puking as many times a week as you are, I'd be down to my college weight, too."

McKenzie flashed me a smile.

"I'll pack something healthy." Lilly took butter and strawberry jam from the refrigerator and set them on the counter. "Carrot sticks and stuff."

I wanted to tell her that we could do without snacks between lunch and dinner, but I knew it would be a waste of breath. "Carrots are fine. No more chips or licorice." I started for the door. "I'm going to jump in the shower, then come back for my coffee."

"Skip the shower." McKenzie began to fold the newspaper. "We'll all go in the water. You can rinse your stink off in the ocean."

Lilly opened the jar of jam. It smelled good, and I realized I was hungry. I was tempted to tell her to put a muffin in for me, too, but I really did need to cut back on the carbs.

"It doesn't make sense to shower, then go swimming in the ocean and come back up and shower again," Lilly said.

Fritz was barking again, now more insistently.

I glanced in his direction, then back at Lilly. "I know, but I feel gross." I made a face. "My underwear is sweaty."

"Eww," Lilly groaned, putting up her hand. "TMI."

Fritz was still barking. Which was weird because he knows better than to sit on the deck and bark at every kid or rabbit that goes by.

McKenzie turned around to look in the direction of the front of the house. "What's going on with him?"

I shook my head. His tone was strange. "Fritz!" I hollered. "Knock it off."

He kept barking. Something about the sound made the sweaty hair on the back of my neck stand up. I walked out of the kitchen and through the living room. I could see him on the deck, his muzzle to the rail. He was still barking. I had never heard him bark like this before. "Fritz! Enough!"

He stopped barking and started to whine.

I stepped out onto the deck, looking in the same direction he was looking.

There was a knot of people crowded around the water's edge, just north of the house; it was maybe seventy-five or eighty yards from the deck, but here, from the second story, I could see pretty well. Some sunbathers were moving toward the clump of activity, others away. On the wind, I caught the sounds of human distress.

"Stay, Fritz," I ordered, walking toward the steps.

"What's going on?" McKenzie came to the doorway.

"I don't know." I looked up from the third step. "Something on the beach. Fritz, stay," I ordered. He had started after me; I had to point for him to go back up to the deck. This was so unlike him. He was never disobedient.

McKenzie glanced in the direction of the commotion. "I'll come with you."

"No. Stay here," I said sharply. Sharp enough that McKenzie stayed where she was.

I hurried down the stairs. I'd left my running shoes in the laundry room, so I was in my socks. I didn't take the time to take them off. As I crossed the dune, I heard the sound of a siren. The frequency of the tone told me it was police. Close, coming this way. I heard another, farther in the distance.

As I went up and over the dune, I looked back over my shoulder. Lilly had joined McKenzie at the rail. Fritz waited at the top of the steps, his whine practically a howl. "Stay there," I called.

I hit the beach at a jog. Closer to the uproar now, I could hear a woman crying. Someone was clearing the area, forcing the crowd back. It took me a split second to realize what I was seeing; the group in bathing suits was standing around someone lying in the sand. I saw bare feet. Long legs. A red one-piece bathing suit. Then I saw the long, wet, blond hair.

I took off at a full run.

At the scene of accidents, I've heard people say that time slowed down for them. That everything seemed to happen in slow motion. For me, as I sprinted the distance, everything was a blur . . . of time and space. The sky whizzed by overhead; the sand moved under my feet. I heard voices, but I didn't hear what anyone was saying. I saw the faces of the people gathered, but they had no features. Not even gender.

"State police," I heard myself call out. "Step back, please."

My back was to the beach house. I faced the ocean. Someone had pulled her just far enough out of the water so that her head was in dry sand. She was almost perpendicular to the water, but her feet got wet with each wave. Her goggles were gone. Her eyes were closed. Like my father's had been.

"Step back! Please!" I barked. I realized I'd come down without my phone. "Did someone call 911?"

"I called."

"They're on their way."

"I hear them."

The voices seemed disembodied.

I crouched beside her. I knew right away that she'd been dead a few hours: Her hands and feet were beginning to slough off skin, she was slightly stiff, and her face and neck looked bruised—

signs of lividity. I pressed my fingertips in the hollow between her windpipe and the muscles of her neck anyway. No pulse in her carotid. She was cold to the touch.

"Should we start CPR or something?" someone asked behind me.

"Here come the paramedics!"

"I see the police!"

I stood and took a step back. I turned to identify myself to the male and female paramedics. I spoke in a low, steady tone. I'd been trained for these types of situations, with the army reserves and the state police.

I provided Aurora's full name. Then I stepped back to give the paramedics room. I heard them going through the motions of a resuscitation, but I knew, as I'm sure they did, that it would be unsuccessful. As I walked toward the first police officer arriving on the scene, in an Albany Beach uniform, I glanced up at the beach house. McKenzie and Lilly were still standing on the deck with my dog.

Could they see her lying on the beach?

I gave my name and Aurora's name to the officer and explained my relationship to her. I pointed to the house, and then I walked away. A part of me thought I should stay with Aurora until she was loaded in an emergency vehicle, but my thoughts were now with the living.

My heart shattered into raw, bloody bits as I trudged over the sand in my socks. Tears ran down my face. I'd seen dead bodies before, even a drowning victim. But my knees were weak, and I felt like I might be sick.

I never saw this coming.

Thoughts blurred in my head. When did she go swimming? Last night? Did she tell me she was going? I couldn't remember her mentioning a swim when we turned in, and I didn't even drink last night. Why did I not hear her go by my bedroom door?

How did this happen?

Did she get a leg cramp and drown? Was it an accident? Or was this something darker, something I could not bring myself to consider right now?

McKenzie and Lilly were waiting for me on the deck. Just standing there, arms around each other, tears running down their faces. They were crying so quietly. Quieter than I expected.

I knew they knew.

I told them anyway.

# Epilogue

# McKenzie

"I don't understand." Janine slid into the plastic chair in the hospital cafeteria and passed me a cup of coffee: cream and sugar. Coffee had finally started to taste good again.

"What's not to understand? It's Aurora."

Janine stared at me. Blinked. She looked cute this morning in jeans and a sweater. It wasn't as if she'd gone full Lilly on us, but I felt like she was figuring out who she was without worrying about what other people expected of her. Not even Lilly and me. She was wearing eyeliner, which I intended to tease her about at some point.

"She left everything to Maura and Mia?" she asked, still dumbfounded.

"Yup." My annoyance was obvious in my voice. I was past the shock I'd felt when I'd seen Aurora's attorney yesterday. Now I had moved on to being pissed. I hadn't broken the news to my girls. I was trying to figure out how I could *not* tell them. Of course, Aurora's attorney had said that wasn't possible. "No trust, nothing. My girls turn eighteen in March, and they inherit"—I took another sip of coffee—"somewhere around one point seven million dollars, *each*."

"Holy shit." Janine took a sip of her black coffee. And again,

"Holy shit." It had become one of her favorite phrases—picked up from Aurora, I was sure.

"Right."

Janine stared at me across the table, her gaze flicking to the clock on the wall. We'd both been in the hospital for hours. We'd even been in to see Lilly before things got down to the wire. We'd already talked to Matt twice since the birth. The birthing center in the hospital had some rule about no visitors being allowed in until the baby was an hour old. (Like we were *visitors?*) We only had to wait eleven more minutes. I planned to hit the elevators in five.

"I didn't know Aurora was . . ." Janine was at a loss for words.

"That rich?" I asked her.

"That rich or that stupid." She put her hands together on the table. "Why did she leave it to them and not you?"

"Obviously she assumed I was going to die before she did." Someone called a code something-or-the-other over the loudspeaker almost directly over our table. I waited until Janine could hear me again. "The will was written in April. It was done perfectly legally; everything's in order. I was dying. She thought she was doing a good thing."

"And Jude?" Janine asked.

I shook my head. "He's not mentioned in the will. I talked to Hannad last night. He seems fine with it. He says Jude is fine."

"That's a lot of money *not* to leave to your only child."

I glanced at her over the rim of my paper cup. "I suspect Hannad is worth far more than that."

Janine glanced away, beginning to get fidgety. "I should call Jude. I haven't talked to him since the funeral."

"You should," I encouraged.

She drew her lips back in a sad smile. "I don't know. I got the impression when we said good-bye that he just wanted to let that part of his life go. Let us go, go with her."

We were both quiet for a minute. Lost in our thoughts. So

much had happened in the last few months that I felt as if I could barely keep up. How could life change so quickly?

The new drug was working, my lungs were looking better every month, and I was seriously considering going back to work part time. Aurora was gone. Things were going well between Janine and Chris. The beach house was on the market. My girls were going to be millionaires in six months. And Lilly had a baby this morning.

I studied Janine across the table. She looked good. Her attorney expected the lawsuit against her to be dropped before it went to court. She talked about Chris like he was now a permanent thing. I'm so happy that she's so happy.

She glanced at the clock again. "We should go. If we're one minute late—"

"I know." I rose. "We'll be in trouble."

We both ditched cups still half-full of coffee and followed one hallway, then another to a bank of elevators. We took the elevator to the maternity floor and then followed signs to the birthing suites and checked in with a young nurse dressed in bright pink scrubs.

Matt met us at the door to Lilly's room. He was dressed in khakis, an oxford, and an argyle sweater vest. Despite a twenty-two-hour labor, he didn't seem to have a hair out of place. He was grinning as hard as any new father could.

"Thank goodness you're here." He kissed the top of my head, then Janine's. "I was afraid I was going to have to come looking for you."

"You said an hour," Janine pointed out, checking her cell phone.

"I know, but according to Lilly, it's been sixty-two minutes." He stepped aside. "Go on in. I'm going to run downstairs, get some coffee, and make a couple more phone calls. She keeps taking the phone out of my hand while I'm trying to talk to people."

I laughed as I lifted up on the toes of my knee-high boots and kissed him on the cheek. "Congratulations, Papa." Then I pushed through the half-open door.

The room was nice. More like a hotel room than the kind of hospital room I'd stayed in after having Mia and Maura. Lilly was sitting in a leather recliner, dressed in a pale blue kimono-style bathrobe. Her hair was combed, and she was wearing pink lipstick. Of course she was. The only sign that she'd pushed out a baby an hour ago were the crinkles of fatigue around her eyes. And of course, it was obvious she'd been crying.

She squealed when she saw us, and then she offered the white bundle to us.

I took her first. "Oh my God, Lilly," I breathed, gazing down at the tiny, sweet face. Her skin was pale like Matt's, but she had jet-black hair and brows. "She's gorgeous."

"She is, isn't she?" Lilly grabbed a tissue from a box and dabbed at her eyes.

Janine peered over my shoulder. "You know I don't know much about babies, Lilly, but I'd say this one is pretty damned cute."

Lilly cut her eyes at Janine.

"Sorry!" Janine apologized. "I forgot. No freakin' cursing around the kid."

I rocked the baby against my chest, remembering the feel of Mia and Maura in my arms when they were this small. I closed my eyes and smelled her heavenly scent. "She's perfect," I whispered. "Our baby is perfect."

"So what's her name?" Janine asked, taking a chair near Lilly. It was the question that had been on both our minds since Matt had called us an hour ago to say she'd been born.

"I hope it won't upset you . . . either of you," Lilly said slowly.

*Aurora.* She was going to call her Aurora. Janine had been sure of it. I hadn't.

"She's your baby," Janine said. "You can name her what you want."

Lilly looked at Janine and then me. She held my gaze for a moment. "I'm going to call her Joy."

"Joy," I murmured, looking down, pressing a kiss to her soft cheek.

"Not Aurora?" Janine said softly.

Lilly turned to her, shaking her head slowly. "No. Matt and I talked and . . ." She looked down and then up again at Janine, tears in her eyes. "We decided that was too big a burden for our daughter, to carry that name."

We both watched Janine.

"I'm sorry if that hurts you," Lilly told her.

Janine looked up. Tears in her eyes. "No," she whispered. She rose and came to me and put out her arms.

I handed the baby to her, pretty sure she had never held one of my girls when they were newborns.

"Joy deserves her own name," Janine said, awkwardly cradling the baby in her arms and looking down at her.

I walked over to Lilly and leaned down to hug her. "I think Aurora would agree."

# AS CLOSE AS SISTERS

## Colleen Faulkner

## ABOUT THIS GUIDE

The suggested questions are included to
enhance your group's reading of
Colleen Faulkner's *As Close as Sisters*.

# DISCUSSION QUESTIONS

1. Would McKenzie, Janine, Lilly, and Aurora have continued to be friends beyond middle school had it not been for Buddy's death? Why did they grow closer together, rather than further apart?

2. What do you think of the way McKenzie is handling her terminal diagnosis? Do you think it's realistic? If you were McKenzie, how would you respond differently?

3. Do you think that Janine has recovered from the sexual abuse by her father or does that abused child still live in her? Did what Aurora did to Buddy really save Janine?

4. What are your thoughts on McKenzie's relationship with her ex-husband, Jared? Is he a good father?

5. Do you think it's odd that Janine chose to be a police officer like her father? Do you think it gives her the control she didn't have as a child? Is law enforcement something that's "in your blood"?

6. Why do you think Lilly was a part of the group? What does she add? Is she in the inner circle? Were you surprised by her secret that only McKenzie knew about? Is it always better to share secrets with those you love?

7. Do you think Aurora is a brave woman? Is she selfish or unselfish? Do you think her strength is real or a facade? Do you know someone with similar characteristics?

8. Did you think McKenzie's daughters, Mia and Maura, behave selfishly? Did you think they'd be okay after their mother's death?

9. If you could choose two of these women to spend a girls' weekend at a beach house with, which two would it be? Why?

10. Do you think what happens to Aurora is an accident? Why or why not?